W9-BKI-558

Guilty conscience . . .

Maggie wasn't sure exactly how long she had been in the shower, but her stress began to melt away. She stood there imagining what her life was going to be like with her new fortune. So what if Arthur fired her when she got back?

The bathroom door creaked open, ending her monetary fantasies.

She cautiously stuck her head out of the shower to see if she could hear anything. Nothing.

She shook her head. Would guilt always make her this nervous?

She was rinsing her hair one final time when she stiffened at the unmistakable sound of the deadbolt being latched. Or was it?

She stepped out of the shower with the water still running, careful not to rustle the shower curtain, and wrapped a towel around herself. There was nothing in the bathroom to arm herself with . . .

A TAX
DEDUCTIBLE DEATH

**MORE MYSTERIES FROM THE
BERKLEY PUBLISHING GROUP ...**

CAT CALIBAN MYSTERIES: She was married for thirty-eight years. Raised three kids. Compared to that, tracking down killers is easy ...

by D. B. Borton

ONE FOR THE MONEY	TWO POINTS FOR MURDER
THREE IS A CROWD	FOUR ELEMENTS OF MURDER
FIVE ALARM FIRE	SIX FEET UNDER

ELENA JARVIS MYSTERIES: There are some pretty bizarre crimes deep in the heart of Texas—and a pretty gutsy police detective who rounds up the unusual suspects ...

by Nancy Herndon

ACID BATH	HUNTING GAME
LETHAL STATUES	C.O.P. OUT
TIME BOMBS	CASANOVA CRIMES
WIDOWS' WATCH	

BENNI HARPER MYSTERIES: Meet Benni Harper—a quilter and folk-art expert with an eye for murderous designs ...

by Earlene Fowler

FOOL'S PUZZLE	GOOSE IN THE POND
KANSAS TROUBLES	MARINER'S COMPASS
DOVE IN THE WINDOW	SEVEN SISTERS
IRISH CHAIN	ARKANSAS TRAVELER

HANNAH BARLOW MYSTERIES: For ex-cop and law student Hannah Barlow, justice isn't just a word in a textbook. Sometimes, it's a matter of life and death ...

by Carroll Lachnit

MURDER IN BRIEF	A BLESSED DEATH
AKIN TO DEATH	JANIE'S LAW

PEACHES DANN MYSTERIES: Peaches has never had a very good memory. But she's learned to cope with it over the years ... Fortunately, though, when it comes to murder, this absentminded amateur sleuth doesn't forgive and forget!

by Elizabeth Daniels Squire

WHO KILLED WHAT'S-HER-NAME?	WHOSE DEATH IS IT ANYWAY?
MEMORY CAN BE MURDER	WHERE THERE'S A WILL
IS THERE A DEAD MAN IN THE HOUSE?	FORGET ABOUT MURDER
REMEMBER THE ALIBI	

A TAX DEDUCTIBLE DEATH

MALINDA TERRERI

BERKLEY PRIME CRIME, NEW YORK

If you purchased this book without a cover, you should be aware that this book is stolen property. It was reported as "unsold and destroyed" to the publisher, and neither the author nor the publisher has received any payment for this "stripped book."

This is a work of fiction. Names, characters, places, and incidents are either the product of the author's imagination or are used fictitiously, and any resemblance to actual persons, living or dead, business establishments, events, or locales is entirely coincidental.

A TAX DEDUCTIBLE DEATH

A Berkley Prime Crime Book / published by arrangement with the author

PRINTING HISTORY
Berkley Prime Crime mass-market edition / September 2001

All rights reserved.
Copyright © 2001 by Malinda Terreri
This book, or parts thereof, may not be reproduced in any form without permission.
For information address: The Berkley Publishing Group, a division of Penguin Putnam Inc.,
375 Hudson Street, New York, New York 10014.

Visit our website at
www.penguinputnam.com

ISBN: 0-425-18183-9

Berkley Prime Crime Books are published
by The Berkley Publishing Group,
a division of Penguin Putnam Inc.,
375 Hudson Street, New York, New York 10014.
The name BERKLEY PRIME CRIME and the BERKLEY PRIME CRIME
design are trademarks belonging to Penguin Putnam Inc.

PRINTED IN THE UNITED STATES OF AMERICA

10 9 8 7 6 5 4 3 2 1

Acknowledgments

Special thanks to Rennie Triplett, Bill Ferry, Mike Terreri, and Jim Conway.

Chapter 1

"**H**ow do I loathe thee? Let me count the ways," said Arthur Riley, narrowing his dark eyes.

Maggie glared up at him as he sat on his throne of a chair. Arthur had purchased new office furniture and amputated three inches off the bottom of the visitors' chairs and love seat so his squatty five-foot frame would tower over anyone sitting in front of him. From where she sat she couldn't see his feet but guessed they had to be dangling inches off the floor.

"Does this mean you didn't call me in here to give me that personal assistant I'd been hoping for?" She crossed her legs so they would stop shaking and noticed they needed shaving. "With your birthday a few days away, I thought you might be in a good mood. For a change."

"Ah yes, my birthday, let's talk about that. You know what I would like to see for my birthday?"

"Your girlfriend having her first orgasm?"

"Oh Maggot, what happened to that little rule we discussed? The one that goes: engage brain before operating mouth? Let me just make a note in your employment file that you continue to display behavior unbecoming a financial consultant." He made a production of opening the folder centered neatly on his desk. "And while I have your file open, let's just review what has happened since our last chat twenty-eight days ago. Back then your assets under management were down 34%, now they're down 41%. You've managed to open up four new accounts, but our goal was fifteen. And—surprise, surprise—your production income is down 32% and it was supposed to be up 10% by now."

Maggie looked at the floor. Four of her wealthiest, most actively trading clients all happened to have been over eighty years old, and all happened to have died within the last six months. It devastated her numbers. Even worse, all of the deceased clients had left their estates to charitable organizations, so there weren't any heirs to prospect.

"If my records are correct," Arthur said, "and they always are, your eight-year employment anniversary with Hamilton Securities is on Wednesday."

"Is that what this is all about?" She returned Arthur's smile. "I don't see how my review concerns you since the home office put a freeze on your firing of any more brokers."

"You must improve your source for office gossip. It's true I'm not supposed to fire any more brokers because of personality differences, but I can still boot anyone who does not meet their production standards. And you are one step away from feeling my shoe on the back of your ass."

"Truly a fate worse than death," she said, raising her hands in mock self-defense.

Arthur shook his head. "You know Malignant, you remind me of one of those little, yappy terrier dogs—the kind that prances around with a bow on its head and doesn't think twice before attacking some dog ten times its size."

Maggie tucked in a strand of red hair that had escaped from her French braid. At least there wasn't a bow.

"And one of these days," Arthur said, "you're going to discover that when you mess with the big—"

His intercom beeped. "Excuse me, Mr. Riley, but Greg King is on line one for you. He said it was urgent."

"I'll take this call, but hold the rest until I tell you differently."

Arthur answered his call and discussed a takeover rumor with his client. While Arthur and the client gossiped, Maggie surveyed the newly decorated office. In a thirty-by-thirty space, Arthur had managed to combine an art deco orange credenza and small conference table with a mahogany desk and had highlighted the ensemble with various pieces of Oriental art.

The only redeeming quality to the nauseating decor was the magnificent view of downtown Clayton. From where Maggie sat, she could see the St. Louis financial district bustling about its business. Unfortunately, the beautiful view was wasted on a man with the sensitivity of a rabid pit bull. She wished he would finish his call. A seven o'clock Monday morning meeting with Arthur was as pleasant as being strip-searched by a gang of bikers.

"I'll put you down for a thousand shares. Thanks for the call, Greg." Arthur hung up, filled out a buyer's stock order, and dropped the order in a pneumatic tube. "Now, Maggot, where were we?"

"I think you were going to tell me what a big dog you are, or maybe you were trying to explain that size doesn't matter, I'm not sure."

"I was about to say that you, my dear, have become one sorry excuse for a financial consultant. On Wednesday, if you haven't met the goals we agreed on last month, you'll need to move out of your office and take the cubicle I've reserved for you back by the bathrooms. By this time next month, if your production is still down, you will be fired." He leaned back in his chair and cracked his knuckles. "It's too bad unemployment checks don't go very far these days, especially with the high cost of your parents' retirement condo."

"Arthur, not even you can ruin my good mood today," she said. "And knowing how deeply concerned you are about my career, I'll tell you why. It just so happens that at ten o'clock this morning I have a new client coming in who recently sold his business and has about nine-and-a-half-million dollars to invest. Between the stocks, bonds, and annuities I've selected, it should easily generate about $250,000 in commissions. And that's just the first installment from the sale." She paused to admire her manicure. "I would venture to say this account might become one of the bigger accounts in the office."

"Buy a clue at Wal-Mart, Maggie," he said. "Bad bluffs don't become you. At the very least, you're going to lose your private office. You'll be lucky if you still have a job next month. And with the reference I'll give you, you'll be fortunate to get a job scraping dead animals off the street. Why don't you make it easy on yourself and just quit? I'll let your new employer know you just decided to make a career change and give you a glowing recommendation. Otherwise, here's what's going to happen. First of all, you will start attending the rookie cold-calling clinics. I'm scheduling the sessions for Thursday nights, Saturdays from ten to three, and Sundays from noon to four. Secondly, I want you to make at least two hundred cold calls per day. You are to provide me with a copy of the prospecting list you're calling from so I can do random checks and make sure you're making your calls. And finally, I am taking you off the Broker of the Day rotation, so say goodbye to free walk-in accounts. How does that sound? Are you sure you still want to be part of my team?"

God, how she wanted to quit, but being a broker is all she had ever wanted to be. Opening the Goldwyn account would get Arthur off her back and then maybe she would start enjoying her job again.

"Really, Arthur, all this special attention isn't necessary. Tomorrow morning you're going to see my name next to the biggest commissions on your production run.

Besides, it doesn't make sense for me to quit now; I just reordered some business cards." She spoke with such conviction she almost believed it.

He drew a big red circle around June fourth on his desk pad. "I guess we'll see. One other thing, if you miss any of my educational cold-calling gatherings or the Wednesday sales meeting, you're fired. If you fail to make a thousand cold calls each week, you'll be fired. Now please just sign here to show the HR idiot that I've explained the terms of your employment while you're on probation."

Maggie scrawled her name where Arthur indicated at the bottom of the list of edicts.

Arthur's intercom beeped again.

"I told you not to bother me."

"I'm sorry, Mr. Riley, you asked me to notify you when that radio show was going to start," the secretary said.

"Thank you."

"While I have you, the Operations Department called and needs to talk with you about some overdue margin calls on your account."

"That's all."

"And the police called. Apparently your convertible Corvette wasn't stolen, the bank—"

Arthur hit a button on the speaker and hung up on the secretary. "And now Maggie, if you'll excuse me, I have more important business to attend to."

After Maggie left, Arthur put his phone on "do not disturb" and turned on the stereo he kept tucked in his credenza. While he waited for the radio show to begin he leaned back in his Herman Miller chair and propped his feet on his desk. Tormenting the little redhead was the ideal way to begin the week. He smiled and reviewed his perfect plan. By the end of the day, all of his financial problems would be solved, and the two people he hated most would be dead—with Maggie the first to go.

Chapter 2

Tim Gallen backed his car out of his driveway and headed to work. At thirty-eight years old, his life had become as boring and predictable as the government-issued Buick Regal he was sitting in. He reached over and turned on the radio.

"... would-be murderers, put your guns and knives away and stay tuned to find out how you can bump off that wealthy aunt, irritating boss, or maybe even that IRS auditor with something you have in your very own kitchen, garden, or garage."

Great. Being an IRS special agent was about to become more hazardous.

Tim turned onto Lindbergh Boulevard as commercials for Schnuck's Grocery Stores, Blockbuster Video, and Burdis Toyota all professed great service, selection, and prices.

"Good morning St. Louis," the radio jock said. "It's 7: 20 a.m. on a BEAUTIFUL Monday morning and this is Scott Calhoun with news talk 880 A.M. Today, as promised, we begin our week-long salute to St. Louis writers. This morning I have with me Larry Brandon—the author of the new book: *Poisons: A Writer's Reference.* Larry, as I understand it, you have put together a how-to book for writers."

"That's correct," Brandon said.

"Well, I found your book fascinating, and I'm not even a writer."

"Thanks. I tried to make it easy for the layman to understand. For each poison I provide the medical name, the toxicity level, the form it comes in, method of administration, effects, symptoms, reaction time, antidotes, and treatments, as well as case histories."

"That way authors won't make the mistake of trying to poison someone with tear gas," coached the host.

"You're right. Tear gas burns, it doesn't poison."

Terrific. Just what the world needed, more information on how to kill people. Tim waited at a stop light.

"The case histories were the most intriguing," Scott said. "What are some of the more unusual cases of poisoning you discovered?"

"There are real-life case histories, like the lab technician who wanted to get back at his boss for scheduling him to work third shift."

"A situation I'm familiar with," Scott said, laughing. "What did he do?"

"The lab worker put a mercuric compound on the lights in his boss's office. The heat from the fluorescent bulbs caused the mercury to give off fumes that slowly made the boss go insane. The man's family admitted him to a hospital where he recovered, away from the fumes. But when he returned to work, it started all over, and he shot himself to avoid a life of insanity."

"I hope my station manager is getting all of this."

"My book also provides literary cases of poisonings. One of the best examples is from author Penny Miller, in her book *Centerville Cookout.* She uses an oleander branch in a barbecue scene. The murderer gives the victim the tree branch, notched, so the poisonous sap releases when the victim roasts her hot dog with it."

"There's a timely tip for those summer picnics that are upon us. That brings up another point. When I think of poisons, I think of the typical ones like arsenic and cyanide, but there are really many different kinds."

"Scott, for the creative writer, the possibilities for using poisons are really endless. There are poisons that can be added to a victim's jacuzzi so they're absorbed through the membranes. You could put poison on the back of a postage stamp to be licked by the victim. Even using the victim's allergy to certain foods can be construed as poisoning."

"You must be popular at parties."

Tim stopped at a 7-Eleven for his morning dose of caffeine and slid back into his car just as the show returned from a commercial break.

"If you just tuned in, this is Scott Calhoun and we're talking with Larry Brandon, author of *Poisons: A Writer's Reference*. The phones have been lighting up, so let's take some of your calls. Okay, Vicki Merrill from Crestwood, you're on the air. What's your question?"

"Hi, I love your show; and Larry, I can't wait to buy your book. I'm a writer with a severe case of writer's block. I'm looking for a way to have a character killed that will leave an unusual clue. Any suggestions?"

"What does your killer do for a living?"

"He is a magician. He performs a lot at children's birthday parties."

"Oh, that opens up all sorts of possibilities. The first thing that comes to mind is phosphorus. It's used in manufacturing explosives and smoke bombs among other things, so it's possible that a magician might have some up his sleeve. The reason you may want to use it is that any exposure above two parts per million in the air will cause a decrease in red blood cells, skin irritation, and nerve and testicle degeneration."

"There's nothing like a little testicle degeneration to ruin your day," Scott said.

"My chapter on industrial poisons fully explains it."

"If you are an up-and-coming writer and have a question, give us a call. The number is 555-6293. All right, go ahead caller."

"Hi Larry, I'm so glad I got through."

"What's your name?"

"Uh, my name is Arthur."

"You don't sound like a Martha."

"Not Martha, Arthur."

"Okay, Martha/Arthur, what's your question?"

"Here's my situation; I have an ordinary guy as a character who is trying to kill his rich father-in-law while he's visiting for dinner. My character doesn't have access to any drugs or fancy industrial poisons so I was thinking about using something from the garden or yard. I want to make it look like an accident."

"You might want to consider English nightshade. It's an ornamental plant with dark, dingy-purple, bell-shaped flowers and large, simple leaves. Everything on the plant is toxic, especially the roots, leaves, and berries."

"Could you tell me a little about its symptoms and how it might be administered?"

"It has some interesting symptoms—blurred vision, hot dry skin, dry mouth, disorientation, hallucinations, and a heartbeat audible at several feet. It eventually causes convulsions, coma, and then death. Now, if your victim is suffering from a flu or maybe had a bit too much to drink one night, the caring son-in-law might accidentally use the nightshade to make an herbal tea."

"Thanks, you've been a lot of help."

"I'm glad I'm a coffee drinker," Scott said. "Now we have Dave Vance from Fenton. What's your question, Dave?"

"Am I on the air?"

"You sure are, what's your question?"

"My neighbor's dog barks nonstop. What could I use to shut it up permanently?"

"That's not the purpose—"

Tim turned the radio off and stopped at the next light. The cross traffic passed back and forth. He rolled down his window hoping to allow a little breeze into the sweltering car.

Maybe he should pick up a copy of the poison book. Actually, he didn't even need to buy the book. According to the author's description, the plant growing outside Tim's temporary office was English nightshade. He could use Martha/Arthur's plan, only instead of poisoning a rich father-in-law, he would poison a certain Cleon Cummings. Life would be a little different if he controlled Cleon's estate. All $139 million of it. No more working seventy-plus hours a week dealing with people who were always trying to get one over on the system. He glanced at the pile of paperwork beside him that had been his only companion over the weekend. Yes, $139 million would certainly change his life. Heck, even a couple million would do the trick.

On second thought, poisoning someone he was investigating for tax fraud would probably end up making the news and seriously impairing his career. Especially if he was caught.

The truck behind him honked. He took his foot off the brake and started forward and then instantly hit the brake again when a bag lady stumbled in front of his car. The pickup behind him did not react as quickly and rear-ended Tim's Buick.

Tim checked his rearview mirror to see who hit him as the bag lady reeled around to his driver side and thrust an umbrella in through the open window, the point pushing into his neck.

"The cat is wet!" the hag shrieked, her hair knotted and mangled. "Now you've done it! The cat is wet! She'll never sleep tonight!"

"Listen, ma'am." He carefully raised his hand to keep

the dirty umbrella point from pushing farther into his neck. "I'm sorry, but you just darted in front of me."

The pickup behind Tim honked and passed him on the right side. Other cars followed.

"Look," he said. "I don't think I actually made contact with you. I'm sorry if I frightened you. Please, I need to get that truck's license plate before he—"

"Puss! Puss! The cat is wet. The cat is wet and it's all your fault!"

Her voice shrilled through the morning air. A crowd began to gather on the sidewalk to watch. Including, he noticed, a roving Channel 12 camera crew. Par for the course.

He turned back to the hag. "Well, maybe what we should do is—"

The smell of urine and body odor drifted in through the open window and stopped him in midsentence. He looked at his side mirror to see the woman urinating partially on her leg and partially on his car.

"Please don't—"

"The skies will darken, the stones will choke your breath, Puss, Puss, sorrow and death. The cat is wet and it's all your fault. Puss will never sleep tonight!"

She concluded her hex and spit a glob of warm, yellowish saliva on his face that dribbled onto his shirt and tie. He pawed at his face, trying to remove the disease-infested goo. When he looked up again, she was gone.

Chapter 3

Maggie walked through the checkerboard of sixty identical cubicles that made up the Hamilton Securities boardroom. Each cubicle, with its standard-issue desk, filing cabinet, and rookie stockbroker super-glued to a phone, added to the neurotic buzz in the air, further intensifying Maggie's jittery nerves.

Flanking the outer edges of the bullpen were the private offices, including Maggie's near the lobby entrance. The private offices were really nothing more than three and a half walls that went three-quarters of the way to the ceiling, but compared with the bullpen they were luxury unparalleled and a sign of distinction, or at least an aptitude for sucking up to management. Maggie got her office after only three years with Hamilton. At the time she was twenty-four and the youngest female broker to be awarded a private office in Hamilton history.

But for everything that had gone right during her first years, something had gone wrong this year and now she was in danger of losing her office and possibly her job.

Hopefully, Mr. Goldwyn would change her luck.

She nodded at her secretary, picked up her *Wall Street Journal*, and quickly made her way into her doorless office to regroup. Inside there was barely room for two client chairs, her desk, and a credenza, but the office had a nice window overlooking the main lobby. Every flat surface held piles of important information that needed to be read, filed, mailed to a client, or trashed if she ignored them long enough that they were out-of-date.

She dropped into her chair. Arthur's threat had been unnerving, but it would be meaningless by this time tomorrow. She pushed aside a stack of unread annual reports to clear a space on her desk. Now she could calm her nerves with her customary morning Pepsi and Oreo cookies. Thankfully, three sadistic workouts a week at the gym kept the Oreos from sticking. A couple hundred dollars worth of designer skin care products and makeup concealed any occasional skin irritations caused by her love of chocolate and provided a Cover Girl complexion. She was twisting the Oreo ends perfectly apart, dusting the open Goldwyn file with black crumbs, when her phone rang.

"Mag, it's Laurie on line one," Stacy yelled through Maggie's doorway.

She popped open the can of Pepsi and answered the phone.

"Laurie, 7:30 is a little early for you to be in your office. Didn't the blind date go well last night?"

"If I have another date like that one I will seriously consider either becoming a lesbian or lifelong celibacy," Laurie said. "I can't believe we're old maids and we're only thirty."

"Hey, I've got another seven months before I reach old maid status," Maggie said. "So what went wrong this time?"

"We had dinner at Portofino's, which was nice enough. But this guy kept droning on about himself, how good he looked for being thirty-seven, how much money he had, how often he worked out at The Club, how he went out on dates four times a week. Then he went to run his fingers through his toupee for the umpteenth time in an hour and accidentally pulled it off."

"Oh, God."

"Mag, it was so embarrassing. I mean, I didn't like this guy but I felt so bad for him."

"What did you do?" Maggie ate another Oreo and glanced at her watch.

"What could I do? I told him I had to call the sitter and check on the twins."

"Not the twins routine again."

"I tell you, this guy started stammering more at the thought of college tuition for two than the fact that his rug was on lopsided. By the time I got back from the phone—oh, that obscene message on your machine last night was from me—he'd already paid the bill. I was home by nine."

"Maybe next time."

"Yeah, right. But that's not why I called. I wanted to wish you luck. Today's the big day, isn't it?"

"It will be in about a couple of hours."

"What's wrong? You sound a little down."

Maggie sighed. "I shot my mouth off at the Tiny Terror Tot this morning and now he wants me to make two hundred cold calls a day and start attending these bullshit cold-calling sessions. If there's any problem with this new account, my employment here may be drawing to a close."

"Don't let Arthur get to you. Tell me how you're going to spend the Goldwyn money instead."

Maggie gazed back at the file. She knew every entry without needing to look. "Well, we're going to start with a block of munies I've reserved with staggered maturities beginning—"

"Don't talk stockbroker mumbo jumbo to me. I don't care how you spend his money. I'm talking about how you're going to spend your commission money, you idiot."

A nervous smile returned to Maggie's face. "Laurie, I can't say that. It'll jinx me."

"Oh for God's sake, I know you. You've had that calculator of yours on overtime figuring up the commission and you already know how you're going to spend every penny of it. You were the same with the proceeds from those damn Girl Scout cookie sales, so clue me in. I love a good shopping spree."

"Okay, I guess it doesn't matter since I've already let the cat out of the bag. I'm using part of the money to help my parents move into a retirement community in Florida. All their friends are there, and they're so excited. It's more like a resort than a retirement home."

"You already told them?"

"I've already given them the money. They were having some financial problems arranging for admission, so I explained about the Goldwyn account. It was such a Kodak moment. I haven't seen them so proud since I was potty trained."

"Well, at age twelve that was quite an accomplishment for you. How did you give them the money already? When did Hamilton start fronting commission checks?"

"Hamilton didn't. I took out advances on every Visa and MasterCard I could."

"Oh Mags—"

"Now don't say a word, I don't want to hear it."

"I guess since your folks have the money, it's too late to talk you out of it."

"Just a little."

"And here I thought you were going to do something responsible like buy boob jobs for all your friends. What a disappointment you turned out to be."

"Laurie, you've got to be kidding. Fake boobs went out with the eighties."

"I don't care. I've wanted bigger boobs since Todd Dinkins made me president of the 'itty-bitty-titty committee' in the sixth grade. What about the rest of the money?"

"Most of it is going into investments, but I was thinking about spending some on a prospecting campaign to attract new clients. I haven't decided. I hate to jinx myself too much by spending all the money before it's in the bank."

"Jinx, shminx. But speaking of bad luck, have you found a date for the Fourth of July party yet?"

"No, and I'm not looking. I don't need the distraction. Not until—"

"I know, not until after you make your first million dollars. You know, there's more to life than stocks and bonds. Ever heard the saying 'love makes the world go 'round?' "

"Yeah, but money keeps it spinning." She had decided a long time ago she wasn't going to get involved with anyone before she was financially independent. She had seen too many women compromise their goals in the name of love.

"How about taking a vacation to Europe? I know this great little inn—"

"No, Laurie. I've never been out of the country, and if I did leave, I probably would just want to go sit on a beach some place with an umbrella drink and a *Wall Street Journal.*"

"And probably get skin cancer. I hate to tell you this kiddo, but I think my grandma has more excitement in her life then you do."

Maggie's other phone line lit up. "Cleon Cummings on line two," Stacy yelled.

"Hey, I've got to go. I've got a client on the other line. I'll call you later and let you know how everything went."

Maggie smiled as she pushed the button for her second line. She had been assigned walk-ins on her first day at Hamilton when Cleon strolled in to open a checking account with ten thousand dollars and an investment account with three million dollars. Only after she opened the accounts did she discover Cleon was Arthur's father-in-law and that the two men had dedicated their lives to hating each other.

"How's the only stockbroker I know with a great pair of lamb chops?" Cleon boomed. "Any chance you remembered to shave them this morning?"

Maggie held the phone away from her ear. "Hi, Cleon. No, as a matter of fact I forgot, but thanks for asking. You could say I've had better mornings. I just finished my recommended daily dose of humiliation courtesy of your evil son-in-law."

"Is Arthur a little cranky today? Or is that redundant?"

"I'd say his impression of a human hemorrhoid keeps getting better every day."

Maggie assumed Cleon opened the investment account to torment Arthur because, except for the occasional purchase of CDs, she had never been able to persuade Cleon to invest any of the money. That meant that the three million didn't generate any real commissions, but at least the account looked good for assets under management.

"So what's up?" she said. "I don't suppose you called to let me invest that money you've had sitting around earning a pittance in the money market. I've got some great Missouri triple-A bonds available. Double tax-exempt, and I know how you feel about paying taxes."

"No thanks on the bonds. But speaking of taxes, would you believe I'm sitting in the office of my IRS agent waiting for the big shit to show up for work? I decided to use his quarter to call and see why I haven't received my check."

Maggie pulled up Cleon's account on her computer. "What check is that?"

"I called last week and told your secretary to close my investment account and send me the proceeds. Didn't she tell you?"

"Stacy was on vacation for a few days last week. You must have talked with the temp, and she never said anything. Why, Cleon, what's going on?"

"It's nothing you've done, and actually I meant to call

and say goodbye, I've just been really busy with preparations. I have what they call an inoperable heart problem. The doctors say that with drug therapy I might make another couple of months."

"Oh Cleon!"

"The truth is, I could go any time, whether I'm in a hospital or not. So I told them to stick their drugs and treatments up their money-sucking asses."

"I'm so . . . so. . . ." She choked on the words as her tears quietly made black stripes out of her mascara.

"I've sold Stuffing Stuff. Practically gave the damn business, including my pig farm, to my manager."

Cleon originally purchased the farm because he needed the space for his taxidermy operations, but he quickly fell in love with the animals. Maggie remembered her visit to the farm last year, right after a contagious disease had forced him to destroy most of his pigs. Cleon was heartbroken.

"I didn't think you still kept any pigs after that . . . problem you had."

"I don't." His voice softened. "I didn't want to go through that again. Probably just as well. The way my taxidermy business took off, I wouldn't have had time to keep running around catching escaped pigs." He paused. "I'll never forget, right before that happened, I installed this new-and-improved electric fence to try and keep those rascals in their pens. Would you believe they actually loved the shocks? Used to rub their spines up against it. I think they were just trying to run up my electric bill."

Maggie had heard this story several times before, but she laughed again anyway. How could Cleon be dying?

"But enough about those damn pigs," he said. "You'll never guess what I'm doing for my final exit."

"Dare I ask?" She looked for a tissue but couldn't find one, so she wiped her nose with Arthur's memo announcing the new cold-calling sessions.

"I'll tell you but if you leak this to anyone, you'll . . . you'll never have another orgasm again."

"The way my love life is going, that's not much of a threat, but I promise."

"You swear?"

"I swear."

"You swear and hope to never have another orgasm if you lie?"

"I do."

"No, you have to say it."

Maggie rolled her eyes. "Okay, I, Maggie Connors, being of not-so-sound mind and only a twenty-nine-year-old body, swear and hope to never have another orgasm if I lie."

Maggie finished her oath just in time to spot her sales manager staring in her office door. He flushed, ducked his head, and moved on.

She shook her head. "Okay, so what's up?"

"Maggie, I've put together the master plan to end all master plans," Cleon said in an excited whisper. "In one magnificent fell swoop I will eternally screw both Arthur and the IRS."

"I'm listening."

"Wait, let me make sure no one is coming." There was a few seconds' delay, then, "I'm taking all of my money with me."

"How on earth are you going to do that?" Had he finally found a company to launch his mummified body into space with suitcases of cash by its side?

"I'm cashing everything in and shredding it."

Maggie switched the phone to her other ear. "What exactly do you mean, shredding it?"

"Arthur called me last week begging for money, and I turned him down. The piece of human waste then messengered me a paper shredder and told me I could shred all my money and stick it up my ass. So I decided to take him up on it, except for the part about up my ass." Cleon chuckled. "For the last few days I've been turning hundred dollar bills into pieces of white and green paper."

Maggie froze. She wasn't sure of the exact figure, but

Cleon was worth something like $150 million. And he was turning it into scrap?

"Magpie, are you still with me?"

"Cleon, you're insane! I can't believe. . . . Can we talk about this? Isn't there something better you can do?"

"Keep your voice down. Remember the orgasms."

"Isn't there something better you can do? Donations to charity or something?" Or give it to her?

"Oh, I've given my share to charity, and I'll give more before I'm done. But if I leave anything behind, one way or another either the IRS or Arthur or both are going to wind up with money I've worked a lifetime for. Neither of them deserve it, and I'm going to see to it they don't get it."

Maggie wasn't sure how the eccentric had amassed his fortune; he certainly didn't do it being a taxidermist or a pig farmer. Over the years Cleon had made references to being a scuba instructor, a commercial developer, even a restaurant owner, but he always avoided identifying the real source of his millions.

"Cleon, you're wacked." She frowned. "Why are you so excited?"

"If you were my age, you'd understand." His strong voice faltered and he paused a moment to compose himself. "When Arthur—that goddamn drunk—killed my wife and my only daughter, he took too much. I'm tired of trying to hang on to life. I'm tired of getting out of bed each morning and hating Arthur for what he did. I'm just. . . ."

Maggie sighed. Who was she to judge him? And it was his money. Besides, the thought of helping to screw Arthur was not without appeal.

"Okay," she said. "What can I do to help?"

"I've depleted my checking account, but what arrangements do I need to make to have my investment account paid out today in cash?"

"We can have a check waiting for you—"

"No, I need it in cash."

"We can't do a cash disbursement," she said shaking her head. "Maximum cash payout on an account is $100. We can give you a certified check and make arrangements with the bank across the street to cash it for you, but they may need some notice to come up with that much money. Let me see what the delay was on sending out your check." She changed screens on the computer to check the account's history. "It looks like there's a hold on your investment account because you never returned your W-9 form, but that must be a clerical error."

"Or Arthur. Can you override it or something?"

"Sure. I'll just have the Operations Department check their files. But, I still can't have your account paid out in cash. Does it have to be today?"

"Yeah, I'm afraid if the IRS finds out about my plan, they'll find a way to freeze the account. The last thing I want to do is die leaving something for Arthur to get his grubby little hands on. I can't believe I didn't check on this earlier."

Maggie almost said, *So many millions, so little time*, but stopped herself.

"Why don't you wire the funds to my bank in the Caymans?" he said.

"The Caymans? Why send the money to the Caymans?"

"Hiding it is the next best thing to shredding it," he said. "You know there's something delightfully ironic about sitting in an IRS office and arranging to have money sent out of the country. Now here's what I want you to do with my account. . . ."

Cleon gave Maggie the bank's name, routing number, and his account number in the Cayman Islands. She assured him she would take care of the transfer, asked him to keep in touch, and they said their goodbyes.

As she reached over to hang up the phone, her bra strap broke.

Jesus Christ! What did she do to deserve all of this?

Chapter 4

Tim Gallen stomped into the lobby of the Federal Building, took the elevator up to the second floor, trekked down a long, nondescript hallway, and then took an access elevator down to the first floor, which opened to the Annex. With each step he became less pissed about the bag lady's sticky spit on him and more fed up about the inconvenient route required to reach his relocated office in the Annex.

The Internal Revenue Service's Examination and Criminal Investigation Division offices were normally located on the tenth floor of the Federal Building. Four weeks ago, Exam and CID were relocated to the Annex so renovations could be completed on their offices. The remodeling was supposed to take three weeks, but the discovery of asbestos changed that.

Tim stepped off the elevator and went into the Annex men's room to wash the homeless hag's mouth muck off his face and clothes. Ed Granger, his group manager, was standing at a urinal.

" 'Morning, Gallen," Ed said. "Interesting way of washing your car."

"Very funny. How did you—"

He shook himself and zipped his fly. "I was waiting to make a left on Washington. Quite an entertaining little show you put on."

"It was all worth it, if it made your day a little brighter."

Ed washed his hands, still laughing to himself. "I'll see you at the group meeting. Try to look presentable. Walking around looking like a human blotch isn't going to help the Service's reputation," he said before leaving the rest room.

When Tim was satisfied he'd disinfected his face, he blotted his shirt and tie with a paper towel. The paper towel disintegrated as he rubbed, leaving white bits of lint ingrained into the wet spot that now covered the entire front of his shirt. He threw the towel toward the trash can, missed, and left the men's room in disgust.

CID's makeshift office was located inside Exam's temporary offices, in the far corner of the Annex. Tim punched in his number code at Exam's main door, passed through the small lobby, and turned down the hallway to CID. The door to CID was already unlocked. He entered and made his way to his office in the back corner, where he noticed his light was on. When he hurried through the door he found Cleon Cummings just hanging up his telephone.

" 'Morning, Timmy," Cleon bellowed. "It's about time you got in—having kind of a late start aren't you?"

"Mr. Cummings, how did you get in here?"

Cleon Cummings sat comfortably with the morning paper spread on his lap. Wearing khaki pants and an orange polo shirt he looked more like a grandfather ready to play golf than a multimillionaire facing criminal charges for tax evasion. A wet cigar jutted from his smiling mouth.

"Oh, I've just been sitting here reading the morning rag and admiring your fine collection of 1960's green, metal office furniture." Cleon nodded at the window in Tim's office, almost completely obscured by the plant growing outside. "What did the government do, cut the pruning budget? Get it? Cut, pruning?"

"Mr. Cummings, this is a federal office and a non-smoking facility. You can't—"

"You really should buy yourself some clippers and fix that plant. I've never seen such dull flowers. It's downright depressing. But on second thought, I guess it goes with the decor."

One benefit of working in the old Annex was that the windows actually opened. Tim took advantage of this, hoping the outside air might relieve the cigar smoke.

"Mr. Cummings, you can't just walk in here and make yourself at home. How did you get past the—"

" 'Fraid I'm going to find out something I shouldn't?" Cleon smiled a happy, bald man's smile. "Have a seat. I'd like to discuss something with you."

Tim remained by the open window. He was used to giving orders, not taking them.

"Don't go getting your knickers in a twist, son. Look, I even brought doughnuts." He put out his cigar on the bottom of his shoe and set it aside to be finished later. Then he picked up a paper bag sitting next to his chair and lifted out two doughnuts and placed them neatly on the desk. "Would you like the one with sprinkles or are you a glazed man? My guess is you're a glazed man."

"Mr. Cummings, I—"

"Come on, you're a bachelor, I know you haven't had breakfast, sit down and let's talk. By the way, what's that attractive drizzle all over you?"

Tim straightened his tie, still covered with wet blotches, and sat down at his desk.

"Never mind that. What do you think you're doing?"

"Do you have any hot water? I brought the most delicious tea." Cleon placed a small tin of tea on the desk while still chomping on his doughnut. "Are you a coffee or a tea man? I'm a tea man myself. I don't know why. I think the entire world discriminates against us. Ever notice that waitresses are always so quick to refill your coffee, but if you need more hot water—forget about it. Here, look, I even brought a tea strainer because I figured you weren't expecting to entertain. How about that hot water?"

"Mr. Cummings, I don't have any hot water, and I'm not a tea drinker. May I ask how you got in here and what you want?"

"In life I have found that attitude is everything. I waited for somebody to punch in their secret code at the Exam entrance and I simply barged right in behind them. Then I made my way back here where I found CID's door unlocked—somebody probably went out for an early coffee and forgot to lock up behind himself. I meandered around until I saw that very official-looking piece of masking tape on your door with your name written on it in black marker. I just turned the door handle, and a remarkable thing happened: it opened. I guess your operation guy hasn't bothered installing an elaborate security system since these offices are temporary digs."

Tim didn't respond.

"And being Monday morning, your secretary must be dragging ass a little so no one was around to flag me down."

"Mr. Cummings, what do—"

"Timmy, you're a bottom-line kind of guy and I appreciate that, so I'll get right to the point. My attorney called me Friday and said the grand jury gave you the indictment you wanted on me. I'm scheduled to be arraigned at 8:30 tomorrow morning."

"I'm aware of that."

About two years ago Tim's supervisor gave him the revenue agent's notes from Cummings' preliminary audit and asked Tim to handle the joint investigation with the Exam Division. Although Cummings was one of *Forbes*'s 500 richest men, he had paid less than $14,000 in taxes over the last seven years. It was the largest net worth case Tim had ever worked.

"Let me ask you this," Cummings said. "How long have you been working on my case? Two years is it? Poring over my bank statements, my tax returns, my receipts. You name it, I think you've looked through it. Plus, I think you've interviewed everyone I ever did business with as well as anyone I ever talked to, except maybe my first grade teacher."

"A funny thing happens when we talk to the people you do business with, we discover and document all sorts of expenditures you've made." Tim pulled Cleon's file from his desk drawer and placed it on his desk, but didn't open it. "For instance, when we first took on this case, my partner and I took a ride out to your pig farm to get a look around. At the time, you were doing a renovation that would make Bill Gates envious. We talked to the contractors and asked each how much you were paying them. We talked to the suppliers and asked what you were paying them. We asked each person we talked to if they remembered who else was working there at the time. Slowly, phone call after phone call, we documented over $740,000 you spent in one year on a new pond, a new dock, a new barn, a new heated driveway—"

"I don't like shoveling snow."

"And then for sixty days we monitored who was sending you mail. That enabled us to identify your accounts with banks and other financial institutions, which helped us discover sources of unreported income. We also monitored your mail to unearth some of your other expenditures, and I gotta tell you my favorite is your annual $130,000 payment toward having your body mummified and launched into space when you die."

"I know that sounds expensive, but it does include the invitations to the launch event as well as a video tape."

"Mr. Cummings, you can stretch a buck better than anyone I've ever met. You declared an annual income of under $50,000, but we documented your annual expenditures at over two million. That's a great trick if you can do it, but I'd like to know how." Tim stretched back in his chair and clasped his fingers behind his head.

"It doesn't really matter any more." Cleon took a break from his doughnut-eating to look pensive. "The time has come to put this behind me. My doctor tells me my dance card only has about one punch left. I'm ready to make this thing go away. I'm tired of having it hang over my hairless head."

"Sir, you've got a big tax problem, and the only way to make it a smaller problem is to cooperate, tell the truth, and get it over with. If you are interested in a plea arrangement, I suggest you have your attorney contact the U.S. Attorney's office. I can't help you with that. But I can tell you this, I've never written up a special agent's prosecution report where the guy didn't plead guilty or get convicted at trial. The reason I'm telling you that is because you and I both know one thing: you're guilty of income tax evasion. You know it better than I do."

"No, Timmy, you misunderstood. I don't want a plea arrangement, I want to make this tax situation disappear."

Tim stared at Cummings. He didn't need his notes, he knew Cleon's case so well he could site Cleon's social security number in his sleep.

"You're being charged with tax fraud, which is a felony offense under Section 7201. Conviction under this statute could result in your imprisonment for not more than five years and/or a fine of not more than $250,000 for each of the years for which you get convicted.

"As far as I can tell, you owe Uncle Sam almost $14 million. That doesn't even include pending civil penalties. Now how are you going to make that, and the thousands of man hours this investigation has taken, go away?"

"Let me show you something." Cleon licked a few sprinkles from his fingers and moved the uneaten glazed doughnut, the tea, and the strainer off to the side of the desk. He picked up the briefcase that had been tucked by his chair and laid it in front of Tim. "Go ahead, open it. But let me shut your office door first."

Tim waited until the door was closed and then leaned

forward and flipped open the locks on the briefcase. It was full of neat stacks of hundred-dollar bills.

"That's right, Timmy. Guess how many glazed doughnuts you can buy with two million in cash? How old are you? Thirty-seven, thirty-eight? Why, you're the proverbial 'tall, dark and handsome,' but yet you haven't had the time or the money to settle down with a wife and kids in a big West County home."

Tim stared at the cash in front of him and did the math. Even assuming the maximum annual raise every year, he wouldn't make two million in his entire career. Well maybe if he took a late retirement but after taxes—

"Don't you get tired of seeing all your friends in the private sector pass you by?" Cummings said. "You should be out on the golf course with them, not getting bloodshot eyes looking at bank statements. You've worked hard the last fifteen years. This could make things right for you. You could even buy yourself a decent shirt and tie. All you have to do is help me make this case go away."

Tim glanced down at his blotch and then his eyes darted back to the money. He felt as though he had just drank an entire pot of coffee. "Mr. Cummings, it's a little late in the game to be offering this." He spoke slowly and concentrated on keeping his voice calm. "Even a two-million-dollar bribe wouldn't go far with the Service. I would have to pay off my partner and everyone else involved in working or monitoring your investigation, which includes my Group Manager, Centralized Case Manager, Branch Chief, Division Chief, District Counsel, the Assistant U.S. Attorney, and probably even the clerical staff who input my daily log activities into the computer."

"Well, let's talk about that. My heart is having problems but my memory is still sharp as a tack. I was thinking about that initial interview you did with me when you came out to my farm. As best as I can recall, you never read me my rights."

"I certainly did Mirandize you. My partner witnessed

it, and I noted that I did in my report on that interview."

"Timmy, I'm sure your report says you read me my rights because that's what you are supposed to do. You probably automatically included it in your report without even thinking about it. But when you get up on the stand, your memory might be better focused. You might remember the truth, which is simply that you forgot to do it."

"I guess that would kill the case, but everyone would know I was lying."

"With two million bucks in your bank account, what would you care?"

"Under 18 USC 201(b), bribery is a felony punishable by a fine of not more than three times the monetary equivalent of the bribe, or imprisonment for not more than fifteen years, or both."

Cleon picked up the glazed doughnut he had brought for Tim and began eating it. "Bribery is such an ugly word. Let's say this is a payment toward my back taxes and I don't need a receipt. And how in God's name do you know all these statute numbers? Instead of sleeping with the tax code you should find yourself a woman."

The stacks of bills with their promise of financial freedom mocked him.

This must be God's punishment for coveting Cleon's money in the car that morning.

Cleon leaned forward in his chair and lowered his voice. "Son, with this money you could start enjoying life for a change. Take some advice from a dying man, the last thing you want to do is assume that there will always be a tomorrow."

"I don't know what to say. No one has ever made an offer to me like this before. I'd be taking money illegally and depriving the government of your tax dollars."

"Timmy, let's take a moment to think this through. Social Security is almost bankrupt. The Welfare system is a joke. And each year our taxes are going higher and higher as the services rendered by our government are getting more screwed up." Cleon waved the half-eaten glazed doughnut as he spoke. "So you tell me, why on earth should I give this government any of my hard-earned money when it has shown a consistent history of fiscal irresponsibility?"

"Mr. Cummings, it's not my job to defend the government. I share some of the same concerns you do."

"Well then let's talk about the IRS. Even after the Reform Act, you guys can't live up to the same scrutiny you inflict. In fact, the last audit by the General Accounting Office found that the IRS cannot, and I quote, 'reconcile the accounting records it keeps on individual taxpayers with the $1.9 trillion in revenues it collected.' Could you imagine what would happen if I kept my books the way you guys do? I would have been playing butt buddies at the friendly, local penitentiary a long time ago, courtesy of your fine organization."

"I'm aware of our accounting problem, but clearly two wrongs—"

"But, let's say how you keep your books isn't important. That your $51 million in accounting errors found last year by the GAO don't matter. Let's just say the American people are willing to give you a big mulligan on that one. How do you justify the fact that the IRS employs over 100,000 people, twice that of the CIA and five times that of the FBI—and I gotta tell you that doesn't make me feel very safe—yet tons of the computerized notices you send to taxpayers contain errors?"

"If someone has a question about a notice—"

"They can call you? Are you kidding me? According to the GAO, one-third of the poor saps that call the IRS for help can't get through, and if the taxpayer does get through there's still no guarantee he'll get the right information. In fact, the IRS gives wrong tax information to millions of people each year."

Cleon popped the remaining bit of doughnut in his mouth.

"In an organization of our size there are bound to be

some problems," Tim said. "I don't make the rules. I just enforce them."

"Come on, Timmy, I expected better than that from you, but that's exactly my point. Why should I entrust almost $14 million to government employees with the mental agility of a tank? Hell, if I ever saw one of you guys, just once in your nine-to-five careers, demonstrate an ability to solve a problem or invent a better method of doing something, I would gladly hand over the thirteen million, eight hundred and seventy-three thousand dollars you think I owe."

Tim sat stunned in his chair as the fat man in front of him licked glazed icing off his fingers.

"Mr. Cummings, I happen to think playing by the rules is what keeps it safe for people to go to sleep at night and wake up the next morning. Without rules, we would have anarchy."

Cleon shook his head with a look of profound soundness. "Games are not always won by playing by the rules."

"Maybe, but without the rules to define it, there's no game. Associate Justice Oliver Wendell Holmes once said, 'Taxes are the price we pay for a civilized society.' "

"We've lost our focus here. Let's not try to solve all the government's problems, let's just focus on solving mine. I don't want to spend my remaining days sitting in a court room, or even worse, sitting in jail. I thought rather than spend a couple of million on legal fees, why not cut to the chase and invest that money in you?"

"Are you working with any law enforcement agency in conjunction with this offer?"

"Now you're talking. No, I'm not. Cross my heart and hope to die," he said, crossing his heart and then raising his right hand.

Tim just stared at the money, so Cleon continued with his sales pitch.

"Think for a moment what you could do with two mil-

lion dollars. If you want to save the world, this could be
your start-up money."

"Mr. Cummings, this is a lot to think about. I don't
know what to say."

"Say you'll take the money, which will help refresh
your memory concerning my Miranda warning."

"But my partner was at that interview. I'd have to involve him in this."

"Would he join us?"

"He would if I told him to."

There was a rap on the door. Tim's secretary walked
in, and Tim slammed Cleon's briefcase closed.

"I'm sorry, Tim. I didn't realize you were in a meeting." She retreated and yanked the door shut behind her.

"Do you think she saw the money?" Cleon said.

"No, I closed the briefcase in time. Why the hell didn't
you lock the door?"

"Hey, if I was a smart guy would I be sitting here in
the first place?"

"Mr. Cummings, my office isn't the best place to talk
about this. Give me a few days to think things over and
then we can get together somewhere else and discuss this
further."

Cleon shook his head no. "Unfortunately, the clock is
ticking. As I said, my arraignment is tomorrow morning
so I need to know now if you're in or out."

"I just can't make a snap decision. I need to talk to my
partner, and he's not in this morning. I really need some
time."

The two poker players assessed each other.

"Timmy, why don't you and your partner come out to
my farm tonight? Say around seven o'clock? It's so
blasted hot out, perhaps the three of us could take a swim
in the river and chat without worrying about interruptions."

Tim agreed.

Cleon picked up his briefcase and waddled out of the
office.

A few seconds later Tim's intercom buzzed, causing him to jump slightly in his chair. Evidently a two-million-dollar bribe made him jittery.

"Yes, Donna?" he said.

"Mr. Cummings would like to know if he could have his tin of tea back."

"You're kidding me."

Through the intercom Tim heard Donna ask Cleon if he was kidding.

"He says he isn't kidding and not to forget the strainer either."

"Thank you Donna. I'll bring them right out."

Instead of returning the tea to Cleon, Tim picked up the phone and called John Corbin, the chief of Inspection. Inspection was the IRS's Internal Security, with exclusive jurisdiction to investigate bribery allegations involving the Service. While the phone rang, Tim replayed in his mind what had just happened. A voice mail chime snapped him back to his call.

"John, this is Tim Gallen at CID," he said into the phone. "I just had an unexpected meeting with Cleon Cummings, a taxpayer I've been investigating for tax fraud. The grand jury gave us our indictment on Friday and he's scheduled to be arraigned tomorrow. He came into my office this morning and offered me a two-million-dollar bribe if I would get on the stand and say I forgot to Mirandize him. He had a briefcase filled with cash. As we've been trained, I played along as best as I could. I told him I'd have to involve my partner, Dwight Buckley. We set up a meeting for tonight at his farm. I tried to stall for more time, but he wants to finalize this before his arraignment. He also said something about the three of us taking a swim in the river to discuss this further. I'm sure he suggested that as a precaution so I'm not wired. Per procedure, I won't say anything to anyone until I hear back from you. Sorry if I sound a little rattled, but this—"

The voice mail beeped and then disconnected him. Tim hung up the phone, and his intercom sounded again.

"Mr. Cummings would like to know if he could have his tea back today," Donna said.

Tim opened his office door expecting to give the items to his secretary but instead found Cleon standing there.

"Thanks, Timmy. I'll save this for our next tea party." Cleon tucked the tea and the strainer into his paper bag.

"I didn't know you drank tea," his secretary said.

Cleon gave her a conspiratorial wink and then whispered loudly, "Your boss is a closet tea drinker, the worst kind."

Tim ducked back into his office. He couldn't explain why he felt guilty even though he had no intentions of accepting Cleon's offer. Before he closed his office door he heard Cleon yell, "Don't forget to shut your office window, we're supposed to get rain later on."

Tim called John Corbin again at Inspection.

This time when John's voice mail answered Tim paid attention to the message: John was in today, but away from his desk.

"Hi John, Tim Gallen again. Just wanted to make sure you got my message to call. I'm going into a group meeting soon, so please page me if you don't reach me in my office."

into the air, bobbled the catch, and watched it drop and roll to the middle of the room.

The wire operator turned back to her computer.

Normally Arthur would have left the tube for someone to trip over, but today, with the magnanimity born of the potential three million dollars in his pocket, he decided to retrieve it. After a few more minutes of pretending he had a reason for being there, he walked out of the Ops Department knowing he was one step closer to controlling some of Cleon's money.

It was hard for him to keep from skipping back to his office. He couldn't believe today he would finally get back at the old man. Arthur never forgave the eccentric asshole for missing dinner that one winter evening. If Cleon had met them like he promised, Cleon would have driven his wife home, and there probably wouldn't have been an accident. Instead, Arthur got stuck chauffeuring his mother-in-law back to her place. The roads were so icy even a sober person wouldn't have been able to avoid the truck veering head-on for them. Arthur's wife had been sitting beside him in the car, his mother-in-law in the back seat. Both women died in the crash and everyone blamed Arthur, which made their loss even worse.

Well, now Arthur was getting even.

He had hired a private detective and knew Cleon was dying. Immediately he had contacted an estate attorney who assured him that with the right legal team—and enough billable hours—they could negotiate a settlement from Cleon's estate even if he was disinherited. But a settlement would be months, if not years away, and he needed the money now. He was behind on his mortgage payments. His checking account was overdrawn. His option account had unsatisfied calls. He needed at least $250,000, and he needed it fast.

When Arthur's detective discovered Cleon's ridiculous plan to shred his money, Arthur panicked. But then he realized it was the answer to his financial nightmare. His new plan was so simple. Maggie would have an accident tonight so she wouldn't be around to dispute his changes to Cleon's account. Then, tomorrow morning, he would close Cleon's account, issue a check in Cleon's name, forge the signature, and cash it. The IRS and Cleon's estate administrator would both assume the balance had been shredded with the rest of Cleon's money. Conveniently arranging for Cleon to die tomorrow night would keep him from contesting the forgery.

The radio show had been very helpful. Now it was just a matter of arranging for a couple of timely, untimely deaths.

Chapter 6

Ed Granger, Tim's group manager, was shuffling papers and trying to bring the group meeting to order when Tim arrived. Tim took his usual seat at the conference table, causing Bill Merriefield and Roger Kipp to retreat from their seats to the other side of the table, leaving Tim alone to face the other seven agents in his group.

"All right," Granger asked, "why isn't anyone sitting by Gallen?"

"Rumor has it that he's been hexed." Merriefield pushed his glasses up and looked at Gallen like he had the plague.

"Hexed?" Tim said.

Merriefield pushed his glasses up again and grinned. "A buddy of mine over at Channel 12 called me a few minutes ago. He said one of his stringers shot some footage of you getting pissed on and hexed by some bag lady this morning. Got the sound and everything."

"She didn't piss on me. She pissed on my car."

"Channel 12 is using it as the opening footage for their

upcoming story on how the public hates the IRS."

"They're going to do what?" Granger yelled. "Gallen, if you have any influence over there, you'd better use it."

"Way to go, Gallen," Rick Garrety said with a sneer.

Tim returned his sneer and watched as Garrety blew another irritating bubble with his gum. He wondered if Garrety set up the whole incident with the bag lady. The woman was probably Garrety's girlfriend.

"Merriefield, Kipp, get back over to your chairs," Granger said. "This place is more like Romper Room than a division of the United States Treasury."

Merriefield and Kipp reluctantly returned to their usual seats.

"Okay, guys, settle down, we've got some new procedures I need to review with you, but before I do, I want to update you on some administrative issues. As you know, we were supposed to have moved into our new offices by now, but it looks like the asbestos removal is taking longer than expected. So, today security will be installing a pass card lock on the CID entrance. You will each get a pass card, which you'll need to open the door. A little reminder: just like the pass cards we used in our old offices, there is a fifty-dollar fee to replace a lost card.

"Additionally, budgets have been real tight around here, and I'm sorry to say that the investigative aides we were hoping to hire were not approved."

General groans came from the group. They'd heard this news before.

"So I need you all to make an extra effort to keep your expenses under control. Fewer requisitions are going to be approved, and I don't want to hear any whining about it."

"Great," said a voice from underneath Bob Schaefer's mustache. "We're out there busting our humps trying to get major drug players off the streets while Congress flies around the country on golf junkets. Yet we're spending too much money. Look at this place. These prehistoric yellow chairs belong in the Smithsonian. This Annex is a dump, and we get no respect."

"Hey," Kipp said, "if you wanted respect, why'd you join the IRS?"

"Yeah," Merriefield said, "nobody pisses on FBI cars."

"Or if they do," Kipp said with a grin at Tim, "they never do it twice, and it never makes the six o'clock news."

"If Abbott and Costello are finished?" Granger said. "I am pleased to report that our very own Tim Gallen had the lowest expense report in the region last month."

Tim stood up and patted himself on the back.

"Yeah," Merriefield said, "but your No-Doz expenses to stay awake and read all those financial statements set a new world record. You've got to get yourself back into the action, Gallen!"

"Hey," Tim said, "just because I haven't kicked in a door lately doesn't mean I'm not doing my part for God and country."

"All right, all right, let's all play nice, shall we, and remember we're special agents for a few minutes?" Granger said. "I can't believe they give you guys guns. The bottom line is that the last few major cases we've prosecuted have fallen through for one reason or another."

"Well, if we could get a surgeon to remove the broomstick that's stuck up the Assistant U.S. Attorney's ass," mumbled Kipp who had just lost a case that had so much evidence the defendant should have been convicted even if the prosecutor didn't show up.

". . . and we could use some good publicity. So Gallen or Garrety, if either of you need help on your cases that are about to go to trial, let me know."

"This is all Gallen's fault, isn't it?" Merriefield said. "He's the one who got the hex this morning, and now it's affecting the whole damn department."

Merriefield was still sitting precariously on the edge of his chair. With a quick nudge, Tim sent him toppling to the floor. Granger ignored the hoots and hollers that followed.

"Additionally, the semiannual workload reviews are coming up, so I want to remind you that your diaries detailing your daily time and activities need to be up-to-date."

Ed passed out copies of the Service's new computer security policy to each of the agents. For the next thirty minutes he updated them on the changes that would be implemented. Finally, he said, "If no one has any further questions, then I've got to run to a presentation I'm giving this morning—"

"To encourage voluntary compliance," the agents yelled in unison.

"I'll be back in about two hours, if anyone needs me." Ed grabbed his notes and left.

Meetings at CID were the exception rather than the rule since undercover work and surveillance caused the agents to work such varied hours. After Ed left, most of the agents stayed to swap the latest stories and finish their coffee. Tim didn't mention the bribe to anyone, but he wished he could have talked to Ed.

He chatted briefly with some of the agents, but he couldn't concentrate on what anyone was saying. He mumbled something about needing to check his messages and returned to his office. He had a few voice mail messages but nothing from Inspection. He called John Corbin again.

This time John's voice mail message said he was out of the office until this afternoon.

Tim hung up the phone without leaving another message. He was surprised a two-million-dollar bribe didn't warrant an immediate return phone call.

Tim turned on his computer and typed in his statement concerning Cleon's visit while the meeting was still fresh in his mind. He saved the file and shut the computer down.

He called John Corbin again, left a third message ask-

Chapter 7

Behind Maggie's desk the squawk box, a direct audio connection to Hamilton's New York office, started the 10:05 morning call. Various Hamilton analysts explained why their recommendations from yesterday didn't happen and what to expect from today and tomorrow.

"Bonds were trading lower in response to interest rate pressure. Several blue chip stocks were off . . . and utility stocks were responding to. . . . Even a pregnancy takes nine months, so don't give up on your holdings now."

Maggie reached over and turned the sound down. Across the aisle she could see a few of the older brokers mulling about and exchanging analyses. The younger brokers didn't have time for trends and projections. They needed trades they could do today.

Stacy stuck her head in Maggie's office. "Your mother is on line one."

Maggie picked up the phone. "Hi, mom."

"Hi, honey, your father's on the extension."

"Hi, dad."

"What's wrong? You sound down."

"It's nothing," Maggie said. "I'm just having a bad day. No, make that a bad month. Oh, what the hell, I'm having a bad year."

"Now, Maggie, I'm sure it's not that bad," he said.

Maggie switched the phone to her other ear and checked her watch. She was sure her parents didn't want to know that a meeting she was about to have would determine whether she lost her job and went to debtor's prison or became broker of the year and went shopping at Neiman's. She offered the most benign excuse for her mood she could think of. "I broke my bra strap and I think it's affecting my perspective."

"Well, I think you're just working too hard," her mother said. "But we have some news to cheer you up. We got settled in over the weekend, and would you believe we even walked down to the beach this morning? It's just gorgeous here. We're playing bridge later today with the Higginbothams. Remember them? I think you went to school with their youngest girl."

"We can't thank you enough for your help," her father said.

Earlier in the year Maggie's parents lost the majority of their life savings to a con artist who convinced them that exporting Texas longhorn cattle to China was the wave of the future. Not wanting to bother their daughter with the knowledge of their venture, they entrusted over $500,000 to a man named Rob Stahl. Maggie always wondered where *60 Minutes* found senile seniors who gave away their nest eggs and now she knew. Honestly, Rob Stahl? He sounded like a Dick Tracy villain.

As an only child, it was up to Maggie to help fill in the gaps for her parents' financial loss.

Her mother had been talking nonstop, and Maggie tuned back in to hear, "You're just going to have to stop working so hard and come down for a visit."

"Mom, I'm really kind of in the middle of something right now. Can I call you back tonight?"

"That's fine. We were just trying to use your 800 number at work so you wouldn't have to run your phone bill up. We love you, honey."

"We sure do," her father said.

"Okay, I'll talk to you tonight."

Maggie hung up the phone and was going to go the bathroom to fix her bra strap when Stacy told her Mr. Goldwyn had arrived. Maggie straightened her Donna Karan beige suit and checked for Oreo remnants in her teeth while Stacy went to gather refreshments for the meeting. Then Maggie walked with lopsided breast support to greet the account that was going to save her career.

Standing in the middle of the lobby dressed in a white polo shirt, green plaid shorts, and black knee socks, Stanley Goldwyn was an orchestra of nervous tics. Maggie shook his soft, clammy hand and then escorted Mr. Goldwyn to the conference room. She closed the door, took a deep breath, and sat down beside him.

"Well, Mr. Goldwyn, after months of research I think I've put together a portfolio plan that will diversify your $9.5 million in a conservative manner while still giving you growth opportunities." Maggie tried to remain calm and hoped she didn't have drool coming down her chin in the shape of dollar signs. "I've reserved a block of municipal bonds with the muni-traders. If you'll endorse your check, I'll have it deposited. Then I'd like to start updating you on the current annuity rates and review some limit orders on the stocks we've been talking about."

Mr. Goldwyn rubbed his knuckles, unable to meet her eyes. Something was wrong.

"I sure do want to thank you for all your time and effort you've spent on this," he said in a feathery, southern voice. He gestured at the master plan sprawled across the conference table. "It really has been fun putting it together."

"That's what I'm here for, but the fun part is just beginning."

Mr. Goldwyn's hands were trembling now, and she noticed his eyes starting to water up.

"There's . . . there's something I've got to tell you," he said. "I've tried several times, but I've got to do it today or else."

"Mr. Goldwyn, what is it? What is there to get upset about? Everything is going to work out just like we planned." She threw all her effort into getting a smile on her face. "We've selected some very conservative investments, so if it's the market volatility you are concerned about—"

"No," he whispered. "Maggie, I don't know how to tell you this."

"Is there a problem with the sale of your business? Do you want me to contact the attorney? If it's just another delay we can work around that."

Please God, not another delay.

Mr. Goldwyn was silent for a long time. Then, focusing what seemed like all his effort, he said, "There is no attorney," and crumpled onto the table in tears.

"Mr. Goldwyn, calm down. Everything is going to be fine." Feeling the need to do something, anything, she stood beside him, gently rubbing his frail shoulders. "Now take a deep breath, count to ten, and tell me what you're talking about."

Slowly his breathing became more regular. She returned to her seat and waited for him to speak.

"Maggie, there is no attorney," he said at last. "I don't own a business. There aren't any sale proceeds. I don't have nine-and-a-half-million to invest."

"But all these months. . . ."

"I'm sorry. It started by accident. The first time I came in here . . . I had some time to kill and thought it would be fun to pretend I was loaded." His words picked up speed as he spoke. "But you were so excited and so helpful, I couldn't keep myself from coming back. And then I started gambling down at the riverboats, spending everything I owned, trying to win a big jackpot so I could have some money for you to invest. And. . . ." He took a big gasp of air, "now I'm broke and somehow I have to explain to my wife that our retirement money, our money for a rainy day, everything, is all gone. My God, I've taken out a second mortgage on our home, all because of my gambling. I just couldn't stop myself. I kept thinking that after all that money, surely the next game would be the winner. I don't know what to do. I'm going to have to declare bankruptcy."

He dissolved into tears again. The clocks on the wall ticking the time in New York, Chicago, Los Angeles, and Japan all refused to stop ticking.

"This means I'll be fired," she said.

"Oh, no, I can't let you lose your job. I'll talk to your boss and explain it's all my fault. I promise I'll fix it."

Sure, Arthur would understand.

Chapter 8

Tim met with the reporter and her producer at Channel 12. He pleaded with them not to include the bag lady footage in their IRS report. They responded with the mercy of a snake with a mouse in its mouth. Part of the footage was already airing as a promo.

Before going back to work, Tim decided to make a quick trip to a Smoothie King for one of their fruit concoctions. Unfortunately, the closest Smoothie King was about fifteen minutes away in the opposite direction from his office. The healthy refreshment was worth the drive because after the morning he had, he needed rejuvenating.

He checked his voice mail using his cell phone, and there was still no message from John Corbin. He called Corbin again and left a fourth message saying he was surprised a message concerning a two-million-dollar bribe didn't deserve a return phone call. He flipped his phone shut, which ended the call. He started to regret the sarcastic tone of his message to the chief of Inspection, but then the Smoothie King drive-up speaker interrupted his thoughts and asked him what he wanted to order. He asked for a black cherry, papaya, and banana drink mixture. Usually the fruit drink helped him clear his mind and relax.

He took several long drinks while he steered his car back onto the highway. He reached cruising speed, and then traffic slowed as road construction forced four lanes into two. Another mile and traffic stopped completely. Ten minutes passed and nobody moved. Concrete construction barriers on both sides of the highway prevented anyone from escaping the traffic jam. A fire truck and several ambulances raced by, using the now empty, oncoming lanes of traffic.

He turned on the radio and waited for a traffic report. Twenty minutes later an announcer said a tractor trailer carrying chickens had jackknifed along with two other trucks in the "cattle chute" section of the highway. He turned the radio off when the radio show host started making fowl traffic jokes. He picked up his cell phone and called his voice mail once again. No message yet from Corbin. He tossed the phone on the passenger's seat and then drank the last of his fruit drink. He wasn't going anywhere for awhile.

At twelve o'clock Tim was still stuck in traffic.

"Ah, monsieur, we have your favorite table waiting for you as always. Are you dining alone?" he said as he grabbed a rumpled brown bag from the passenger's side floor.

"Yes, Louie, alone as usual," he answered himself.

"Monsieur, do not fret, for today our chef has prepared one of your favorites," he said, lowering his voice teasingly. From the bag he removed two napkins, an apple, and an insulated sandwich container. He draped one napkin over his lap and set the other on the passenger's seat.

"He has prepared a naughty little peanut butter and jelly sandwich that is to die for," he said, popping his mouth twice. He opened the container and removed the sandwich, then wiped out the container before putting it back into the bag. "Bon appetit."

He sank his teeth into the slightly stale sandwich. One of the downsides of being a bachelor was that he never seemed to finish a loaf of bread before a green growth appeared.

The sandwich devoured, he rubbed the apple on his shirt and contemplated the man he would be sending to jail for income tax evasion and/or bribery. Tim surprisingly found himself liking the old scoundrel. It was almost a pity to put him away, assuming he didn't die before he got convicted.

Cleon, like so many others before him, had brought this mess on himself. The facts of the case didn't tell him much. Cleon seemed to have led an ordinary life for such a rich man. He didn't surface in the St. Louis papers until five years ago. It was then Cleon had started selling his assets and making huge donations to charities. Cleon sold several vacation homes, a Kansas City restaurant famous for its ribs, a dozen fine paintings, and all of his other business interests except for his taxidermy business in south St. Louis, which included the Stuffing Stuff showroom and the farm where he did the actual mounting. Cleon appeared to be systematically liquidating the holdings he had taken a lifetime to acquire while filing obviously false returns.

Tim tossed the apple core back into the brown bag.

Yes, Cleon had all but hung himself. And now he had made his situation even worse with the two-million-dollar bribe. Hopefully, Cleon's conviction for bribery would repair any damage to his career caused by the homeless woman television footage.

Tim picked up his cell phone to check his voice mail again. He punched in the number but when he pressed "send," the phone went dead. He fished around in the back seat for his phone charger that plugged into the cigarette lighter. Nothing. He felt under the seat. Still nothing. He drummed his fingers on the steering wheel and tried to remember where he had last seen the charger. It was in his briefcase, which was back in his office.

He got out of his car and tried to get a look at what was going on down the road, but he couldn't see anything except other drivers doing the same thing. Although it was a bright, sunny day, he half expected to get hit by a renegade bolt of lightning while he stood there. Getting struck by lightning was the only thing missing from the banner day he was having.

He got back in his car, slammed the door closed, and suddenly became extremely anxious. Why hadn't Inspection returned his calls? Had Cleon made a doughnut delivery to someone there as well? Inspection usually wanted to work with an agent for several days before an agent went to a pay-off meeting. They needed time to brief the agent and role-play all sorts of situations as well as get the clearance necessary to use surveillance equipment and scout the meeting location.

With Tim's meeting less than six hours away there were a million things that needed to be done. And he was stranded in traffic. Right when he thought his frustration level would induce a brain aneurysm, traffic began to inch forward.

It was after two o'clock when Tim made it back to his office. Donna was away from her desk and the office seemed quiet. He opened his door and found John Corbin sitting in his chair. Arliss Thomas, an Inspection agent Tim knew of but had never met, was sitting where Cleon had sat this morning. Ed Granger was leaning on Tim's desk. The two men from Inspection looked hostile; Ed looked plain worried.

John Corbin spoke first. "Is there something you would like to tell us?"

"Yeah, you suck at returning phone calls."

The inquisition began: Who scheduled the meeting with Cummings? How did Cummings get into Tim's office? What exactly did Cummings say? How did Tim respond? Why did Tim leave this morning? Where did he go? Who could substantiate his visit to Channel 12? Why did it take so long for him to get back? How could he have been stuck in traffic when the accident was north of the station? Who could vouch for his visit to the Smoothie store? Why didn't he answer his cell phone? Why didn't he tell Ed about the bribe this morning?

Tim carefully answered each of their questions but couldn't figure out why the men were acting as if he was guilty.

"Why did you wait until your third message to Inspection to mention the bribe?" Corbin said.

Tim's voice exploded in the small office. "I left four messages! My first message to John was a very long, detailed account of my meeting with Cummings. I made that call the moment Cummings walked out of my office. My message was so long that the system even cut me off at the end."

"I never got it," Corbin said. The other Inspection agent nodded in confirmation.

"After my first message, I called a second time to confirm that you received my first message. Then, I called a third time and left my cell phone number since I hadn't heard back from you. Finally, I left a fourth message saying how surprised I was that a two-million-dollar bribe didn't warrant a return phone call."

"I only got the last three," Corbin said. "When I called your cell phone it just rang and rang."

"Then how did you know it was Cummings who made the bribe—"

Ed Granger joined the conversation. "Donna told me she walked in on your meeting and saw a briefcase filled with cash. We called the station, and they said you left around nine-thirty. When the hours passed and we couldn't locate you, we became a little concerned."

Tim's mouth gaped open in shock. "So that's what this is about? You think I took the money and then disappeared?"

Granger stood up. "Let's slow down everyone," he said, raising his hands in the air.

"Thanks for the goddamn vote of confidence."

"We never got your first message," Corbin repeated.

Granger became the voice of reason. "A bribe is always unnerving. And one this size makes everyone a little on edge. I'm sure someone at Smoothie King will corroborate your visit and making that visit on Service time is something we can discuss later."

Tim started to say something in defense but Granger kept talking.

"It's unfortunate, Tim, that your first message wasn't received. Although I did tell you to go to the station and see what you could do about the footage, I'm not sure that was the best course of action given the circumstances." Granger looked around the room to make eye contact with each man as he spoke. "I'm at least comfortable that Tim did follow procedure. Right now I think what we've got to focus on is that we've got a limited amount of time to prepare for this meeting and the only way we're going to get Cummings on bribery is if we all work together."

Corbin, whose vote was really the only one that mattered, nodded his head in agreement.

Tim spent the next half hour providing everyone with background information on Cleon's tax situation and recent indictment. Then he turned on his computer and printed out his notes from this morning. Again he repeated all the details he remembered from the meeting.

The three men absorbed everything Tim said, asking questions occasionally to clarify, but basically letting Tim talk. When he finished they reassured Tim that he said the right things to Cummings.

Tim recounted his meeting with Cleon in an affidavit, and they began developing an investigative workplan.

Corbin picked up the phone to call the U.S. Attorney's office when Dwight barged into the office.

"This woman from Shearson I've been trying to get a

date with called me," Dwight blurted out. He didn't seem to care that Ed and the guys from Inspection were in Tim's office.

"We're in the middle of something here, Dwight," Ed said. "Can you save the Casanova report for another time? But we need to talk to you—"

"She called because she saw that promo of Tim running on Channel 12," Dwight said, still out of breath.

Tim glared hard at Dwight. "Thanks for sharing that with me. It really puts my day—"

"If you would shut up for a minute. After she saw your promo, she remembered processing some subpoenas for you on Cleon Cummings's accounts."

"And. . . . ?"

"And she called to tell me that Friday, Cleon liquidated his holdings, all forty million dollars of them, and made arrangements with a bank to have them paid out in cash. I queried the Currency & Banking Retrieval System. In a three-day period, there are a dozen Suspicious Activity Reports of Cleon withdrawing just under ten thousand in cash. Then, five days later, there are about twenty Currency Transaction Reports showing Cleon Cummings having millions of dollars paid out in cash. I'm sure more CTRs will show once the fifteen-day filing deadline gets closer. I checked with the rest of the banks and brokerage houses we subpoenaed, and, from what I can tell, all the accounts we requested statements from are closed. Zero balances. All paid out in cash wherever possible."

"All of them?" Tim's voice broke slightly.

"All of the ones I've contacted so far. I think he's even sold the taxidermy showroom and his farm. I haven't been able to find out anything on the Hamilton Securities account or the account he has up in Kirksville."

Tim sat there digesting the news. If Cleon closed all his accounts then he was probably on this way out of the country by now, taking the remaining shreds of Tim's career with him. But if he planned to bolt, why offer Tim the bribe?

Granger asked for Cleon's home phone number and dialed it. The phone rang twelve times without an answer. At least the phone wasn't disconnected.

Maybe there was still time.

Chapter 9

There *are few things more disgusting than getting sick in a pubic bathroom*, Maggie thought as she held on to the toilet paper dispenser and tried to keep her French braid out of the way of her vomiting. The cold sweat that ran down her back began to dry as the retches subsided to dry heaves.

She flushed the toilet handle with her foot, covered the seat with toilet paper as she had been instructed to do since she was five, and sat down, holding her head in her hands. She could hear the sound of the auctioneer's gavel bringing the crowd to order as bidding began on the sale of her parents' condo. Her mother and father stood on the front lawn, underneath the palm tree, like the one pictured in the brochure.

"What will the neighbors think?" her mother would ask.

Her father would respond flatly, trying not to be emotional. "They're not our neighbors anymore."

Maggie would want to be there to comfort them, but

she would be in jail for having $25,000 on her credit cards and no way to pay it.

She stood up, wiped her mouth, tossed the paper, and then flushed again. She couldn't spend the rest of the day sulking in the bathroom. She stood at the sink scrubbing her hands and surveying her face. Her tears had washed away most of her makeup, leaving white blotches accented with a red nose and eyes.

She splashed some cold water on her face and began to repair the damage. Arthur was not going to win.

Ten minutes later she was at her desk, staring through her open doorway at the bullpen. Most of the cubicles were empty, a testament to Arthur's lousy leadership and the difficulty of being a broker.

There had to be a client who could do some business for her. She paged through her holding book, which detailed each client's transactions. But as she turned the pages, she could hear each client's objections in her head: "The market's too high. I think interest rates are going higher. I'm waiting for Saturn to align with Mars. I saw on the Internet that. . . ."

She leaned back in her chair. That indomitable attitude had not lasted long. How many boxes would it take to pack up her office?

The telephone interrupted her self-pity.

"Magpie, it's Cleon again." His voice was strained.

"Hi, Cleon, what's up?" She pulled his account up on the computer. The wire transfer hadn't taken place.

"I just checked with my bank in the Caymans and they're telling me they never received the money."

"I'm sorry, I'm looking at your account now and for some reason it didn't go through." Maggie checked her watch. It was almost four o'clock and any transfer now would not be credited until tomorrow. "Cleon, hold on, let me check with the Operations Department."

Maggie called Ops and listened to three different wire operators tell her they didn't know what she was talking about. No one had received the wire order.

"Cleon, Operations doesn't know what happened." She fidgeted with a letter opener and chipped her manicure. "We can send the wire again, but it's after hours. It won't get credited to your account until tomorrow."

"Tomorrow is too late. I need to get that account out of my name today. Is Arthur still in?"

"No, he went to a seminar this morning and hasn't come back yet. Why? Do you think he's involved with this?"

Cleon didn't answer her. "Do me a favor. Would you switch to the phone in one of your conference rooms? I'd rather not have anyone overhear our conversation."

"Cleon, your privacy is protected. I don't need to switch phones."

"Please, Maggie. Just do this one thing for me."

She agreed and transferred the call to a conference room.

"Anyway," Cleon said, "wiring the money tomorrow will be too late. What else can we do? I've got to make sure that account is zeroed out today."

"I'm sorry, I don't know. I'm not up on the latest money laundering techniques."

"Hey, that's an idea. How 'bout if I transfer the money to you for a few days and then you could transfer it back to me? That might work."

"Except the Securities and Exchange Commission would have this place crawling with people. They generally frown on brokers commingling their clients' funds."

"Okay, how about this? Transfer my balance into a new account in the name of Penelope P. Penderpot and make sure it happens today. Then, first thing tomorrow morning, wire the funds to my Cayman account."

"Cleon, Penelope P. Penderpot was the name of your favorite potbellied pig."

"Damn it, Margaret, what are you, the oldest freaking girl scout?"

Maggie caught her breath. Cleon raising his voice was

about as common as Mother Teresa participating in wet T-shirt contests.

"I'm sorry Cleon, I—"

"Look, we're talking about a good bit of pocket change. I'd rather not see it fall into the wrong set of grubby little hands."

"I don't understand. Whose grubby hands? Tell me what's going on."

"I'm going to say this one more time." His words were slow and deliberate. "Transfer my balance into a new account and title it in Penelope's name. Then, no matter what happens, tomorrow I want you to wire the funds to the Cayman account I gave you. Promise me, no matter what."

Maggie looked at the Goldwyn file Stacy had returned. Maybe what Cleon was asking didn't matter. Of course it violated a variety of Hamilton and SEC rules to knowingly falsify an account, but the way her career was going she wouldn't be around to suffer the consequences.

"Fine, hold on for a minute and I'll get an account number for you." She put Cleon on hold, called the Operations Department for a new account number, and then returned to Cleon. "All right, fax me a letter of authorization saying you want to transfer the balance of your account number 685-49934 to a new account number 685-76601. You should state in the letter that you absolve all ownership of the assets."

"It's on its way," he answered and hung up.

Ten minutes later Stacy gave Maggie Cleon's fax. Maggie looked at the letter, said goodbye to Cleon's three million, and handed it back to her with instructions to make sure the transfer was done today. Stacy disappeared to handle the transfer, and Maggie started searching her desk for a new account form. While she was searching for Penelope's form, Christine Sable and Bill Farley moped into her office and dumped themselves into chairs.

"We saw your name on Arthur's required attendance list for his cold-calling sessions," Christine said. "Did you forget to give Arty his morning blow job? Is that why he's so cranky?" She looked like she had just walked off the tennis court with a perfect tan, perfect legs, and perfect blond hair.

"Arthur's got me on a new boot camp program to increase my production."

"You've got to stop prospecting those nursing homes so your clients will stop dying on you," Bill said.

"Very funny."

"You know," Christine said, "all last week I had this I'm-going-to-win-the-lottery-on-Saturday attitude, and it's making this Monday particularly unbearable."

"Hey, maybe you're onto something, Chris," Bill said. "What if we sold our clients out of their holdings and moved them into lottery tickets?"

"You'd only do it if there was a four-percent commission on lottery tickets."

"I've had enough gambling and lottery talk for one morning. Can we change the subject?" Maggie said.

"God, what's wrong with you? You're acting like you ran out of tampons at two in the morning."

"Nothing. Nothing is wrong." Maggie realized she was out of new account forms and stopped looking. "Chris, do you happen to have a safety pin in your purse? I broke my bra strap."

"God, I hate that," Bill said. "There's nothing worse than losing a good bra."

Chris dug through her purse a moment, then triumphantly displayed a four-inch diaper pin. "Tah dah."

"What am I supposed to do with that?"

"It's all I could find. Sorry."

"Great! With my luck I'll probably puncture my lung." Maggie flung the Goldwyn file into the trash and headed toward the bathroom. When she returned she verified that Cleon's balance had been transferred into the new account. Tomorrow she would write up the paperwork for the new Penelope account and make sure the wire transfer went through. Tomorrow she would also have to make up for the two hundred cold calls she didn't make today. And hope that one of them just happened to have a couple of million to invest.

But for now she was going to put a fork in this day and head to the gym.

As Maggie walked out the back door, Arthur walked in the front door of Hamilton Securities. He had attended a seminar on how to handle people with tact and skill, or at least that's what his alibi would be. Ten minutes into the seminar he excused himself to use the rest room. With more than one hundred boneheads in attendance, no one noticed whether or not he actually sat through the mind-numbing lecture. He returned five hours later when the speaker was handing out worthless certificates of completion to everyone.

He snatched his phone messages, grabbed a stack of confirmations from trades placed earlier, and shut himself in his office. He rushed to his computer to make sure Cleon's balance was where he left it. Arthur typed in the account number and waited for the balance to appear.

Zero.

He retyped the account number.

The zero balance stayed the same.

A ringing telephone interrupted his shock, and he responded by hurling it across the room. Or at least halfway—the cord snapped taught and the phone fell in a jumbled mess in the middle of the carpet.

His secretary burst into the office. "Mr. Riley, is everything all right?"

"Get out!"

"But Mr. Riley—"

"I said get out!"

"But Operations needs to talk with you about your overdue margin calls."

Arthur yanked his stubby body to his feet, pursed his mouth into a Tasmanian devil snarl, and pointed toward the door. The secretary retreated from the office.

He punched in a series of key strokes on the computer and located Cleon's money. Maggie had transferred Cleon's balance into a new, unnamed account. He collapsed into his chair. He had spent the morning running errands and making arrangements with Mr. Smith, but Maggie's account transfer changed everything, for the better. She had just made stealing Cleon's millions a little bit easier.

Chapter 10

"**This** is 911, what is your emergency?"

"I've been poisoned! He poisoned me and stole all of my money. You've got to help me."

"What is your name, sir?"

"Please, you've got to help me. He's poisoned me and taken all of my money."

"Okay sir, calm down. We'll send a medical unit out to you, but I need your name and address first."

"It's Cleon Cummings. I live at 9605 Silver River Drive in South County, but you've got to hurry."

"Okay, Cleon, help is on the way. What kind of poison did you take?"

"The kind that kills, you idiot. Oh my God, I'm a dead man. The iris poisoned me and now I'm a dead man."

"Cleon, listen to me. Are you listening? It's going to be all right. Now what form of poison did you take? You say it's an iris, like the flower?"

"He must have put it in my tea. Oh my God, my heart

is going to pound out of my chest. Can you hear it? Please! You've got to help me."

"Cleon? Cleon! Listen to me. You're going to pull through this. We'll do it together, but you've got to pay attention—"

"I'm sooo hot and my mouth is so dry."

The phone clamored to the floor.

"Cleon, are you there? Pick up the phone."

"Please make my heart stop beating like that. Can you hear it? My God, it's so loud. It's going to explode out of my chest. Please somebody, make it stop. Damn him for poisoning me. I knew he wanted my money but I never thought he'd do this. . . . don't let Arthur get the money!"

"Cleon, pick up the phone!"

"Essie, is that you? Please help me, Essie, I'm so hot."

"Sir, you've got to try to vomit if you can."

"I've got to have water."

"Sir, calm down. Help is on the way. Sir? . . . Hello? . . . Hello?"

Chapter 11

The five-man IRS team, joined by the efforts of every agent they could commandeer help from, accomplished in a few frantic hours what normally took days or weeks to get approved through the system.

The plan was simple. Tim and Dwight were each outfitted with a wireless video camera disguised as a pager. The two agents would meet with Cleon and try to get him to repeat the bribery offer while inside Cleon's home. If Cleon would only discuss the bribe if the men went swimming, Tim would explain that they were on call and it would arouse suspicion if they didn't respond to a page. If Cleon wouldn't allow them to bring the pagers and insisted on swimming, then the two agents would rely on the Inspection surveillance team. The Inspection team would be camouflaged and positioned across the river. They would record the bribe offer using an omnidirectional microphone and a parabolic dish. This was the least favorite option since outside noises—an airplane, the river, etc.—made recording conversation much more difficult.

If Tim and Dwight managed to get Cleon to repeat his offer, bribery would be added to the many counts against Cleon, and he would be arrested. If, for some reason, they were unable to get the offer recorded, Cleon would be arrested for smurfing—making multiple withdrawals from banks of just under $10,000 in cash, to avoid causing the banks to file currency transaction reports. The structuring laws under Title 31 made smurfing punishable by a fine and/or imprisonment. Cleon's case would be considered an aggravated case with an enhanced penalty carrying a fine of not more than $500,000, imprisonment of not more than ten years, or both.

All of these charges were in addition to the felony tax evasion charges he faced and the huge tax bill he still owed.

One way or another, Cleon was going to jail tonight. Assuming, of course, that their little convoy made it to Cleon's in time.

The telephone repair truck in front of them contained the Inspection team that would be doing the undercover surveillance. Then there was Tim and Dwight's car. Behind them was a white cargo van with four more agents who would assist when it was time to make the arrest. No one had mentioned the Ford Taurus, three vehicles back, that had been trailing along since they left the office.

Tim checked his watch for the fifth time in as many minutes.

"Give your wrist a break," Dwight said. "We're going to get him, stop worrying."

Tim didn't answer. He guessed Inspection had probably bugged the car. It was standard procedure to keep an agent under surveillance before, during, and after a bribery meeting.

He cracked his knuckles to relieve some of his tension. The afternoon had been nonstop faxes, phone calls, forms, and meetings. Everyone broke bureaucratic land speed records so Tim and Dwight could make Cleon's meeting. The moment the arrest warrant was issued and the electronic monitoring approved, the entire crew bolted to their vehicles only to have Tim and Dwight stopped by three Inspection agents. Tim and Dwight were searched as was Dwight's car. All personal items and monies were inventoried in a statement Dwight and Tim each signed. The delay made them late for the meeting. It didn't help that the surveillance crew also got a late start caused by some equipment malfunctions.

Dwight turned onto Silver River Drive as the summer sunset pulled storm clouds in to fill its absence. The white back-up van followed them a little way and then eased to the side of the road. For now, Tim couldn't see the Ford Taurus but guessed it wasn't too far away. The telephone repair truck had continued down the main road so they could set up across the river.

"What's the address we're looking for again?" Dwight said.

"9605."

Dwight steered the car around a sharp curve. "It's probably the one with the squad cars and ambulances jammed in the driveway."

"What?"

"Cleon's house looks like OJ's place on the morning after. So much for our grand plan." Dwight let out a long whistle and parked the car on the front lawn near the rest. "Boy, that's some industrial-sized-hex you have. Even Channel 8 News is here."

Tim went searching for the officer in charge of the scene and found Sergeant Tom Zahorchak being interviewed by a Channel 8 reporter. Tim waited with his back to the pair, pretending not to listen. A paramedic approached carrying the red tackle box of his trade and motioned Tim to leave the property.

Tim flashed his credentials. "I'm here to arrest Cleon Cummings."

The tired medic laughed. "Well, as soon as we pull his

body out of the river, we'll give it to you to cuff."

"He drowned?"

"He went down like the *Titanic*. When we got here he was jumping around on the dock down there. From all his ranting and raving I think he was hallucinating pretty badly. He jumped in the river before we could get to him. By the time we dived in after him, the current must have sucked him away. They've got dogs going up and down the banks without any luck. There are scuba divers down there looking too, but we're about out of daylight. If they don't find him tonight, I'm sure he'll float eventually."

Tim looked down at the river bank quietly being engulfed in darkness. "When did this happen?"

" 'Bout an hour and a half ago."

Sergeant Zahorchak finished his interview and started toward the house when Tim caught up with him. "I understand Cleon Cummings is presumed drowned."

"What's it to you?" the sergeant said, rubbing his stomach and looking eager to get home for dinner.

Tim explained the circumstances surrounding the warrant for Cummings as they walked toward the house. Before the officer and Tim entered the home they put on rubber gloves to maintain the integrity of the crime scene.

"Don't touch anything in here, we're still dusting."

Inside, officers scurried like ants at a picnic—taking pictures, dusting for fingerprints, and recording measurements. But even amidst the noise and hustle, the house seemed eerily empty. Boxes filled with everything imaginable and labeled accordingly stood guard in deserted rooms. All the pictures had been removed from the walls. The furniture was covered with white sheets, waiting for the Salvation Army truck.

A mounted deer's head in the family room stared at the men working in the kitchen. The kitchen was spotless except for the sink, which held a tea cup, saucer, and tea strainer. The contents from the cabinets and drawers had already been boxed up and moved out.

A man wearing gloves took the cup from the sink and

carefully drained the few remaining drops of tea into a vial. Tim turned in time to see another gloved man carrying an opened tin of tea. As the man walked by, Tim got a glimpse of the container's purple-black contents. It looked like the same tin from his meeting with Cleon.

"As you can see," the sergeant said, "our victim wasn't a big eater."

"Any suspects?"

"Not yet."

"We passed an office off the living room. Do you mind if I take a look?"

"Go ahead. There's a computer on in there, an Apple. I happen to be an IBM man myself."

The sergeant led him to the office. Like the rest of the house, it had been packed up. The file cabinets were empty and draped with white sheets. The contents of the shelves had been cleared off and boxed up. The only life in the room came from computerized fish swimming across the monitor.

Still wearing his gloves, Tim moved the mouse and awoke the computer. He clicked on the hard drive icon and scrolled through the applications: Solitaire, Minesweeper, Jungle Adventure, Flight Simulator, and a host of other games. The only serious programs were UPS tracking software and the word processing application that came with the computer. He clicked on the word processor and got an error box stating the computer didn't have enough memory to open the application.

Tim's shoulders sagged. "I guess it was too much to hope for an accounting package of some kind. I don't see anything here, but you'll probably want to have someone take a more thorough look."

"Have you eaten?" the sergeant said.

Tim shook his head.

"If you have a strong stomach, there's something you gotta see. We've already searched the rest of the property and haven't found anything unusual, although those animals in the barn waiting to get stuffed are kind of creepy.

But this . . . it's the worst crime scene I've ever encountered."

Tim rubbed the stress collecting in his temples. "Lead on."

The sergeant escorted Tim to the back bedroom. "There."

All the room's furniture had been pushed to the corners. In its place was a huge mound of clear trash bags filled with shredded paper.

"What's the big deal about some shredded paper?" Tim said.

"Take a closer look."

Tim walked to an open trash bag beside the shredder, then dropped to his knees and ran his fingers through bits and pieces of paper. Here and there he could make out a serial number, an eye, or a nose. Cash. It was cash. The room was filled with bag after bag of shredded hundred dollar bills.

Tim realized he was now sitting down on the floor. "Who in their right mind would do such a thing?"

"I think the key words are 'right mind,' " the sergeant said.

"There's got to be millions and millions of dollars here."

The sergeant agreed. "More money than everyone in my department will make in our combined lifetimes. I'm not even sure how you'd get an exact count of the amount. Are you all right? I don't think I've ever seen an IRS agent so white."

"I'm fine."

Tim's beeper sounded. He recognized the page. It was Ed, and he wanted to see Tim immediately. Tim dusted the money shreds from his hands and left the house. He would be back once the police released the crime scene to check for any signs of traceable cash. Right now he needed to get back to his office and salvage his career.

Chapter 12

"**R**esist. Resist. Keep those tummies tucked in."

Maggie glared at the sadistic aerobics instructor wearing a dental floss leotard. The minute hand on the clock had stopped moving. The other women in the class seemed to be sucking all the air out of the room with each stomach crunch. Everyone was clad in cute little spandex outfits except Maggie, who was sporting on old pair of fuzzy shorts and a faded T-shirt promoting a marathon. She hadn't run in the marathon, but she had slept with a guy who did and, while she didn't remember his name, it was one of her favorite T-shirts.

"Three more," the instructor shouted above the belligerent bass from the overworked workout tape. "Three, two, one, and one more. That's it. Keep it going."

Learn to count.

"Last one. That's it everybody. Thanks for a great session." The instructor bounced to her feet, congratulated everyone and disappeared.

Maggie collapsed on the floor. In a feat more courageous than climbing Mt. Everest, she had dragged her butt off the couch and jogged the mile and a half to the gym. God, was the daily war against her two favorite foods—cheese and chocolate—really worth this punishment? All she wanted to do now was grab a quick shower and then boil herself in the hot tub. Soaking in the hot tub almost made the torturous workout worthwhile.

In the locker room, she dropped her clothes like a fireman and stepped into the shower. As she lathered she realized her legs were really getting hairy, but she didn't have a razor. She dried off and put on her favorite one-piece blue and white striped suit. It flattered her small waist while providing the support she needed at other spots. She glanced at her legs again. The gym was closing soon and there was a good chance the hot tub would be empty. She could risk a public viewing.

She left the locker room and walked toward the smell of chlorine. The tiled alcove with the hot tub wasn't empty. There was a man in his early thirties, soaking, his head tilted backward and his eyes closed. Moisture from the steam collected on his beard and mustache. Maggie quickly stepped into the hot tub and let the pulsating water envelop her. The splashing of the water caused her companion to sit up and open his eyes.

"Good workout?" he said.

"I'm not sure there is such a thing."

"Yeah, I know what you mean. If it weren't for those damn automatic membership payments getting charged to my Visa there's no way I'd be here."

Maggie winced remembering one more charge she couldn't pay. She closed her eyes and tilted back her head. Maybe he'd get the hint and let her brood in peace.

No such luck.

"Did you just finish the abs class?" he said.

Maggie pretended not to hear him over the sound of the bubbles.

"Did you just finish the abs class?" he said louder.

She kept her eyes closed. "That's right."

"You know, you should really be replacing your electrolytes after such an intense workout."

"I'll probably get a cheese pizza when I get home and call it even."

"I've got something you should try."

He stood up and reached for his gym bag. As he dug in the bag Maggie noticed the farmer's tan on his left arm didn't match his right. He handed her a plastic bottle of juice, and she accepted it as though it contained live bait.

"Go ahead," he said, "try it."

Maggie opened the bottle and sipped the lime-green liquid. It started off bitter but tasted better the more she drank.

"And this is?"

"It's a new drink called SportsAid. I drive a truck and deliver it to grocery stores and sports events like marathons. Every once in a while, a case breaks and I pick up some freebies."

Maggie looked at the bottle closer. "You know, I think I've tried this before and I don't remember it tasting like this."

The truck driver looked at Maggie as though she had divulged a corporate secret. "This is their new formula. It's not available to the public yet."

Maggie set the empty bottle aside and closed her eyes to avoid any further conversation with her hairy blue-collar companion.

"Well, my time is up," he said.

Maggie listened to him crawl out of the water and towel off.

"Have a good night," he said at last.

She nodded absently without opening her eyes. With no one else around, she could unwind and enjoy the pulsing bubbles. She couldn't remember when the hot tub had been so relaxing or she had been so tired. All the tension in her body felt like it was being pulled into the tub's filter. She slumped down to let the water flow over her shoulders.

Her hairdresser had said something about keeping her newly acquired "natural" auburn hair away from chemicals for another forty-eight hours, but she wasn't sure what day it was anymore. The warmth rose up her neck and around her chin. She tried to open her eyes and check the time on the clock but her body no longer responded to commands from her brain.

The water jet aimed at her lower back pushed her body out of the formed seat and into the center of the tub. There were no more thoughts of her hair turning green, her parents' condo deposit, Arthur, or Visa bills. Her head dropped into the water as she was pulled into a dark, peaceful place.

Someone was pounding on her stomach. In reaction her body tried to cough up the water that filled her stomach and lungs. That made it hard to sleep.

Hands from nowhere rolled her on her side, and the retching grew worse. Each convulsion made her stomach ache as though every rib was broken.

Finally she forced her eyes open and saw she was lying on the floor next to the hot tub, coughing and spitting in front of a small crowd. She really should have shaved her legs.

It seemed to take forever for her to regain her normal breathing. "What happened?" she whispered at last.

"Mike found you floating face down when he came to shut down the tub," the manager of the gym said. "He pulled you out and started doing CPR."

Someone wrapped a beach towel around her. She struggled to prop herself up.

"The ambulance is on its way," the manager said.

She pulled the towel closer. "No, I don't need an ambulance. I haven't eaten anything all day and I must have just passed out. I'll be fine."

"Look, I'm no doctor, but your pupils are as big as quarters. Something's wrong. You should have some medical attention."

Maggie thought about the $500 deductible her insurance required and opted to take her chances at home. "No, really. I'll be fine."

One of the women helped her into the locker room and waited while Maggie took a cold shower to try and shake the grogginess. Someone else gave her a ride home and by midnight she was in her own bed.

By morning the experience was a blurry memory.

Chapter **13**

His lungs filled with water.

The fight to breathe ended. His opened eyes and mouth formed a contorted grimace. He drifted silently, the scales on his body occasionally breaking the water's surface. A scuba diver below him continued a search for hidden treasure, oblivious to the death that had occurred inches above his head.

Tim peered into his fish bowl.

"Well, this is just great. I think this is the third goldfish I've killed." He turned the air pump off, allowing the scuba diver to rest. "And I really liked this one."

Ed Granger raised a questioning eyebrow.

"It did seem like he was trying to avoid me lately."

"Occupational hazard," Ed said.

Tim left the floating fish and sat down at his desk. It was almost midnight and the office was strangely quiet. No phones ringing. No agents arguing. Just mounds of paperwork and case files patiently waiting for their owners' attention in the morning.

Ed rubbed his eyes. He looked like he was trying to think of some encouraging words to offer Tim after tonight's disaster, but it was late and the coffee was probably no longer stimulating his brain.

Besides, there was no consolation. Cleon Cummings had turned $139 million into a ton of confetti.

"What's your schedule for tomorrow?" Ed said.

"I'm not sure. I'd like to do some follow-up. I'm not convinced all the money is gone." He prayed there was some left.

Ed sat for a moment drinking his coffee. "The two South County detectives working the Cummings case would like to talk to you in the morning. They reviewed the 911 tape, and they're now classifying it as a murder. Cummings told the 911 operator that he didn't want some guy named Arthur to get away with his money. He said his tea had been poisoned with iris. I guess you could hear Cummings's heart beating on the tape—he must have been really screwed up."

Tim tried to keep his voice level. "Poisoned?"

"Yeah, I'm sure in the autopsy they'll figure out exactly what kind of poison killed him."

"And you could hear his heart beat?"

"Not the way I'd want to go. Any idea who Arthur is?"

His mind raced as he thought about the visit from Cleon and his bribe. Cleon had brought tea to his office.

"Any ideas?" Ed said again.

"Arthur Riley is Cleon's disinherited son-in-law. Arthur killed Cleon's wife and Cleon's only daughter—Arthur's wife—in a car accident."

"Well, that will certainly get you disinherited. And that seems like a good reason to off a father-in-law. Although I guess anyone who knew what Cleon was up to would have a pretty good motive with all that cash sitting around waiting to be shredded." Ed handed Tim a business card. "Do me a favor and give this detective a call tonight and let him know where he can pick up the son-in-law. It's a good break that Cummings implicated his son-in-law before kicking, but because of his bribe offer, the detectives will probably want to interview you as well. Be prepared for their questions."

Tim nodded.

"This still seems odd. Here's an old coot who never once broke the law, and then all of a sudden he tries in a bizarre way to screw the IRS and it costs him his life." Tim was getting more uneasy the longer he thought about the case. "What makes someone do that? This guy was so clean he only had one parking ticket in his life . . . and he got that three weeks ago in Baltimore."

Ed was nodding sagely, but Tim could tell he was no longer listening. He had called Tim in for this late-night meeting, and Tim was still waiting to find out why. It was probably coming now.

Both men were quiet as Ed summoned the words he had to say.

"The really bad news is since we don't have Cleon to prosecute, the investigation into your actions this morning is probably going to be heavier than I'd hope," he said. "It's just too bad John didn't get that first voice mail from you."

Tim nodded but the word "poison" still gnawed at him.

"This has become a very high-profile case and I'm afraid of what the Keystone cops in Inspection might do from here. I'll do what I can to protect you, but you know how excitable they are. When all is said and done, you may find yourself reassigned as a case reviewer."

There it was, finally out in the open. It was time for Tim to start considering other career opportunities.

Ed said good night and left the office. Tim called the detective and left a voice mail message with Arthur's home phone and address. He should go home himself but instead he sat for about twenty minutes staring at the dead fish floating in the bowl. Something in the Cummings case was missing. . . .

He picked an empty coffee cup out of the trash to scoop out the fish's carcass. Just as the fish floated gracefully into the white Styrofoam coffin, Tim dropped the cup and grabbed the phone book. He ripped through the pages looking frantically for his bank's bank-by-phone number. He dialed the number and punched in his account code. The recording asked if he wanted to check his balance, transfer money, or some other function. Tim pressed one to check his balance.

"Two million, fifteen hundred dollars and seventeen cents. Thank you for banking with Federal Savings Bank. Goodbye."

The fifteen hundred hundred dollars was right. The two million wasn't.

He hung up and redialed.

"Two million, fifteen hundred dollars and seventeen cents. Thank you for banking with Federal Savings Bank. Goodbye."

Tim hung up the phone. He wouldn't have to wait for a lab to come back with the test results on Cleon's stomach. The bits of purple stuff he saw in the opened tea container at Cleon's was English nightshade. It had to be. The author on the poison radio show had described nightshade as causing audible heartbeats. How many things did that?

The detectives were misinterpreting what Cleon said on the 911 tape. Yes, Cleon didn't want Arthur to get the money, but it wasn't the iris he was blaming for the poison. It was the IRS.

Chapter **14**

On Tuesday morning, Maggie dragged her pounding head into the office to find a man she had never seen before sitting at her desk, scouring her account books. His face was so intense that if he was wearing a cowboy hat and jeans instead of a suit and tie he could have been a natural for a Marlboro man billboard.

Stacy's desk was empty even though it was after 8 a.m.

"Excuse me!" Her voice detonated the early morning stillness, and she cringed at the aftershocks ringing through her temples. "May I ask what the hell you're doing?" she said more quietly.

The man looked perfectly comfortable at being caught. "Good morning. My name is Tim Gallen. I'm a special agent with the Criminal Investigation Division of the Internal Revenue Service." He smiled and exposed two dimples that contrasted strangely with the small scar over his right eye. Then he presented his badge and picture ID.

"I don't care who the hell you are, you don't have the

right to help yourself to confidential information in my office. Now get out."

Two brokers walking by with coffee stared at Maggie losing her temper so early in the morning. She ignored them and walked past the agent to close the books he had opened.

He didn't leave. Instead, he took a seat next to her desk.

"Mr. Gallen was it?" she said. "Maybe I didn't make myself clear. I want you out of my office, out of this building. Now."

"Really Maggie, I just want to—"

"It's Ms. Connors."

"Okay, Ms. Connors," he said, leaning hard on the surname, "all I want to do is to ask you some questions about Cleon Cummings's account."

Cleon? Maggie's gut clenched. She assumed the agent was here to investigate Vito Barruso, a client the IRS had visited her about previously.

Gallen took a pen out of his shirt pocket and opened a note pad. "Now, how long was Cleon a client of yours?"

"You seem to be missing the point here, Mr. Gallen." Her head throbbed with the echo of each syllable. "Cleon hasn't authorized me to disclose any information to you."

"It's hard for a dead man to authorize anything, isn't it?" He cocked his head, raising his right eyebrow and the scar at her.

She collapsed into her chair. "Dead? Cleon?"

"But here is the authorization you need." He handed her a subpoena for Cleon's account records. "You can review it with your Ops manager if you need to."

"How? What happened? Was it his heart?"

"He drowned in the Silver River behind his house last night."

Maggie listened to the words without really hearing them. Cleon drowned? She looked down the hall to see if Arthur had arrived yet, but there was no sign of him. She thought about her last conversation with Cleon and her chest seized. Compounded with the headache she was still suffering from last night, her temples ruptured with each gasp for air.

"How is that possible?" she said.

"The investigation is still under way. Ms. Connors, I'm sure this is a shock, but I'm really in kind of a hurry, would you mind?"

Maggie looked at the papers but it was entirely too early for this kind of confrontation. Her mind was still fuzzy from her own brush with death the night before. She needed some time away from the agent to collect her thoughts.

"Would you mind giving me a moment? I'd like to get something to drink."

She checked something on her computer screen, cleared it, and then excused herself and walked past the board-room toward the cafeteria.

With Cleon dead, was she still obligated to wire the money to the Caymans? Or should she tell the agent about it? *Regardless of what happens*, Cleon had said. Did he suspect Arthur was up to something?

She wiped her eyes and tried to dismiss it. Surely her promise didn't apply now.

She had checked Cleon's account before leaving her office, and his balance had been transferred into a new account, legally transferred. But because she hadn't turned in the paperwork, it still read as a no-name account.

She put fifty cents into the soda machine and a can of Pepsi emerged. Maybe she wasn't going to debtor's prison after all. Perhaps she had found a way to acquire several million dollars for her very own. Maybe it was time to admit that life as a broker wasn't for her. She smiled through her tears. Cleon would certainly rather that she have the money than the IRS or Arthur.

She returned to her office with a Pepsi and tissues, feeling more anxious than when she left. She scanned the subpoena, set it aside on her desk, and blotted her nose.

"What is it you want, specifically?"

"How long was Mr. Cummings a client of yours?"

"No, Mr. Gallen, I mean what statements do you want? I believe your subpoena only instructs me to provide you with copies of account records. I see no reason to volunteer any other information."

"Do you have something to hide, Ms. Connors?"

"Yes, I believe I do. An absolute disgust for an agency that thinks it's so omnipotent that it can go around and destroy people's lives. If you weren't hounding Cleon so hard, he might very well be alive today, but I'll bet that doesn't keep you from sleeping nights. Did you even know Cleon? Did you know what a great guy he was?"

"I visited him at the pig farm as part of my investigation. Although as I recall, it was a pigless pig farm."

"Well, that pig farmer was one of the sweetest guys I've ever met. If you didn't see any pigs it was because they caught some disease and Cleon was forced to put them all down, including thirty-five potbellied pigs. But you know what he did? He stuffed the potbellied pigs and set up a kind of fake barnyard inside his barn for inner-city school kids that visited. He even had a motion sensor that triggered when you opened the gates to their pens and played oinking noises." Maggie's chest tightened as she remembered her last visit and started to sniffle. "That's the kind of man you've been harassing. He wasn't just an overdue tax bill."

"I'm sorry. I didn't know."

Maggie's phone rang. A client needed yesterday's closing prices on a few stocks. She took her time giving the quotations to him, sniffling occasionally, and then asked about his family. While the client was giving her an update on his plans for a summer vacation, Maggie covered the phone and asked Tim to wait in the lobby. He shook his head. Maggie turned her back to him and continued talking with the client, drawing out the conversation as long as she could. She even placed an order for three candy bars his daughter was selling for a fund-raiser.

"Getting back to Cleon's account," Gallen said as soon as she hung up, "what's his current balance?"

Maggie pulled up the cash balance screen on her computer and turned the monitor toward him. "As you can see, both his investment account and his checking account have zero balances."

He'd asked just the right question. The particular account screen Maggie showed him would not document the investment account's money transfer as the transaction screen would.

"Can you pull up a transaction history on the investment account for the last thirty days?"

"I could if there had been some activity, like deposits, withdrawals, or stock trades. But this computer won't show inactivity," she lied. "It will take a while to photocopy his previous statements. Would you mind waiting in the lobby?"

"Okay." He stood up but didn't leave. "I'm sorry we got off on the wrong foot. Could I try and make it up to you?" He reached across her and retrieved the subpoena from her desk.

"What did you have in mind?"

"How 'bout I buy you lunch? But I must warn you, a bag lady put a hex on me yesterday and I haven't quite been able to shake it, so you couldn't order anything flaming. I'd hate to add burning down a restaurant to my list of casualties this week."

It had been so long since she had been asked out, it caught her completely off guard. Thank God she had put her hair in a French braid again to avoid a threatening bad hair day.

"We could go to a place that doesn't serve pork," he said.

She turned to say "absolutely not" and noticed again that he was quite attractive. He was easily ten years older. With his crooked nose, inquisitive gray eyes, and sandy brown hair that looked like it had been cut with hedge clippers, he had a boyish appeal with a menacing undercurrent. The scar over his eye could have come from a brawl with an unhappy taxpayer or from banging his head on a communion railing. He was too hard to read. Yesterday she might have dropped everything to have lunch with him, even her non-dating rule. He certainly would be an enjoyable distraction.

But today she had three million to protect.

"Is having lunch with a person one of your techniques for getting information from them?" she said.

"As a matter of fact it is, but that's not why I asked."

She studied his eyes for a moment.

"I'm sorry, I'll have to pass," she said softly.

"I understand. Maybe another time. I'll just wait in the lobby."

Maggie watched him leave without saying anything. When he turned the corner to the lobby, she quickly checked the transaction history for Cleon's account on the computer. The final entry listed the transfer of Cleon's assets to the new nameless account. She cleared the computer screen and walked to bookkeeping to request the back copies of Cleon's statements but stopped in the lobby when she noticed the agent had already disappeared. Stacy was just coming back from the mail room.

"Here's your mail," she said. "I'm going for more coffee, do you want anything?"

Maggie shook her head. "Do you know what happened to the man who was waiting here?"

"The good-looking IRS agent? He came in this morning before you did and asked for back copies of Cleon Cummings's statements. That's where I've been for the last half hour. I pulled the statements and gave him a printout of the past thirty days' transaction activity."

Maggie's eyes widened. *Damn.*

"Why?" Stacy said. "Shouldn't I have? He had a subpoena for them, so I thought it was okay. Julienne wasn't in yet, so there wasn't anyone in Operations I could check with. Did I do something wrong?"

"No, you didn't do anything wrong." Maggie faked a smile worthy of a Miss America Pageant. "In fact, you saved me from digging through all those statements. Just don't mention anything to Julienne or Arthur. I've got enough problems with management. I don't want them to think all of my accounts are in trouble too."

"No problem, my lips are sealed."

Stacy headed to the cafeteria to refill her coffee. Maggie waited until Stacy was out of sight and then ran for her office. With Cleon dead there was an opportunity to make some changes, but she had to work quickly—it wouldn't take long for the agent to discover the account transfer.

The paperwork Cleon faxed authorizing the transfer of his investment balance into the new account did not include the name for the new account. It was, in effect, like signing a blank check. Maggie typed in the new account number on her computer, then sat mesmerized by the three-million-dollar balance flickering on the screen. It would certainly pay for her parents' bills. Maybe it didn't matter if the agent traced the balance and found it, and she was sure he would. Was there anything illegal about Cleon giving this money away right before he died?

Probably. And Cleon had said she should transfer the funds regardless of what happened. Besides, Arthur would have an epileptic fit if he knew she'd taken the money.

But if her plan worked, he would never know. No one would.

She slipped out the back door of the Hamilton office and walked down the street to a Mail Boxes Etc. For fifteen dollars a month, she arranged to have the mail of Terry Stevens received at one of their post office box numbers. Maggie signed a few forms assuring them she was Terry Stevens, and the gum-chewing clerk handed her a box key without asking for any identification or even reviewing her forms. The transaction took less than ten minutes and she made it back to her office before anyone missed her. Next, she filled out the new account form for Cleon's no-name account using the name Terry Stevens, a fake social security number, and the new address.

Stacy walked into Maggie's office to let her know the Ops Department was looking for the account form for the new account she opened yesterday. Maggie handed her the completed form and instructed Stacy to cash out the account and mail the proceeds today to Terry. If Hamilton mailed the check today, it ought to be in the Terry Stevens's rented box by Thursday at the latest. That was just enough time to buy some nontraceable bearer bonds from a rookie broker at one of the largest bond houses. She looked up their phone number and made the call.

"Janey Fitzgerald Securities. How may I direct your call?"

"Hi," Maggie said, "I'm returning a call to one of your brokers, but I don't remember his name. I know he just started with your firm."

"That would probably be either Dave Milanovits or Joe Michaels."

"I'm not sure. He's a younger guy. I don't think he has much experience."

"That's Joe Michaels. I'll transfer you now."

"Joe Michaels, how may I help you?" a voice said a second later.

"Joe, my name is Terry Stevens. I'm interested in buying a large quantity of bonds, and I'm hoping you can help me."

"Ms. Stevens, you've called the right place. Janey Fitzgerald Securities is headquartered here in St. Louis and has one of the largest inventory of bonds in the region."

"Great. I'm interested in buying three million dollars worth of bearer bonds with their coupons attached."

"With coupons?"

Maggie sighed. "Yes, along the bottom of a bearer bond are little squares called coupons. You cut them out periodically and mail them in to the issuer. The issuer then sends you back a check for that period's interest."

"I know what coupons are," said the broker. "I'm just surprised you're looking for bearer bonds with coupons still attached."

"I realize most bearer bonds issued in the 1960s have long since been redeemed; I was hoping you might make a market in foreign bearer bonds. I could have the funds deposited with you on Thursday at the latest. I'll need to take possession of the bonds by Friday morning."

"I'd be happy to help you with that. Unfortunately, bearer bonds—domestic or foreign—usually take several weeks to deliver. I really don't think we could have them for you by Friday."

"Joe, I called your competition about an hour ago with the same request. That broker was going to do some checking and call me back. I got tired of waiting so I called you. If you're really interested, why don't you put me on hold and talk to your manager right now to see if it's possible."

"Thanks. I'll be right back."

Maggie listened to the on hold music while the rest of the Hamilton office started waking up. Most of the secretaries had arrived and were exchanging stories about Monday night's bar activities. The brokers were wandering to their desks to read the *Wall Street Journal* over coffee and try and figure out how to generate some business for the day.

"Ms. Stevens, this is Scott Humphries. I'm the senior sales manager here at Janey. Joe tells me you're interested in a three-million-dollar purchase of foreign bearer bonds."

"That's correct."

"Bearer bonds aren't as popular as they once were because if they're lost or stolen it's like losing cash. And if you lose them, it's finders keepers, losers weepers. Since they're not registered anywhere, there's no way to replace them."

"I'm very familiar with how a bearer bond works."

The manager remained silent.

"Look," she continued, "I realize we're in an electronic age and a bearer bond is kind of a financial antique. But it happens to be what I want."

"May I ask then, why you want bearer bonds specifically?"

"Mr. Humphries, without going into all the gory details I will tell you that my ex-husband, whom I have a re-straining order against, is a broker at Hamilton Securities. He's taken my inheritance and churned it until all that's left is this three million dollars."

"Churning is a pretty serious accusation."

"Last month he bought and sold the same mutual fund twice in my account to generate the additional $50,000 in commissions he needed to qualify for some training junket to New York. If that's not churning, what would you call it?"

"Would you mind if I called him to confirm this?"

"I'd rather you didn't. In fact, Stevens is my maiden name, and I prefer not to tell you his name. Besides, he's in New York with his secretary. I think he called it an advanced training program but that doesn't quite explain why the secretary is along, now does it?"

"I would still prefer—"

"Mr. Humphries, I don't think you understand. The point of this exercise is to close out the account without his knowledge. I'm buying bearer bonds because they won't leave any paper trail for that man to follow. He has sent me to the hospital more times than I care to admit, and I'm not going to let it happen again."

There was a long pause. Maggie could tell the manager was weighing the improbability of her story against the commissions from the bonds.

"Is the account in your name or is it in joint names?" he said at last.

Maggie gave him the Terry Stevens account number and told him he could confirm hers was the only name on the account. "Listen. I don't care what the bond maturities are or what country they come from. And, I'm willing to double your usual commission. I just want the bonds and then I want to get out of town. As far as I know there is nothing illegal about doing this. Are you going to help me or not?"

"Ms. Stevens. We may be able to help you. Give me a

minute to check something and then I'll put Joe back on the phone."

A few minutes passed before the music on hold stopped and she heard Joe's voice.

"Ms. Stevens—"

"Call me Terry."

"Okay, Terry. My manager told me one of the brokers here in the office has a client who is planning on bringing in about two million in foreign bearer bonds next week to sell. The client isn't comfortable with the risk."

"Who are the issuers?"

"They're from all over, Costa Rica, Venezuela, some from the UK. I'll try to track down a complete inventory for you, but they are all what I would consider risky issues. Are you okay with that?"

"I'll be comfortable with whatever you can find."

"Well, the broker believes he can persuade the client to sell early. If so, we shouldn't have a problem locating the balance. If this client doesn't agree to sell, then there just isn't any way we'll be able to get the full amount for you in such a short time, but we'll do what we can. Of course, all of this will be dependent upon you having the funds to us by Thursday. In the meantime I'll need to get some new account information from you."

Maggie proceeded to give him the Mail Box address, her real home phone number, and some other miscellaneous details. They agreed to talk again on Wednesday and she hung up.

She walked toward Hamilton Securities' front door. She no longer felt a part of the office—absconding with three million must have that effect. The usual chaos in the boardroom seemed to have an unfamiliar undercurrent to it. She imagined the stares and whispers, usually directed at the new kid on the block, were now focused on her.

She opened the front door feeling as if she had tucked the back of her suit skirt into her pantyhose.

Chapter 15

Tim sat outside the Hamilton office in his "new" car, a rented, beat-up Chevrolet with mismatched hubcaps, a huge hole where the radio should be, and a stench emanating from the back seat that hinted a family of German shepherds recently called this car home. In his dark suit and starched white shirt he felt as out of place as an opera fan at a monster truck rally.

He looked at his watch. Right now he should be meeting with the South County detectives to provide some background on Cleon Cummings, but if they hadn't already reached the conclusion Tim was the killer, it was only a matter of time before they did. Instead, he waited for Maggie Connors to leave her office and lead him to some answers.

He drummed his fingers on the dashboard. How could his life have changed so drastically overnight?

After his meeting with Ed last night he drove home, making sure no one from Inspection still had him under surveillance. He stuffed a duffel bag with his passport,

some toiletries, one dress suit, a few pairs of jeans and
shirts and, most importantly, five thousand dollars in
emergency money he kept inside a fake shaving cream
can. Then he drove to the St. Louis airport, where he
parked his Buick in the long-term parking lot. Next he
took the Metro-Link shuttle downtown where he managed
to rent a drug dealer special from Bubba's 24 Hour Car
Rentals and Bail Bonds. For the low, low price of three
hundred dollars a week, the rent-a-wreck came with free
mileage, a car phone, emergency flares, and no questions
asked. A one-thousand-dollar security deposit on the heap
had relieved Tim of the usual credit card requirement and
gave him fifteen minutes of prepaid cell phone use.

He tried not to shift his weight for fear one of the seat's
springs might pop loose and rip his only pair of dress
pants. In less than twelve hours he had gone from the
hunter to the hunted, but he wasn't sure why. To com-
plicate matters more, he knew every newscast in the country would soon be flashing his face and accusing him of
murdering Cleon Cummings. And the really frightening
thing was the report would make sense.

First, a fingerprint analysis would identify Tim's fingerprints on the tin of tea and on the tea strainer. Eventually, detectives would search Tim's office, and it
wouldn't take long to notice the deadly plant growing
outside his window. When they interviewed Tim's secretary, she would tell them Cleon had been in Tim's office
that morning and had forgotten his tea. She would remember that it took a while for Tim to return the tea tin.
The detectives would probably ask if the delay was long
enough for Tim to open his window, pull some flowers
from the plant, and put it in the tea. The secretary would
say it was. She might even remember Cleon's reminder
to Tim to close his office window.

Maybe she would mention the briefcase of cash, or Ed
would. One way or another, news of the bribe would leak,
which would add to the avalanche of circumstantial evidence. Then someone, probably from Inspection, would

discover the two million dollars in Tim's bank account, which would be hard to justify on a government employee's salary.

Perhaps it was time for him to start believing in hexes.

Of course, Arthur would fall under some initial scrutiny, but Tim learned from Maggie's secretary that Arthur had been at a seminar most of the day and at work the rest. Tim confirmed Arthur's arrival and departure times with the front desk receptionist and the parking garage attendant. Without any witnesses to the actual poisoning, a prosecutor would have Cleon's 911 tape along with the circumstantial information pointing at Tim. The evidence against Tim was so well orchestrated that if Arthur did murder Cleon and frame Tim, he was sure Arthur's seminar alibi would check out.

But Maggie didn't seem as composed. If Tim was right and she was working with Arthur, it would be easier to get answers from her. From his experience in interviewing tax evaders, he knew how to tell if someone was lying, and Maggie was obviously hiding something. At least she hadn't been able to tell the difference between a real subpoena and a fake one.

It was too bad she didn't take him up on his lunch offer. If he could get someone to relax and start talking, usually the person would accidentally divulge enough information to incriminate themselves. Happened all the time in taxpayer interviews. Lunch would have been a great opportunity to find out what she was up to.

A patrol car drove by and he slumped down in his seat. He had considered turning himself into the police. It was the ethical thing to do. But he knew the local police would relish the opportunity to have an IRS special agent as a perp. Rather than show any favoritism, they would railroad this case as fast as they could to make the six o'clock headline news. No other suspects would seriously be considered.

He was getting too old for this shit.

Chapter 16

By 9:30 a.m., Maggie was standing in the kitchen of Joann and Peter Stevens's home, across the street from Maggie's childhood home. Although it had been more than ten years since Maggie lived with her parents, she was still the one the Stevens trusted to water their plants when they were out of town. Maggie wasn't quite sure why she had this honor, because the plants always got worse under her care.

Maybe it was because Maggie was the same age as Terry, the Stevens's only daughter. The two girls had grown up together, and from a distance the two could pass as twins. That is, until a closer look at Terry revealed her telltale blank stare, flailing arms, and garbled speech, the result of brain damage that prevented Terry from mentally maturing.

The Stevenses didn't travel much except to explore new therapy options for Terry. Their trip over the weekend to Quincy, Illinois, had been the exception. Yesterday, at the

site of the National Special Olympics, Terry had run in
the track and field competition.

Maggie smiled. Her thoughts were about Terry, but not
about Terry's recent accomplishment. She filled the watering can and watered the spider plant hanging over the
kitchen sink. The water slipped down the plant's long,
thin leaves and drained back into the sink. She put down
the watering can and began searching the secretary desk
in the kitchen. There were dozens of food coupons, bits
of wrapping paper, appointment books, a telephone book,
and miscellaneous items, but not what she was looking
for.

She stopped. Was that the front door opening? She listened to the empty house for a few minutes and took a
deep, calming breath.

Next she went to the study and checked the stacks of
papers on the desk, searched through desk drawers, and
went file by file through an antique filing cabinet. Nothing. She watered the rubber tree plant and started to water
the fig tree before she remembered it was fake.

Upstairs, she refilled the watering can in the hallway
bathroom before making her way into the master bedroom. Again she found nothing except an interesting book
titled *How to Have Better Orgasms*, tucked discreetly in
the nightstand. Who would have guessed? She flipped
through the pages before replacing it.

A creak downstairs froze her, but again it was followed
by silence. Maggie tried to ignore her overworked guilty
conscience as she walked into Terry's room. Like the rest
of the house, it too was very tidy while still being homey.
But again, nothing. She watered the fern hanging in front
of Terry's bedroom window, accidentally dribbling a little
on the carpeting.

She returned to the kitchen where she emptied the watering can and replaced it on the counter. She walked
through the dining room, study, living room, and family
room again, looking for anything she might have missed.
Nothing. There was no place else it could be.

She flopped on the family room couch and pulled her license from her wallet. Was there some way of altering it? No, she had tried unsuccessfully in college, and there was no reason to believe she could do it any better now.

It was then that she spied it. A pink book nestled among other books on the shelf. *Terry's Treasures*. Maggie had seen the faded scrapbook many times as a child. When her mother had brought her to visit, Terry had dragged this scrapbook out and they'd looked at the same pictures over and over. Maggie had dreaded those visits.

She grabbed the book and began paging through it. On the first page was a letter Mrs. Stevens had written to her unborn child. On the next page was a hospital wristband with Terry's name on it next to a picture of Mrs. Stevens with baby Terry. Then she turned to the next page.

The birth certificate was there, just as it had been so many times before. Terry Sue Stevens, born January 14, 1966, at 6:52 p.m., to Joann Eshelman Stevens and Peter Joseph Stevens at St. Joseph's Hospital. Eight pounds, three ounces, twenty-two inches long. Dr. Jim Groff, attending physician. Stamped on the back was a set of Terry's tiny, blue footprints. Nothing on the certificate stated anything about a mental impairment.

She freed the worn and tattered certificate from the scrapbook page, then flipped through the rest of the scrapbook. Baby pictures of Terry, family birthday pictures, a Polaroid of Terry and Maggie dressed for Halloween, Special Education report cards, locks of hair, and other memorabilia. Some Special Olympics souvenirs would be going in this book as soon as the Stevenses got back, which meant she would need to return the certificate tomorrow.

Maggie put the book back on the shelf. Now she had the beginning of her new identity, but it was getting late and she had to hurry.

She locked the house and headed for Illinois.

Chapter 17

Ed slammed his phone down, spilling his now cold cup of coffee all over his desk.

"Hold all of my calls!" he yelled to his secretary. "If anyone says a goddamn word to the media, they're fired."

When the South County detectives had called this morning saying Gallen didn't show for their meeting, Ed started to worry. Then an enterprising reporter got hold of Gallen's secretary, who answered way too many questions before the phone could be yanked from her hand. She was immediately suspended from the job and ordered not to talk to the media again or she would be fired. She left the building crying, which the news captured on tape. By noon, calls from the media were clogging the IRS phone lines, and when reporters couldn't get details on the "Death and Taxes" murder, they began making up their own.

Although Cleon had mentioned his son-in-law on the 911 tape—which the media already had—reporters had quickly verified Arthur's whereabouts on Monday and had immediately moved onto the iris implication, which they deciphered as the IRS and, more specifically, Tim Gallen. The reporters had pieced together Gallen's activities from yesterday and no one could account for Tim's time between 9:30 a.m. and 2 p.m. Some reporters speculated that Tim used this time to make arrangements to get out of the country. More imaginative reporters suggested that the four-and-a-half-hour absence was long enough for Tim to drive out to Cleon's and steal additional money from the poisoned taxpayer.

Either way, when Ed picked up his phone he heard, "Is it true that the negative publicity running on Channel 12 caused your agent to flip out and murder one of St. Louis's most charitable millionaires?" Or, "How long was Gallen investigating Cleon Cummings and was he really just wasting taxpayers' money as he plotted his crime?" Or, "Sources say Gallen helped shred some of Cleon's money. Was he trying to get back at you and the government?"

"No comment" was the official agency answer, but the questions kept coming.

Ed ignored his ringing telephone and flipped on the office television in time to see a reporter demonstrate the shredding of a one-dollar bill; the news budget must not have allowed for the drama of shredding a hundred-dollar bill. Then the report cut to footage showing the sixty-two bags of shredded money found at Cleon Cummings's. No wonder the national news picked it up so quickly. It really was great television.

He still couldn't make sense of it. Of all the IRS agents Granger had ever supervised, Gallen was the last one who would ever do something like this. Too many times Gallen had demonstrated an iron-clad ethic, from turning down a hundred-thousand-dollar bribe back when he was a revenue agent to returning a lost five-hundred-dollar winning lottery ticket to the agent who had stolen Gallen's old girlfriend.

He checked the Channel 12 news. They were playing

the hex footage with a new voice-over claiming the bag lady had tried to warn the public about Gallen but no one had listened.

Could Gallen explain his innocence? Ed desperately hoped so. If not, it meant his department was going to come under enough negative publicity to ruin everyone's career. The agents didn't deserve this. They worked long hours, risking their lives for what many people perceived as an accountant's job.

They needed to find Gallen and get some answers. Ed cleared his schedule and agreed to spend the rest of the day letting the police interview him and Gallen's fellow agents. He would do whatever he had to, to help find Gallen and the truth behind this mess.

Chapter 18

Mary Hodgkins sat in her chair staring at the Illinois Bureau of License and Registration's bulletin on fraudulent applications, but thinking about her upcoming vacation. Thursday she would be leaving on an all-expense paid, seven-day vacation to the beautiful Cayman Islands.

A year ago she participated in a radio promotion at a local car dealership that challenged a dozen people to see who could keep their lips on a car the longest. The one who did won the car. After four and a half days without sleep, it was down to Mary and a postal employee. Mary was blearily fantasizing about driving away in the $34,000 convertible when a radio jock asked her a question and she turned her head to answer. It cost her the car, but she won a free trip to the Caymans for second place.

The door to the break room opened and Mr. Tuttle, her supervisor, walked into the room, spraying air freshener in her direction.

"I'm going to catch a fraudulent application," she said,

acting as if she had been studying the bulletin.

"Sure, Mary, whatever you say," Tuttle said.

She shifted in her chair to hide the coffee stains adorning her pink stretch pants. She hadn't wanted to wear the pants again, but she'd overslept as usual and didn't have time to search for a clean pair that probably didn't exist. Thankfully, the day was almost over and she could go home and change into a comfortable pair of sweats.

"By the way, I need you to work Saturdays for awhile when you get back from vacation." Tuttle put the air freshener down on the counter and poured a cup of coffee.

"But I've worked the last five Saturdays in a row."

"It's not my fault you picked the only government job in Illinois that requires Saturday hours," Tuttle said. "Maybe if you would make it to work on time once in awhile or improve your test-passing ratios your work schedule might improve."

"Yeah, right."

"There's that positive mental attitude again."

"You want positive? How about this? I'll bet you I catch a fraudulent application by the end of the week—one the computer will miss."

"Sure you will. You're going to outsmart our new $80,000 computer system."

"I mean it. I'll bet you a month of Saturdays off that I do, and if I'm wrong, then I'll—"

"And if you're wrong, then you'll be working Saturdays for the rest of the summer."

Mary stood. Her cheese curl-created bulk towered over the man. Her pale eyes held his. "You're on."

"You have until Friday at five."

"But my flight leaves on Thursday."

"I'm being generous. I think you'll need the extra time."

Mary returned to her desk and watched the fan on the counter oscillate. Although the fan hummed back and forth, a dank must hung in the room as if the air had not been changed in the three decades the License Bureau had

occupied the office. What had she gotten herself in to?
She hadn't caught a cheater since that fifteen-year-old
three years ago.

Henry Wohlschlaeger sat at his desk next to Mary. He
looked like an original fixture, motionless except for his
eyes. He was probably counting the diamonds in the pattern of the waxy yellow floor to pass the time.

The front door opened and diverted their attention. Two
teenaged girls bounced in wearing matching tennis outfits
and matching permed hair. They made the office decor
seem even duller. Henry immediately walked to the front
desk to help them.

"I'm here to take my test," the taller girl said.

Henry busily began preparing the paperwork he so
loved. He double-tapped the papers on the counter to assure their alignment before taking the paper clip from his
mouth to secure them. Henry was always the first to the
counter to help a pretty girl and save her from having to
parallel park twice—Mary's favorite revenge on beauty
queens.

"I'm a little nervous," the perm said with a giggle.
"May I review the rule book one more time?"

"Of course," Henry said. "Just as soon as we get your
forms filled out."

Oh hell, Henry could have them. They obviously
weren't the cheaters she needed.

Maggie Connors walked through the door of the Hanover,
Illinois, Bureau of License and Registration hoping she
didn't look as if she was about to commit a felony. Ob-
taining a driver's license with false identification was
probably punishable by five years in the Illinois peniten-
tiary, a $100,000 fine, or both. She should have looked it
up on the Internet.

It had taken four hours to drive from St. Louis to Hanover, Illinois. She barely had enough time to take the written and driving test before the office closed. Maggie had
driven to Illinois because this state issued a driver's li-

cense on the spot once you passed the test. Missouri mailed out their driver's licenses, and it took about three to four weeks to receive them.

She approached the counter and removed a plain white note pad and pen from her pocket. She didn't carry a purse.

My name is Terry Stevens. I am mute and I am here to take my driver's test, she wrote on the pad of paper. She then handed the pad with Terry's birth certificate to an immense woman in coffee-stained pink stretch pants.

The woman studied the paper carefully, then picked up Maggie's pen and wrote, *Wait right here*.

Maggie smiled, pointed to the woman's cigarette-stained teeth and then to her own ear.

"I'm sorry," the woman said loudly, with exaggerated emphasis. "Wait right here. I'll be back in a minute."

The woman lumbered back to confer with her supervisor. The two talked in hushed voices while staring at Maggie. The woman handed the supervisor Terry's birth certificate, and they began scanning a regulation book, still glancing occasionally at Maggie. The supervisor stepped into his office and started making phone calls.

Maggie froze, horrified over the flaw in her scheme. She'd decided to act mute so she could get in and out without a lot of questions about her age; it didn't occur to her they might call someone who knew sign language. She should have planned for that. She could have wrapped her fingers like they were broken. She was about to run out of the office when the pink woman walked back to the counter.

"Would you please come with me? We need to confirm something."

Maggie stifled her urge to flee and followed the woman to a desk.

"What is your social security number?"

Maggie nervously wrote Terry's social security number on the pad of paper. She looked around for another exit.

Maybe it wasn't too late to make a run for it. Would they physically tackle her?

The supervisor had taken the birth certificate to the computer and was tapping away on its keyboard. What could their computer system tell them? Did it have a physical description of the real Terry Stevens somewhere in its data file?

"And I'll also need your address."

845 Landis Avenue, she wrote, and then stopped. She had no idea what the local zip codes were.

"I've never heard of that street, is that in Bedford?"

Maggie nodded her head yes.

"Oh, that must be on the west side. Is your zip 01 or 02?"

Maggie held up two fingers.

"Okay, now please complete the top portion of this form. My supervisor is confirming your birth certificate. We're really screening license applications for people your age who don't have a previous license for identification."

Maggie tried to look puzzled.

"When someone your age hasn't had a license before, we cross-check the name to make sure there isn't a death certificate on file for them. We use a new computer system being tested in our office to catch folks who get a birth certificate of a deceased person and think it's a free ticket for a new license. You'd be surprised at how many people we've already caught. Kids try it before they turn twenty-one so they can buy beer, truckers are in here trying it to spread out speeding violations. You name it, we get it. Makes you wonder how many slipped through the system before."

Maggie frowned her disapproval.

"He's trying to track someone down who knows sign language in case there is a complication with your testing."

Maggie nodded her head. Her tongue seemed to be swelling inside her mouth for no apparent reason.

The supervisor was back on the phone, rubbing his face with his left hand. He found a pimple along his jaw and picked at it. Maggie turned away, unable to watch the outcome of either the phone conversation or the pimple.

"The birth certificate checks out," he yelled from across the room. "I haven't been able to get a hold of the sign language person I'm looking for, but you can begin the testing."

The pink lady waved at him and led Maggie back to the counter.

"Take this test and fill it out. If you don't know an answer, just guess. Take all the time you need. You can sit there."

She motioned to a row of greenish-blue student chair desks that must have been liberated from an old elementary school. Maggie took a seat next to another girl and began working on the test.

And stopped.

How many feet were you supposed to stay behind an ambulance? Fifty? One hundred? Weren't you were supposed to pull over to the right? Which way do you turn your wheels when parking uphill without a curb? Inward? Outward? Maggie always left them straight.

Just as Maggie realized how difficult the test was, the girl beside her practically jumped out of her chair and skipped to the counter with her completed test. Maggie hadn't even had a chance to copy a few answers from her. Damn, why hadn't she reviewed the regulation book before taking the test? It was such a long way to come to flunk. Maggie had picked the little town of Hanover because it was close to the interstate and she was hoping they wouldn't have a very advanced computer system. So much for that plan.

She finished the test as best she could and brought it to the counter. The pink lady snatched it.

"You can wait over there while your test is graded," she said.

Maggie sat in a row of brown aluminum chairs directly

across from the testing desks and watched the woman check her test. The woman went through the test, line by line, occasionally stopping to stretch her waistband, which seemed incapable of any more elasticity. Finally the woman motioned her over.

"A passing grade is seventy-five. Congratulations, you got seventy-six."

Maggie almost yelled in her excitement, something a mute person really shouldn't do.

"Go out to your car and wait for me. I'll be right there."

Maggie sat in her car, tapping the steering wheel. The sky was getting dark again and threatening to rain. The entire Midwest seemed to be condemned to a boiling wet summer.

Within five minutes, the pink woman appeared. She stood in back of Maggie's car and instructed Maggie to turn on the left blinker, right blinker, put the car in reverse, and step on the brakes. Then she checked the turn signals from the front.

The woman then squeezed herself into the passenger seat and wrapped the seat belt around her. Maggie, following the woman's directions, spent the next ten minutes turning left and right through the streets of the small town. The woman didn't make her parallel park. When they returned to the testing office, it began to rain with the enthusiasm of a drunk who had waited too long to use the urinal.

"You failed to come to a complete stop at the second stop sign," the woman said, "and your speed coming down that last hill was a little high, but the rest was fine. Let's go get your license."

Both women unbuckled their seat belts and Maggie grabbed an old *Wall Street Journal* from her back seat and handed the front section to the pink woman to use for protection. They splashed their way to the office and then tried to shake the weather off once they were inside.

Maggie noticed the supervisor was gone, as were the two teenaged girls. A woman with her teenaged son and young daughter were now standing at the counter with the other test administrator.

"Remember, keep two hands on the wheel, one hand at two o'clock and the other hand at ten o'clock," the mother said.

"Ms. Stevens, please stand in the black box on the floor so we can get your picture," the pink lady said.

"Mom, I know where to put my hands. Besides, I'm not really comfortable when I drive with only one hand."

"Neither is anyone else in the car," his little sister said.

"Ms. Stevens?"

Maggie turned toward the pink woman and started to say "What?" but caught herself. She had to focus.

"Please stand in the black box on the floor so we can get your picture."

Maggie did as she was told. Two pictures were taken, one for their files and one for the license. The picture was positioned on the license and sent through the laminating machine. The test administrator handed it to Maggie.

She held the warm card in her hands. There it was. Terry Stevens, age twenty-nine, of 845 Landis Avenue, Bedford, Illinois.

Mission accomplished.

"Good news!" a voice from behind her said. "I've found someone who knows sign language."

Damn. She turned around to find the supervisor striding toward her with a woman trailing reluctantly behind.

"Did you hear me?" the supervisor said. "I've found someone you can talk to. Ms. Stevens, this is my wife Sharon. She's just started taking a sign language course at the YMCA."

Sharon gave Maggie a self-conscious smile. Then, with careful deliberation, she began forming shapes with her hands.

Maggie shook her head. Ignorance seemed like the best defense.

"I'm not sure if I'm doing an A or an E," Sharon said.

"What are you trying to ask her?" her husband said.

"I'm trying to ask her if she's related to the Terry Stevens who's in the paper this morning."

"Ask her something simple," the supervisor said, "like what her name is."

"We already know what her name is." She tried again, forming each letter in her complex sentence slowly and deliberately.

Maggie began making what she hoped would pass for sign language signals, kind of a cross between arthritis exercises and rap signs.

"What's she saying?"

"I don't know, she's going too fast."

Maggie reached for Sharon's hand, shook it emphatically, and then waved goodbye and headed for the door.

Mary sat at her desk in disgust. Here she was, trying to improve her performance, while her boss was busy dragging his wife around like a show poodle. She picked up the paper to read the article Sharon had mentioned. On the front page was a big color picture of a woman with a contorted smile and a distant look in her eyes. The caption read: "Terry Stevens of St. Louis, Missouri, grins after finishing her first one-mile race in the Annual Special Olympics."

"That's odd," Mary said to Henry, who was picking his teeth with a paper clip. "Two women with the same name, both with handicaps."

"Not as unusual as you giving a woman in her late twenties her first driver's license when she obviously drove here by herself. Where was the licensed driver who was supposed to accompany her?"

Mary's mouth fell open. In the excitement of testing a mute person, she had overlooked one of the fundamental checks. She snatched the phone book and looked for a listing for Terry Stevens. Nothing. She called information, still no listing. Mary tried to remember the car's license plate number, but couldn't. She had noticed it was a Missouri license plate, but hadn't thought anything of it at the time.

She dropped into her chair, fuming. Once a person walked out the door with a fraudulent license, there was no easy way to track them down. She could have the police enter a notation in their computers in case Terry was stopped, but Mary had no real proof. She opened her desk drawer and then slammed it shut again. She was going to be stuck working Saturdays.

She picked up the waterlogged *Wall Street Journal* to fling it into the trash can, then noticed the mailing label in the bottom right-hand corner of the front page. The address was blurry but still readable.

Maggie Connors, Hamilton Securities, 10908 Baxter Road, St. Louis, MO 63105.

Chapter 19

The seat belt jerked Maggie backward as her car came to a violent stop.

She sat dazed for a minute, watching the windshield wipers slap back and forth, losing their battle with the pounding rain. What had happened?

About five blocks from the license bureau the right side of her car had plummeted into the street for some unknown reason.

She looked around for help but the intersection was empty. Worried someone might come along and hit her, she put the car in reverse. It responded with metal-screeching-metal resistance.

She turned the car off and got out. There were bruises starting to form along her collarbone. She ran through the drilling storm to the passenger side and found the right front tire jammed in an open manhole.

"Damn, lady! You got yourself a mess," yelled an oil-covered mechanic running toward her from his service station. "But if you were ever going to do something like that, it's best you did it in front of my station. Let's see what we have here." He bent down to survey the damage, unaffected by the cloudburst.

Maggie's shock turned to rage. "What the hell kind of town puts a manhole in the middle of an intersection? And where the hell is the cover? I'm not paying for this."

"The kids have been taking them off as a prank. There was even a story about it in today's paper. The police have talked to the schools and everything, but they're not having any luck."

The police. She couldn't afford an accident report filed right now, not with a fraudulent license still warm in her wallet. She needed to get the car out of the intersection before anyone began asking her questions.

"Can you tow this into your garage and fix it?" she said, looking between the raindrops on her watch. "I've got to get back to St. Louis."

"Little lady, you don't seem to understand. You have completely broken your tie rod among other things. You've got some serious problems that aren't going to be fixed with a Band-Aid. I'll have to order parts, probably from New Cumberland. We're not talking hours, we're talking days to repair."

"Days? I don't have days." She couldn't miss Arthur's nine o'clock sales meeting tomorrow morning.

He rubbed his unshaven face as another mechanic from the garage joined them.

"Dave, how long do you think it would take us to get in a tie rod for a Corolla? Two, maybe three days?"

"Probably. Boy, look at what a hole can do."

The mechanics traded opinions on the parts and labor the car would require. They seemed oblivious to the rain dripping off their Bud Light hats.

"Kenny," she snapped, reading the man's name off his shirt, "can we move this car into your garage before we drown?"

"Naa, we ought to wait for Gerald. He's our sheriff. He'll want to write up a report."

"You gotta have a report for your insurance," the other man said, then they both nodded their heads in unison, convincing Maggie they were sharing the same brain.

"Right now I don't care about my insurance. I want this car out of the middle of the road. Can you do that or should I call another garage?"

The two men put an arm on each other's soaked shoulders. "Lady, we are the only garage," they said in too-practiced unison.

"Yeah, and you guys are probably the ones who pulled the manhole cover off."

"All right now, offending us is not going to help the situation. Dave, go grab the truck, and let's get this thing out of everyone's way."

What had been a desolate intersection was now backing up with pickups since Maggie's car managed to block both lanes. Maggie took shelter in the gas station as the tow truck deftly raised the car from the hole and the men towed it into their garage. She retrieved her wallet from the car, while Kenny replaced the manhole cover that had been leaning against a nearby tree. They reconvened in the service station's dirty office.

"Is there someplace I can rent a car around here?"

Kenny pointed at an old Chrysler parked beyond the gas pumps. "Once again, you've come to the right place."

"Great, there is a God."

"All we need is your license and a major credit card and we can send you on your way."

"Super."

Maggie dug through her purse for her license. At first rummage, she didn't see it. Her Terry Stevens license was tucked safely in her wallet, but her real one wasn't where it usually was. She dumped everything out of her purse: a compact, a tampon, a change purse, Mace, an appointment book, a business card holder, loose change, pens, a brush, lipstick, blush, and another tampon, but no license.

"What did I do with that?" she said aloud.

When had she last had it? It wasn't at the License Bureau. She was about to go search the car when she remembered.

Terry's house. She must have left it on the couch when she was examining it to see if she could alter the name. She could use her new license, but she didn't have any credit cards to support it.

"What if I don't have my license?"

"Then you don't have a rental car," Kenny said.

"Please, couldn't you just make this one, small exception?"

"No. Unfortunately, it's a big policy not to make small exceptions."

"Well, how about a taxi or something?"

"How much cash do you have?"

"About forty dollars, but I have credit cards."

"Lady, the closest cab service is about a half-hour away. You're not going to find anyone who will drive you four hours to St. Louis without seeing some cash up front. Plastic ain't going to do it in these parts."

"Well, can you give me a cash advance?"

Kenny hit a button on the register, opening the cash drawer. "I would, but I only have about twenty dollars in the till. Dave took our deposit to the bank already."

"Well, where's your bank? I'll get a cash advance there."

"No can do. The bank's closed for the day."

"Closed? But it's only five o'clock!"

Kenny shrugged to indicate determining bank hours was not his responsibility.

"What about an automatic teller?"

Kenny shook his head. "A couple of teenagers hooked their pickup up to the only ATM and tried to yank it out of the bank building last week. They ended up ripping off their fender instead but they put the machine out of order."

"Okay, what about a bus?"

"The last bus out of town left around three. Your best bet is to get the 8:30 bus in the morning that runs to East

St. Louis. From there you can either switch buses to St. Louis or get a cab."

She looked from the car and then back to the mechanics and realized her employment with Hamilton Securities was over. There was no way she would make Arthur's sales meeting. Maybe it didn't matter, but it would have been nice to keep an eye on the Stevens account until she got the check.

"What am I supposed to do until tomorrow?"

"I would suggest the Budget Hotel. It's about a mile down the road. Dave can give you a ride over after we finish the paperwork on your car. We'll need your credit card to get started on the work. For $500 we'll deliver your car to you when it's done."

"Who's we?" Dave said.

"Shut up and get the paperwork done so you can give the lady a ride to her hotel."

Dave dropped Maggie off at the hotel for a five-dollar charge. She was going to run the twenty feet to the front door to avoid any more damage to her dry-clean-only suit, but she was already soaked and didn't have the energy, so she plodded through the storm. Her high-heeled shoes seemed to find the deepest part of every puddle.

She dripped at the front desk while the hotel clerk made an imprint of her credit card. The clerk didn't ask to see her driver's license. Finally, something had been simple for a change.

Maggie climbed the stairs to her room and opened the door to find a typical hotel layout. The queen-size bed had the requisite ugly flower comforter, which probably hadn't been laundered in God knows how long. Above the bed was an equally offensive collection of pictures bolted to the walls. A perfunctory oak table with mismatched chairs sat off to the side. A dark rust-brown carpeting pulled the whole room together to create an eclectic atmosphere of bad taste.

She tossed her purse on the bed and phoned her office.

Stacy answered and assured her everything was fine. She gave Maggie four client messages and told her Arthur had also left a message reminding her not to be late for the sales meeting tomorrow.

A cold shiver ran down her spine as she hung up the phone. The monsoon outside had pushed the temperature down unexpectedly. The air conditioning in her room was still running on high, trying to overcompensate for the heat earlier in the day. Maggie switched the freon off and turned the heat on as she made her last call to the hotel office and requested a 7 a.m. wake-up call.

She quickly disrobed in front of the heater and hung her wet clothes up to dry. Goose bumps covered her body as she freed her long hair from its braid. She retreated to the bathroom for a hot shower.

Maggie wasn't sure exactly how long she had been standing in the shower, but her stress began to melt away. The bathroom was completely fogged, and her fingers looked like prunes. Still, she couldn't get herself to shut off the water. Instead, she stood there imagining what her life was going to be like with her new fortune. So what if Arthur fired her when she got back?

The bathroom door creaked open, ending her monetary fantasies.

She cautiously stuck her head out of the shower to see if she could hear anything. Nothing.

She shook her head. How could she still be that jumpy after boiling herself for at least a half hour? Would guilt always make her this nervous?

But then again, this was the kind of town Norman Bates would feel at home in. Had she deadbolted the front door before getting into the shower? She told herself she had and returned to the warmth of the water.

She was rinsing her hair one final time when she stiffened at the unmistakable sound of the deadbolt being latched. Or was it?

She stepped out of the shower with the water still running, careful not to rustle the shower curtain, and wrapped a towel around herself. There was nothing in the bathroom to arm herself with. The mace she carried was buried in her purse somewhere in the room.

The cold draft of air blowing in from the slightly ajar door almost convinced her that her nerves were working overtime, when she heard a shuffling noise. She walked weak-kneed toward the bathroom door. Her heart pounded louder with each step. She put her hand on the doorknob expecting it to fly open with a crazed maniac standing in the doorway with a butcher knife and a look in his eyes like Jack Nicholson on speed.

Nothing happened.

She took a deep breath and opened the door slightly. Each creak of the hinge made her cringe.

From inside the bathroom she couldn't see or hear anything in the room.

It was time to confront this overworked imagination of hers. She was sure she would find an empty room, a locked door, and then she would get back in the shower. She shoved the door open.

Standing in the middle of the room was a man with his back to her, searching her purse.

She screamed and ran back into the bathroom.

The bathroom door didn't have a lock. It didn't have a latch. It wouldn't stop him anyway, it never did in these situations. She braced herself against the door. The man easily pushed it open.

There was nowhere else to hide, no weapon, nothing.

He grabbed her wrist and dragged her out into the room. He threw her onto the bed and pinned her. Straddling her, he held both of her wrists in one hand before she realized she wasn't screaming. She took a deep breath, and he clamped his other hand over her mouth.

Her screams became muffled shrieks.

"Stop it," he said, "I'm not going to hurt you, but you have to shut up."

She struggled and twisted to break his grasp but he was

too strong. She could taste blood in her mouth from the force of his hand.

"Maggie, shut up right now or I'll make you shut up."

She stopped screaming and looked into the man's face for the first time. It was the IRS agent from this morning.

"Okay, that's better," he said. "Now, I'm going to remove my hand, but don't scream. I just want to talk to you."

He removed his hand from her mouth but when Maggie opened her mouth, he clenched his hand over it again.

"Sorry, I thought you were going to scream," he said. "Let's try this again. I'll remove my hand and you stay quiet. If you scream, I'll grab that little towel that's wrapped around you and use it as a gag. As much as I might enjoy that, my guess is you're the type that wants dinner and a movie first."

He took his hand off of her mouth and Maggie remained silent.

"Now, I'm going to get off you, and we're going to sit here quietly and talk. Do you hear me? I'm not going to hurt you, I promise. Believe me, this isn't the way I usually get a woman into bed."

He shifted to get off her.

She jerked her knee up and planted it in his groin.

He collapsed on the bed, pinning her legs. She tried to kick herself free, but even in his pain he moved back on top of her and covered her screaming mouth. The dead weight of his body threatened to suffocate her.

"Have it your way, Maggie. Tell me how you and Arthur poisoned Cleon Cummings and framed me, or I'll call the police and you can introduce them to Terry Stevens and her three million dollars."

Chapter 20

Arthur tried to keep a suitably serious look on his face as he ushered the police detectives out of his office. When he closed the door behind them, he let his smile wrap around his face.

Cleon, the old bastard, was dead.

The detectives had visited Arthur questioning why Cleon had told the 911 operator not to let Arthur get the money. Arthur shrugged and explained they hadn't spoken since his wife's death. He then told the detectives he had been at a seminar most of the day Monday. He gave the detectives his seminar certificate and invited them to confirm his schedule with anyone at the seminar or at Hamilton. The atmosphere of the meeting grew a lot friendlier. They asked if Arthur knew about Cleon's tax problems, and he assured them Cleon's life was a complete mystery. Then they closed their little note pads and told him they were classifying Cleon's death as a homicide and were looking for Tim Gallen for a variety of reasons. Cleon's body had not yet been recovered, which wasn't unusual because of the current, but they were sure it would be found by tomorrow, at which time he would need to identify it. Identifying Cleon's body was something he would do with pleasure.

Arthur's triumph drained away when his cell phone rang. He grabbed it. "What!"

"It's Mr. Smith."

"I know who the hell it is. It's about time you answered one of my goddamn pages. What was Maggie doing at work this morning?"

"She was late getting to the hot tub. She didn't have enough soaking time before they closed it down and found her. That's not my fault."

Arthur rolled his eyes. He didn't have time for mistakes and wasn't sure this hired clown could do the job without landing them both in jail. Unfortunately, he didn't have much of a choice. In his social circles "hit man" was not a common profession.

In fact, it was only by accident they had even met. Arthur had stopped to get some cash out of an automatic teller machine when a man, his leg in a cast, hobbled over on crutches and demanded the money. Arthur told the man to get bent and was walking back to his Mercedes when he heard the unmistakable click of a gun being cocked. He stopped, turned around, and found a gun pointed at his crotch. Whenever his crotch was the focus, it immediately got his attention. But rather than freaking out, Arthur withdrew the maximum from the ATM— $300—and persuaded his new friend to join him at a bar. Three beers later the two had settled on a price for killing Maggie Connors.

"Where is she now?" Arthur said.

"I lost track of her on the highway when I got pulled over for a speeding ticket."

"You really are the consummate professional, aren't you? Thank God they didn't arrest you."

"Your concern is touching."

"Listen, ass-wipe, just do the job. Wait for her to show

up at her condo and then finish what you were hired for. If she's not home by ten tonight, meet me at my house to help with that gas line problem we talked about this morning. You can finish the other job tomorrow. I have your beeper number if I need you, and next time answer my page when I call."

Arthur hung up.

Chapter 21

"**O**kay," Tim said, "why did you and Arthur poison Cleon and frame me?" The anger in his voice paralleled the thunder outside.

She mumbled something into his hand.

"I'm going to remove my hand one more time and like I said, if you want the police, you'll get the police. I'd be happy to let them sort this out. Do you understand me?"

Maggie nodded her head. He removed his hand.

"What are you doing?" she said, still struggling under his grasp.

He shifted his weight to keep her under control. "Just proving my innocence."

"I don't know what the hell you're talking about, and you're hurting my wrists."

Tim loosened his grip on her but still kept her pinned. "Pahleease. I'm the one you're framing for Cleon's death. But I'm not going to let you ruin my career and send me to jail while you disappear off into the sunset with Cleon's money."

"You're not suffering from a hex, you're suffering from delusions! Now get off me! I didn't do anything and I didn't frame anyone. I don't know what you're talking about."

Tim glanced at the door. The police could come through it any minute.

"Every state trooper and patrol officer is looking for me and half the IRS is helping them. I didn't kill Cleon and take his money, but I bet a jury of your peers will believe you and Arthur did."

"Kill him? You said he drowned."

"He drowned from being poisoned."

She stopped struggling and glared at him. "I'm not working with Arthur, I'm probably not even working *for* Arthur anymore. Besides, why would I kill someone who's dying of an inoperable heart problem?"

"I can think of several million reasons to kill Cleon." He nodded at the fake license lying on the floor. "You want to tell me what that's about if you're so innocent?"

"I didn't kill anyone and how's a license going to prove I did?"

"What do you think the police will say when I tell them you transferred Cleon's money into an account in Terry Stevens's name? And then explain how I watched you commit a felony by getting a driver's license using Terry Stevens's identity?"

Maggie started to cry. "I didn't kill Cleon. And I didn't frame you. I didn't even know who you were until this morning. I only transferred the money after you told me Cleon drowned. I didn't think I was hurting anyone and Arthur is firing me and the payment on my parents' condo . . . I don't . . . I don't want to go to jail—"

"All right, calm down." It was clear this hysterical woman wasn't capable of masterminding this crime. He released her wrists but continued to straddle her. "Listen to me, Maggie, I'm not going to arrest you, so stop crying before someone hears you and calls the police."

While she composed herself, he considered his options. If Maggie hadn't done it, then Arthur must have been working alone. Therefore, whatever evidence might exist would either be in Arthur's office or home. Tim could use help getting in and out of both places.

"Look," he said, "I believe you didn't kill Cleon, but someone framed me and I'm going to need your help to find out who. Can I trust you?"

"I thought trust was the foundation of our whole relationship," she said. "Now will you please get off of me? Because for the record, I do generally prefer dinner and a movie before hopping in the sack with someone."

The scared look in her eyes disappeared as she smiled.

"Believe me, your virtue is safe with me," he said.

Maggie looked slightly disappointed.

"Actually, after that move with your knee I'm not sure I even can get off of you. I probably won't ever be able to have kids, either."

"My apologies to your wife."

"I don't have one."

"With your bedside manner I guess that shouldn't be a shock. So IRS man, are you just going to sit on me all day?"

"My name, again, is Tim."

"Tim, if we spend much more time like this in bed—"

"Calm down. You're not my type anyhow."

"Why? No, don't tell me, let me guess. Because my I.Q. isn't lower than my bust size?"

"Given your current circumstances, your I.Q. might actually be lower than your bust size. But I probably shouldn't jump to any conclusions."

"Get the hell off me."

"What's to keep you from running out the door as soon as I do?"

"Well, for one thing, I typically don't make public appearances wearing a bath towel."

"And a pair of the hairiest legs I've ever seen."

"Hey look, I forgot to shave, okay? I've had a few

things on my mind. But if one more person says anything about my legs, I'll. . . ."

"Do what? Shave them?"

"Can we forget about my legs for a minute? You obviously know what I did with Cleon's account so I'll help you get off the hook with the police if you let me keep the money from the Hamilton account. Deal?"

Tim thought for a moment. He had no intention of letting her keep Cleon's money, money that belonged to the IRS. But he couldn't keep her pinned on the bed forever either.

"You help me first, and then we'll see about Cleon's money."

She briefly considered her options. "Deal."

He got off her, careful to avoid her knees. She rolled away and stood clutching her towel.

Tim handed her purse to her, minus the mace. "Maybe you should turn the shower off before the entire hotel runs out of hot water."

She picked up her damp clothes and went to the bathroom. While she changed, Tim retrieved the pillows from the floor and straightened the bed from their struggle. By the time Maggie returned he was sitting at the desk, staring out the window at the rain and wondering whether involving Maggie was a good idea.

"So, what makes you think Arthur did it?" she said. "God, I'd love to help nail that blood-sucking tick."

He turned and noticed her hair was no longer a wet, tangled mess and she had put on some makeup. The effect was not wasted on him. "There was a radio show yesterday promoting a book called *Poisons: A Writer's Reference*. A guy named Arthur called in and asked about a poison to kill his fictional, rich father-in-law. The writer recommended English nightshade and described symptoms that matched Cleon's."

"That's it? A guy named Arthur calls a radio show and you think that's proof Arthur killed Cleon?"

"It's a start. In any crime situation, you look for who

has a motive. Arthur's got some serious financial problems and he's been disinherited. I'd say those are strong reasons to begin our investigation with him, and we've got to start somewhere."

"I still can't believe Cleon's gone." She bent over the heater, shaking her hair to help it finish drying. "You should have heard how excited he was when he called me from your office to tell me about the shredded cash."

"You knew yesterday morning about the shredded cash?"

She stood up and faced him. Her left hand covering her mouth. "Oh God. Now I'm never going to have another orgasm."

"What?"

"Cleon made me promise not to tell anyone about his plan to shred his money. If I did, I would curse myself and never have another orgasm."

"Does your mother know what kind of agreements you enter into?"

She shrugged.

"Since I have been hexed—although not with sexual dysfunction—I would be happy to help you determine if you're still able to achieve orgasm. Consider it a professional courtesy."

"I thought I wasn't your type."

"As they say, 'I'm from the government and I'm here to help you.' "

"Thank you for your kind offer, but my accountant would never forgive me if I started dating an IRS agent."

"Who said anything about dating?"

Embarrassment flamed Maggie's cheeks. She opened her mouth to retaliate with a sarcastic remark but couldn't think of one. Instead, she turned back to the heater to dry her hair and hide her face.

"Not to worry, though, your sex life isn't dead. I already knew about the shredded cash, as does half the world. Haven't you heard the reports on the radio or seen the news?"

"No. I played CDs in my car all the way up here from St. Louis." Her tone was brisk and business-like. After a long pause she said, "Cleon was really looking forward to screwing you and Arthur and I'm beginning to understand why."

Evidently his dating comment wasn't appreciated.

Tim filled her in on the crime scene he found at Cleon's, including the room full of shredded cash. They discussed the circumstances of Cleon's death, and the hostile edge in her voice gradually faded, or at least was redirected at Arthur.

"I would have loved to have seen Arthur's face when he found out about the shredded cash," she said. "Hey, maybe somehow Arthur saw the shredded cash, flipped out, and poisoned Cleon."

"Slow down, Maggie. Poisoning is usually premeditated. But you may have something. If Arthur poisoned Cleon, maybe he also salvaged some of the money." He thought about it after he said it. It seemed to make sense, but he wasn't sure if his desperation to find the monies owed to the IRS and save his job was affecting his reasoning.

"Perhaps a visit to Arthur's home will give us some answers," he said. "Get your stuff together, we better get going."

A flash of lightning punctuated his statement.

"I'm not going out in this weather. Besides, I'm not sure I want to get tangled up in all of this. I could lose my securities license."

Yes, it was definitely a mistake to involve her, but he didn't have any choice. Having his face plastered all over the media severely limited his ability to investigate. He would need help.

"You've got to be kidding," he said. "You steal over three million dollars from a dead man, all easily traceable and provable, and you don't think you're tangled up?"

Maggie shrugged.

"If you'd rather I have the police come and pick you

up now, just say the word." Tim walked over to her and stared down into her eyes. The top of her head was just below his chest and he knew his height added an element of threat. "Decide right here and now if you're going to help me or if you're going to jail."

She blinked first and turned away. "I guess 'C', none of the above, is not an option?"

He smiled. "No, I'm afraid not. But I will give you this, if anything happens and you are in danger in any way, I'll cut you loose and finish this on my own."

She frowned.

"Don't worry," he said. "Nothing's going to happen."

They packed up their few belongings. Tim carefully wiped down every surface in the hotel room that might hold their prints. It took over an hour and a half to sterilize the place, and when they left it was cleaner than when Maggie had arrived.

On the way to the parking lot, Tim handed her the garden gloves he had used while driving.

"Don't you think you're being a little anal?" she said.

"Did you forget you gave the SEC a set of your fingerprints when you started as a financial consultant? If the car falls into the hands of the police. . . ."

She put the gloves on.

Tim wrapped two towels from the hotel around his hands to safeguard against leaving his own fingerprints and settled in on the floor of the back seat for the bumpy ride to St. Louis. Maggie splashed her way across back roads to avoid troopers patrolling the major arteries. They got lost several times and arrived at Maggie's condo just after midnight. She parked Tim's car in her garage, between an unused mountain bike and a set of wicker furniture. Her spare bedroom didn't have any sheets on the bed, and by the time she fixed up his bed it was 1:30 a.m.

Maggie crawled into her own bed and fell asleep before she could worry about the fugitive IRS agent sleeping down the hall whom she had just wished pleasant dreams. She slept fitfully and dreamed Terry Stevens turned her

Chapter **22**

On Wednesday morning at 7:30, Arthur Riley drove his
Mercedes out of his driveway just like he did every
day. This morning, though, when Arthur's car turned the
corner, Tim's car huffed and puffed and, with a thunder-
ous backfire, pulled onto the private drive leading to Arthur's home. He parked the rent-a-wreck next to the
garage where monstrous old pine trees guarding the estate's perimeter effectively hid him and Maggie from nosy
neighbors. He left the car running, partly because he was
worried that if he turned it off it wouldn't start again, and
partly to ensure a quick escape if he triggered Arthur's
security alarm. Maggie slid behind the wheel of the car
while Tim made his way to the brick sidewalk that led to
the back of the house.

Tim pulled on his gardening gloves and prepared for
the next phase of his new life of crime. He walked by the
strategically placed security system warning signs and
peered through the etched windows flanking the back
door. He didn't see a security panel on any of the walls.

It seemed that cheapskate Arthur may have paid for the signs advertising a security system but didn't have one installed.

Two squirrels scrambled up a nearby oak tree looking for a shady spot to spend the morning. The heat had returned and, combined with Tim's overworked nerves, was causing drizzles of sweat to drip down his back.

He made a fist and punched in the window pane parallel with the door knob. The squirrels disappeared into the trees at the sound of the shattering glass.

A moment later Maggie came running around the corner of the house hissing, "Shhh, shhhh!"

Tim ignored her and waited for an alarm to sound but the house remained dormant. Everything was silent except for the laboring noise coming from the wreck Maggie had left running. He reached his arm past the jagged glass and unlocked the back door. Once inside he was immediately assaulted by the smell of gas. He stepped back outside to catch his breath.

"What are you doing? We've got to hurry. I can't miss Arthur's nine o'clock sales meeting," she said.

"Arthur's house seems to have sprung a leak. See for yourself."

"God, the whole house is filled with gas," she said, returning to the fresh air.

Tim debated proceeding into the home. Being blown to smithereens by a gas leak would dramatically reduce his chances of clearing his name.

"You wait here. Let me see if I can find the leak."

Maggie didn't argue.

Tim left the back door open and hurried to the kitchen in search of the leak. The two-story kitchen seemed larger than his entire apartment. He stood momentarily soaking in the opulence of a lifestyle he would never know on his paycheck. A white and green checkered ceramic tile floor, white custom cabinetry with a center island complete with indoor grilling range, even skylights over the three-level sink. He listened for the hiss of gas but the house was quiet. The burners on the stove were turned off and so was the oven.

He was looking for the basement door when the fumes began to make him too nauseous. He stumbled outside to replenish his oxygen.

At the sound of his coughing, Maggie came back from watching by the side of the house.

"I think we're screwed. This thing could blow any minute," he said.

"Could we make an anonymous call to the police about the gas leak?" she said. "Then we could come back after they fix it and it airs out."

"The police will notice the broken glass, and the neighbors will notice the police. Soon the whole place would be crawling with rich, neurotic neighbors trying to find out what was going on. We'd never be able to get back inside."

"Then you've got to get into Arthur's office. He keeps a record of everything, every meal he buys, every purchase that could be construed as a client gift, everything makes its way to his taxes as a deduction of some kind. Hell, he used to brag about writing off his wedding reception as client entertainment. If there's something connecting him to Cleon's death you'll find it in his receipts, I'm sure of it."

"Maybe if I can find the basement and the source of the leak, I can turn it off. You could go to the sales meeting, and we can come back after the house has aired out."

"Sounds like a plan to me."

Tim took deep breaths, hoping not to hyperventilate, and entered the house again. His heart pounded as he found a pantry, a bathroom, and several closets.

Finally, in the main hallway, he located the basement door. He dashed down the steps with the gas stench getting stronger the further he went. At the bottom there was a room with a pool table and bar area, but no furnace.

He opened more doors and, after a few false starts, found the door to the mechanical room. He could hear the noise of gas blowing without a pilot light from the furnace in the far corner.

Six corrugated file boxes were stacked beside it with a cordless telephone lying on top of the box closest to the furnace. He stepped past the boxes and reached down to turn the noxious fumes off. Thankfully, the furnace didn't explode in his face.

By the time Tim fell on the grass outside, he was dizzy and nauseous. He lay on the lawn sucking in the fresh air. Maggie crouched beside him for an update, but he closed his eyes and concentrated on his breathing.

"Hey Mister, are you the one who broke Riley's window?" a timid voice said.

Tim opened his eyes to see three small boys staring down at them. He pulled himself to his feet and tried to look like he belonged there. "Yes, this house has a gas leak. It's not safe, now go home immediately!"

The three darted off, pushing and shoving each other while they fled.

So much for letting the house ventilate.

"The furnace's pilot light was out and I got the gas shut off." He paused to take more deep breaths. "I saw a bunch of filing boxes down in the basement that might help us. Those kids could be back any time with one of their moms. Do you think you can check out Arthur's office while I go back to the basement?"

"I'll try."

Together they went back into Arthur's gas-filled time bomb.

Arthur Riley sat in his Mercedes convertible outside a 7-Eleven drinking his morning java and enjoying the sun. He picked up his cell phone and punched in his home phone number. After two days of mix-ups and mistakes, at least blowing up his house would go according to plan.

He had read in the paper two months ago about some bozo who was using gasoline to clean his garage floor. When the guy's cordless phone in the garage rang it ignited the gasoline fumes. Arthur planned a little recreation in his basement today.

With the St. Louis real estate market for $650,000 homes being so slow, this seemed like an ideal way of collecting some much-needed insurance money and avoiding a real estate agent's commission while destroying any documentation that could ever be requested for a tax audit. He started to punch in the last digit of his home number when his phone rang.

"Hello?"

"It's Mr. Smith."

"This isn't a good time, Smith. I'm trying to make a phone call if you know what I mean."

"That's why I called. Maggie and some other guy are in your house right now. I think she's with the IRS agent that's been all over the news. I'm not sure what they're doing but you could kill two birds with one stone if you know what I mean."

Arthur backed his car out of the 7-Eleven parking lot and drove down the street to his office to avoid being overheard by a morning commuter going into the convenience store.

"This is perfect," Arthur said. "Maybe they'll even be blamed for the—"

"I know what you mean, but you better hurry. They've been in and out."

Tim showed Maggie where Arthur's office was off the main hallway and then returned to the basement. The smell seemed less offensive. Was he getting used to it or was the gas dissipating?

Maggie opened the windows in Arthur's office to let a slight breeze circulate into the room. The garden gloves she bought this morning made rifling Arthur's desk more cumbersome but they kept her from leaving prints.

Arthur's desk was surprisingly void of important papers. There were no copies of tax returns, no bank statements, no family records of any kind. Arthur's office seemed to be missing several things. Indentations on the carpeting betrayed where two chairs had been removed recently, the computer stand was empty except for a pile of blank computer paper, and there were spots on the wall revealing where several pictures had hung.

She stared briefly at the morning paper sitting on the desk corner and tried to determine what her next move should be. What was she was looking for? Where was the piece of evidence connecting Arthur to Cleon's murder?

The fumes were still very strong, and the three boys could return any minute with the National Guard.

She went to the window to check for an approaching SWAT Team. When she pulled back the curtain, she discovered a briefcase sitting on the floor. She stood by the open window and searched its contents. Inside she found a binder of statements charting Hamilton's sales and profits, an address book, several old *Wall Street Journals*, research reports on various stocks, and a stack of past-due margin calls indicating Arthur's serious financial trouble. Then, in the case's file pocket she found a manila envelope marked "CC!" She quickly opened it and found a receipt for some tea and a nursery bill of sale for English nightshade.

Another dead end.

Arthur pulled into his parking spot at Hamilton Securities. He was about to punch the last digit of his home phone number when his phone rang for the second time this morning.

He hit the receive button. "Damn it, what is it?"

"Mr. Riley," Janet said, "I hate to bother you, but there's a Mary Hodgkins on the line for you. She's called several times. She said it's extremely urgent that she talk with you."

"All right, patch her through."

A second later a tentative voice said, "Hello?"

"This is Arthur Riley."

"Mr. Riley, thank you for taking my call. I realize you're a busy man, but I'm calling regarding a potential felony one of your financial consultants may have committed."

Arthur leaned back in his seat. This was the last thing he needed to hear. "Are you SEC?"

"No . . . actually my name is Mary Hodgkins and I work for the Illinois License and Registration Bureau. Yesterday, we had a woman in her late twenties apply for a driver's license under the name of Terry Stevens."

He leaned forward. "Yes?" So this was where the Stevens account came from.

"We believe it was a fraudulent application. The woman was about five-two, skinny, with long red hair. Is there any chance that would fit the description of Maggie Connors?"

"Maggie Connors? Why would you think it's her?"

"The woman left a *Wall Street Journal* behind. The name Maggie Connors and Hamilton Securities with your office address was on the mailing label. I'm just following up on a hunch that it was her. Can you verify her description for me?"

"Mrs. Hodgkins, Maggie Connors is about six feet tall, one hundred and twenty pounds, with short blond hair. She's got a figure that belongs in a MTV video. I don't think we're talking about the same person."

"Oh. I thought for sure—"

"I'm surprised you didn't contact the Missouri Department of Motor Vehicles with your suspicion."

"Well, as I said, it was just a hunch. I didn't want to file any formal inquiries."

Arthur nodded. *So no one knew about it. Good.*

"I'm sorry I couldn't be more helpful," he said. "Now, if you'll excuse me, I'm on my way to a meeting."

"Oh, of course. I'm sorry to have bothered you."

Arthur lit a cigar, grabbed his cell phone, and walked to his office. So little Maggie had obtained an alternative identity. He wouldn't have thought she was capable of

such deception. He almost felt a little attraction for her.
Maybe she had potential he had never seen before.

He tossed his cell phone and caught it. Too bad she
was about to be blown to little tiny bits and pieces.

Tim ran out the back door and climbed into the old
Chevy. He said a small prayer to the cellular god hoping
the car phone would actually work as promised. His
shoulders relaxed slightly at the sound of the familiar ring
as the phone number beamed itself to a cell tower and
connected him to his office.

In the boxes in Arthur's basement he had found a brochure on the Cayman Islands and some notes on Cayman
banks and attorneys. He was sure there was more evidence
in the boxes but it was too much to sort through with the
gas fumes. Perhaps an anonymous tip could lead to a
search warrant for Arthur's home so the police could focus their investigation on the real suspect.

"Criminal Investigation Division," the receptionist said.

Before Tim could respond, an explosion blew the hubcaps off the Chevy.

Arthur's house was engulfed in a fireball.

Chapter 23

Ed Granger grabbed his phone. "Hello?"

"Hi, Granger, it's Detective Brook. I promised I'd call and let you know what we came up with yesterday regarding the Gallen investigation. It doesn't look good for your guy."

Granger sat down at his desk. "Okay, give me the worst."

"We searched Gallen's house yesterday. That place looks like it belongs in a Ralph Lauren catalog."

"Did you find anything?"

"He had some interesting trash waiting to be picked up by the garbage men."

"What was in it?"

"Just a bank deposit slip, with Monday's date, showing a two million dollar deposit."

Granger hung his head as he listened. Damn. Two million.

"I called the bank, but they said the account had been closed first thing that morning. The funds were wired out to a Swiss bank account. From there it went to Greenland. We're not real sure where it went from there; our department isn't up to speed on tracking international money transfers."

"I just can't believe this. There's got to be some explanation."

"Even if your boy has some answers, I'm not sure what good it would do. At this point I think the evidence is so overwhelming that it would be hard to find a jury who would buy any explanation."

"Thanks for—"

"There's more. We found Gallen's car in the long-term parking lot at the airport last night. According to the attendant's records it had been there since two or three Tuesday morning. I think in all likelihood, Gallen fled the country Tuesday morning before the shit hit the fan. He could have been sitting on a plane when he called in the money transfers. Right now he's probably laughing his ass off on the Riviera with a drink in his hand and two mill in the bank."

"Shit."

"I'm sorry, really I am. We'll try to keep these latest developments out of the media, but they're all over this case. I can't promise anything. How's the heat in your department?"

"Trust me. You wouldn't want to be in my shoes right now."

"I'd believe that. But look on the bright side, it's only Wednesday, maybe your week will improve."

"Thanks, and thanks for the update."

Granger hung up. He had a meeting with his boss in an hour, and he still wasn't sure how he was going to explain all of this.

He'd always trusted Tim. How could he have been so wrong?

Chapter **24**

Arthur paced at the front of the room with his hands folded behind his back.

It was five before nine and the Hamilton Securities conference room was slowly filling with brokers. Most had just finished a McDonald's gastrointestinal breakfast delight, which, Arthur realized, hardly put them in the mood to listen to one of his motivational speeches. Some of the more seasoned brokers even brought their own reading material to amuse themselves during the required meeting.

Once everyone was seated, Arthur stepped behind the podium.

"I'd like to begin this morning by thanking everyone for the cards and flowers regarding the death of my father-in-law," he said. "It's been a difficult situation and I appreciate everyone's support." Actually, he hadn't received any displays of sympathy from his employees but a little bit of guilt was always a good way to start a meeting. "Yet, in the middle of the turmoil surrounding dear

Cleon's death, I had a client storm into my office shaking a letter at me. A letter that was sent from this office. I'd like to share it with you."

He put on his reading glasses.

"The letter reads: 'I haven't seen my family, friends, or girlfriend in twenty-one days. My hair has grown long and I now have a beard. People around the office are tired of seeing me in the same blue suit and white shirt. I think the police towed my Porsche away as an abandoned vehicle. Unless my two cats have figured out how to operate a can opener, they have either starved to death or escaped the house in search of food. Why? Because I have been waiting here in my office for your call, the one you promised you'd make three weeks ago. After waiting all this time, I've decided to take drastic action and pen this letter to you. Please give me a call if you have any interest in doing business. If you have no further interest, simply continue as you have these last few weeks. I'll get the hint.' "

Arthur lowered the letter and stared at the brokers assembled before him. "The letter was written by Bill Farley."

He hoped Farley might show a little appropriate remorse, but instead Farley stood victoriously in the back row and took a bow.

"Bill, I'm putting a copy of this letter in your employment file. I expect you to have an apology letter in the mail to your client today."

Farley nodded smugly and signaled an okay sign that transformed into a jerking-off gesture.

"Is this the level this office has sunk to?" Arthur lofted some spittle on the newer brokers sitting in the front row. "You've all become a bunch of—"

He stopped when Maggie walked through the door.

"And to think I almost missed this inspiring meeting," Maggie whispered, gliding into the seat next to Bill. She was exhausted from the adrenaline rush of Arthur's house exploding and then fleeing the scene before the police arrived. She couldn't stop shaking. Had she not gone out Arthur's front door for some fresh air she wouldn't have made it to this or any other meeting. She was dizzy and had been leaning against a huge walnut tree on the side facing away from Arthur's house when the house blew. The tree protected her from the explosion, otherwise she was sure she would be lying in a morgue right now with shrapnel from Arthur's house embedded in what remained of her body.

"As I was saying, you've all become a bunch of vertebrateless Gumby dolls," Arthur said.

"You're just in time," Bill whispered back. "We've just started making up words."

"You've got to remember you're professionals and to push yourselves to do things you've never done before." Arthur pounded his fat little fist on the podium. "If you usually ask for a 200-share order, next time ask for a 400-share order. If you aren't asking for referrals, start asking."

"Mr. Jones, do you know three other people who don't want to invest in the market right now?" whispered Bill to Maggie.

Maggie returned a smile, but she hadn't really heard him. The image of Arthur's house blowing up and almost being killed was all she could think about.

Arthur's speech dragged on. "There is business to be done out there in good markets and in bad ones. Curt Springer did over $20,000 in commissions yesterday, with $7,500 of it in Hamilton's new technology fund that so many of you are turning your noses up at."

"Springer hasn't had any clients long enough to have to explain why they lost their shirts in Hamilton's old technology fund," responded one of the older brokers, loud enough for Arthur to hear. Arthur ignored his comment, not wanting to confront one of the few brokers in the office who was generating commissions.

"I am reinstating our cold-calling clinics on Thursday

nights as well as Saturdays and Sundays. Anyone who was below their production goal last month is expected to attend. I'm very serious about this. It's about time this office started giving some good phone. I was in here a couple of nights last week and only a few of the new brokers were in making calls. That's part of the reason this office is lagging so far behind production goals for the region. You guys can do it. You've got the most valuable analysts on Wall Street supplying you with direction. There's no reason why your clients shouldn't be participating in this market. All you have to do is believe in yourselves. Anything is possible when you apply the sales techniques you've been taught."

"I'm not in the mood for Arthur's Mary Kay impersonation," Bill murmured to Maggie.

"I thought you liked it when Arthur put on that pink dress and pumps."

"Maggie, if you have a sales tip you would like to share with the group, I for one would like to hear it," Arthur snarled.

"No, you're doing just fine. I have nothing to add."

"Really, Maggie, your production this year is about half of what it should be. Maybe you could give some of the newer brokers some advice on what not to do."

He tried not to grin as he watched Maggie sit silently and clench her jaw. She had provided a perfect opportunity to expose her poor performance to the rest of the office. It would be one more piece to justify her suicide when the police conducted their investigation.

"I'm serious when I say it's time for this office to pull its ass out of the slumps and start producing some real numbers." He rubbed his chin and pretended to mull over something of great consequence. "Maggie, if you don't hit the production goals we discussed by close of market today then I want your shit out of that office and in the empty cubicle by the restrooms before the market opens tomorrow morning or you're fired."

He could tell she had been expecting this and was trying to stay calm but her face turned a crimson red.

He scanned the meeting to gauge the brokers' reactions. The older brokers stared at the floor, mortified one of their own had just been publicly flogged. The newer brokers shared conspiring looks. They would take their shot at a private office any way they could.

The sound of his secretary opening the conference room door broke the silence in the room. It was obvious by looking at the woman that she did not want to bear his wrath for the news she was about to deliver.

"What is it now?" Arthur said.

She stood in the doorway wringing her hands.

"I'm in the middle of a meeting. Spit it out for God's sake."

"Your house exploded," she said.

"What?" Arthur reached for the podium as support. "My house has what?"

His secretary began crying. "The police just called. They think it was a gas leak."

Smiles adorned the faces of most of the brokers.

"I can't believe it," he said, shaking his head. *At least one thing has gone right this morning.* He shuddered.

"Oh, Mr. Riley, I'm so sorry." The secretary scurried from the room.

"Thank God my cleaning lady wasn't there today. Oh no, my wedding pictures, everything, it's all gone." His took off his glasses and rubbed his eyes. "I can't believe it."

"I guess what goes around comes around, you fat bastard," Maggie mumbled just loud enough for him to hear.

The meeting adjourned and she returned to her office wishing she had a door to close. A few brokers stopped by to swap theories on who blew up Arthur's home, but Maggie wasn't in the mood. Several of them shared their indignation over Arthur's treatment of her. Although they seemed sincere, Maggie felt they were scoping her office for possible upgrades in furniture.

Arthur's public rebuke was the perfect excuse to quit Hamilton Securities. No one would question her departure, and she could quietly disappear with Cleon's money. Yet Arthur's comments incensed her. She sat in her chair watching the office resume its activity and noticed how everyone seemed to be making an effort not to look at her. There was no point continuing the farce, it would only make Arthur happier. She would come in tonight, after everyone had left, and clean out her office. Now she was going to visit her Terry Stevens mailbox to see if a certain Hamilton Securities check had arrived.

Chapter 25

Every muscle in Maggie's body tensed as she scanned the wall of rental mailboxes at Mail Boxes Etc. She found hers near the middle. She slipped the key into the lock and turned it.

Empty. Nothing but four silver, glistening walls the size of a shoe box.

She checked with the woman behind the counter who confirmed the day's mail had been delivered, then moped back outside and hailed a cab. Maybe it was just as well. She would spend the rest of the day helping Tim with his investigation, and by this time tomorrow he would be gone and the check she needed to pay for her bonds would be there.

Her next stop was the Stevens home. She found her real driver's license where it had fallen between the cushions. She replaced the borrowed birth certificate and checked the plants one last time. They were all still alive, sort of. Then she took the cab home, where she found

Tim sitting at her kitchen table finishing a bowl of Captain Crunch.

Tim put his empty cereal bowl in the sink and leaned against the counter, careful to avoid the blades of the ceiling fan circling within inches of his head. "I've been thinking about it. Arthur must have moved all the papers you said were missing from his office down to the basement on purpose. I think he blew up his house to make it all disappear."

Maggie had poured herself a bowl of cereal and stopped crunching to consider this. "Makes sense. That would also give him an insurance check to solve his short-term financial problems. But with the evidence gone, where does that leave us?" She hoped Tim was going to give up and leave the country or something equivalent so she could concentrate on Cleon's account.

"If Arthur was as meticulous as you say, my guess is he probably keeps a backup of everything. You said his computer was missing from his home office? Maybe we'll get lucky and find a backup disk at his Hamilton office or even a hard copy of something."

Maggie resumed her crunching. She wasn't sure a backup disk was going to prove anything, but getting a look inside Arthur's office might be useful for other reasons.

"Since I'm not on Arthur's A list I don't think I can just stop by his office and rummage through his files."

"We can break into his office tonight when nobody is around."

"Sorry, Mr. Bond, but I'm not proficient at lock picking. My keys will only get us through the main lobby doors. How are we going to get into Arthur's office?"

"Where is it?"

"Tucked down a hallway at one corner of the boardroom. Why?"

"I noticed the other day that your office has a dropped ceiling. If it continues back to Arthur's office I bet I could boost you up through the ceiling tiles and you could crawl over and unlock Arthur's door from the inside. I know it has the flair of a Watergate break-in, but I think it could work." Tim paused to get a Pepsi out of the refrigerator. "Is your computer set up to use the Internet?"

"I have a modem, but I just canceled my ISP service because their access lines are always busy."

"Okay, we'll need to pick up an AOL disc somewhere, and while we wait for Operation Drop In, I'd like to talk to the guy who bought Stuffing Stuff from Cleon. I'm sure the police have finished interviewing him by now and maybe he can lead us to another angle."

"That can't be too safe. Your photo is all over the news."

He rubbed his unshaven chin. "This beard stubble should help a little. And I can wear a baseball cap pulled low."

"Yeah, and maybe you could squint and pass as Asian. What if we get stopped on the way down?"

"You can drive, and I'll get under a blanket in the back seat. Just don't break any traffic laws on the way."

"Look, so far this morning I was almost killed and we barely got out of Arthur's before the police showed up. I don't think this is working out. Maybe it would be better if you just went by yourself."

"Why are you acting so cranky all of a sudden? Is this a bad time of the month or something?"

Maggie jumped to her feet and looked for something to throw at him but didn't see anything she was willing to break. "Get out of my house now!"

"What? What did I say?"

"Monday the client I was counting on to save my career turned out to be a fake and my favorite client was murdered. Yesterday I did who knows how much damage to my car driving into an open manhole and then I got the ever-loving-shit scared out of me when you attacked me in that cheap hotel. And then this morning, I break into my boss's house, almost get blown to smithereens, and, when I make it to the damn sales meeting, Arthur humiliates me by evicting me from my office in front of everyone. On top of all that, I've got my parents' $25,000 down payment for their retirement condo on six different Visa cards and no way to pay it. So if I'm a little cranky, it's got nothing to do with my menstrual period."

Tim didn't move.

"I mean it. Get out of this house and get out of my life now, or I'm calling the police. Besides, what happened to, 'Oh if you're in any danger, I'll do this by myself?' "

"Look, I didn't know about all that stuff and I'm sorry." He walked over and put his hands on her shoulders.

She pushed him away.

"Trust me," he said, "you're not going to get in trouble going to Stuffing Stuff with me. Change into some jeans, put a baseball cap on, and we'll look like two summer tourists."

"You haven't heard a word I've said. I'm not going anywhere with you."

"Maggie, have your forgotten our little deal?"

"You said if I help you, we'd see about me getting Cleon's money."

"Fine, you help me, and I'll let you keep Cleon's money. It would seem that if your career is on the rocks as badly as you say, getting your hands on Cleon's money is probably more important to you now than ever. So, either you continue to help me or I'll call Arthur and let him know who Terry Stevens really is."

She didn't believe he'd honor his part of the deal, but she didn't have much choice. She picked up her empty cereal bowl and flung it at the opposite wall.

"Dish hostility is not going to solve anything."

She stormed out of the kitchen and pounded down the hallway to her bedroom. She slammed the bedroom door so hard two pictures fell off the wall in the adjacent bathroom. She leaned against the door a minute and thought about crying. Then she thought about murder. Then she thought about ducking through the open bedroom window and disappearing. If only she had the check.

Finally, she began looking for some clean jeans.

Ten minutes later Maggie emerged wearing a black Polo shirt and jeans. Her hair was stuffed into a black and red Cardinals hat that, despite her misgivings, helped to conceal her identity. She certainly didn't look like the prim, uptight broker Tim had first seen in her office. She looked more natural now, despite the way she glared at Tim.

They drove to Stuffing Stuff in silence, each wearing their garden gloves from this morning. Tim reminded her not to touch anything while they were in the store. A little before noon Tim used the front of his T-shirt to open the front door of Cleon's former taxidermy showroom.

Every square inch of wall space inside the store was filled with mounted heads. The floor was crammed with various animals ranging from a pair of mallards perched on a mossy log to a grizzly bear poised to attack. The animals were jammed so close to each other it looked like the 5:15 commuter train back to the animal kingdom.

No one greeted them so they followed the narrow aisle to the back of the store. There, behind a counter, they found a man hunched over a keyboard, his face illuminated by the glow of the computer screen.

Tim pulled his baseball cap down tighter. "Excuse me." His voice was absorbed by all the fur in the store. The man by the computer didn't move. "Excuse me," he said louder.

The man looked up from his paperwork. "I'm sorry. May I help you?"

"We were next door at the cafe and noticed your sign and decided to stop in," Tim said. He hoped he and Maggie looked the part of a married couple on vacation. They weren't talking to each other, which helped their role-playing.

"Yeah, I've been hearing that. I put up a new sign last Friday and I think it's really helping." He gave Tim an open, friendly stare. "You look real familiar. Are you sure you haven't been in here before?"

"No. I think I'd remember this store."

Maggie stood off to the side with her arms crossed, not saying anything.

"How long have you had this place?" Tim asked. "I don't remember seeing this store before."

"Well, the store's been in this strip mall for about three years. I bought it from the guy who owned it about a month ago. I've got some new brochures that explain my pricing right here." He pulled several brochures from behind the counter and handed one to Tim.

Maggie bent down to take a closer look at a fox with its front legs standing on a log. "These are so lifelike."

"Thanks. They keep me from getting lonely while I try to make heads from tails with this new computer system."

Tim walked to where the man was standing by the counter. "New sign, new brochure, new computer system. Sounds like you're making quite a few changes."

"Yeah, Cleon—the guy I bought the place from—was a great guy. He'd do anything for anyone and was really well connected, which is how he got all his business. In fact, maybe three weeks ago he rented a huge Ryder truck and personally delivered a grizzly and about a dozen other animals to Senator Cartwright in Washington, D.C. But me, I'm not so connected. I've got to rely on things like brochures and bigger signs to help bring business in." He turned to Maggie who was still admiring the fox. "Would you like to see another one? I have one over by the front door."

Maggie followed the man to the front of the store. Tim waited until they'd stepped around the grizzly then he quickly leaned over the counter. By the time he straightened up, the owner was holding a fox that was curled up as if asleep.

"Is there some room in particular you're thinking about adding an animal to?" he said.

"No, not really. I guess we're just looking."

Tim joined them. "I'm curious. You said you bought the store a month ago, but three weeks ago the owner was still making deliveries?"

"Yeah, I've worked for Cleon for years, so after I officially bought the place, Cleon agreed to stay on for a while as kind of a consultant. He had a tendency to keep everything up here." The owner tapped his forehead. "The downside was there were a lot of details I just didn't know about, like what taxes were paid and where our outstanding receivables were. He never recorded things like that. I think that's one of the reasons he had so much grief from the IRS. Anyway, Cleon was still working full-time to make sure he hadn't forgotten to tell me about something when it happened."

"Oh my gosh, is he the man who drowned a couple days ago?" Maggie asked. "I'm so sorry."

Tim pulled his baseball cap even lower.

The owner nodded his head. "Yeah, it's a real crime. I guess some IRS agent went off the deep end."

The three wandered back to the rear of the store.

"I just got a new computer system myself," Tim said. "What kind are you using?"

"It's the new Windows system, but by the time I figure it out it will probably be the old Windows system and I'll have to start all over." The man turned to glare at the computer and then turned back to Tim. "Cleon thought computers were just big paperweights, and I'm beginning to think maybe he was right."

Tim tucked the brochure into his back pocket. "He never computerized anything? I didn't think a business could operate these days without a computer."

"He tried. About a year ago he read some guy's obituary and remembered he never charged him for a deer head. He sent me to Radio Shack that day and I bought a nice little system—had everything but a modem. It only lasted a week. Cleon got fed up with it and took it home to play the computer games that were on it. Said Solitaire was the only thing it was good for. I sure am going to miss him."

"Yeah," Maggie said with a sigh.

Tim glared at her.

"I mean, he sounds like a really great guy," she said quickly.

"I can't even begin to tell you." The owner went over to his desk. "*The Dispatch* has another story about Cleon today. They're even running a photo of the IRS agent with a $50,000 reward—Cleon was on their board of directors. The paper is around here somewhere."

While the owner searched his desk for the article, Tim and Maggie backed toward the door.

"Here it is, I knew—" The owner glanced from the paper to Tim. "Hey, it's you! It's you!"

They ran to Tim's car trying not to cause a scene.

"That was a dangerous waste of time," Maggie said as they sped out of the parking lot. "Now the police are going to be looking for me, too."

"It wasn't a waste of time." Tim held up four preprinted UPS shipping labels he'd lifted from behind the counter while the new owner and Maggie were looking at the fox. "I'm curious why a man who thought a computer was only good for games had UPS tracking software loaded on his home computer. And to use UPS software on-line required him to buy a modem."

Tim slipped the forms back into his pocket. If his hunch was right, then he might come out of this with his career intact yet.

Chapter **26**

The medical examiner opened the door, and two days of decay hit Arthur in the face. He stumbled back into the hallway.

"My God! That stench is horrendous."

"Warm water has the most devastating effects on a corpse," the examiner said, "and this body has been soaking for almost forty-eight hours. Do you think you can continue?"

"Yes, goddamnit. I wasted most of the morning driving down here. Let's get this over with."

Arthur prepared himself for the smell before the examiner opened the door again, but it didn't matter. Although he clamped his fingers over his nose and breathed through his mouth, the odor seeped in and ambushed his nasal passages. The examiner waited until Arthur signaled he was ready to proceed, then removed the white sheet covering Cleon's body.

Arthur struggled to make sense of what he saw. The dried mud caked in Cleon's mouth and nose contrasted ghoulishly with the blanched, distended skin. He knew it was Cleon, but it looked more like a hideous special effects creation.

And the smell! Arthur covered his mouth to contain the repulsion growing inside.

A sparkle from Cleon's one-karat diamond wedding ring pulled Arthur's eyes away from the face. The jewel was oblivious to the desecration it adorned. Arthur stared at Cleon's bloated fingers. Two of Cleon's fingernails were missing and the others looked ready to fall off at the slightest breeze. But the air was still. There was no movement in the morgue.

He looked again at his father-in-law's face to gain some understanding of what he was seeing when a maggot crawled out of Cleon's nose.

A bottle of smelling salts brought Arthur back to consciousness. He opened his eyes and immediately knocked the offensive bottle from the examiner's hands. It shattered against the floor, adding its own peculiar odor to the room. Arthur ripped open the door and escaped into the hallway. He bent over and leaned against the wall as he tried to regain his normal breathing.

"Seeing a loved one in that kind of condition can cause anyone to faint. It's nothing to be embarrassed about."

"Who wouldn't faint looking at that maggot-infested body?"

"So you can't positively identify—"

"Oh, it's Cleon all right. I'd recognize that diamond ring anywhere. By the way, who gets the rock?"

"Excuse me?"

"Cleon's diamond, who gets it?"

"Once the autopsy and the investigation are complete, his personal effects will be returned to the next of kin, assuming they aren't needed as evidence."

"Can I get some kind of receipt? Just to make sure that when you slice and dice him, or whatever you ghouls do, it doesn't slip off his finger and mysteriously disappear?"

"Mr. Riley, I assure you all personal items are carefully

inventoried so there are no mishaps or surprises." The examiner looked at the clipboard he had been holding. "Because of the condition of the body, the coroner will want to make bite molds and take dental x-rays to conclusively identify it. Do you know who Cleon's dentist was so we can track down his dental records?"

Arthur stood up and straightened his tie. "Do I look like the freaking tooth fairy to you? I haven't talked to this man in years. I don't have the first clue who took care of his plaque." He turned and walked toward the exit.

"Identifying the body conclusively will help us close our investigation sooner. The sooner the investigation is closed, the sooner family heirlooms can be returned to loved ones."

Arthur stopped and turned around. "Cleon's checking account was at my firm. I'll have my secretary search his transactions for a check made out to a dentist. I'll get you the name within the hour."

Arthur drove back to his office and found two detectives waiting to question him about the gas leak. The horror of what he'd just gone through helped him perform his role of distraught homeowner perfectly. He repeated the story he had told the police earlier: he had been doing some house cleaning last night, moving files to the basement, and hadn't noticed the gas smell. He recalled leaving the cordless phone on the top of the last file box he took to the basement. They took down his comments, word for word, and, if they didn't seem entirely satisfied with his story, at least they offered their condolences before leaving.

Arthur's secretary appeared at his door. "Mr. Riley, your insurance agent is on line one, would you like me to take a message?" she said.

"I'll take it."

Arthur picked up his phone and motioned for the secretary to leave.

"Riley here."

"Hello, Mr. Riley, this is Lynn Frick. I'm sorry to hear about your house."

"I'm just thankful the cleaning lady wasn't there."

"Yes, that would have made it an even greater tragedy," the agent said.

Arthur pulled a fingernail clipper from his desk drawer and started clipping his nails.

"I talked with our investigator," Frick said. "He's waiting for the police report to answer some questions. While he was at your place this morning he told me he talked with one of your neighbors, a real estate agent named Sherlyn Harrison. I guess you were thinking about selling your home?"

Arthur stopped clipping. "I was thinking about taking out a home-equity line of credit and wanted to see what the place was worth. Getting a market value from a real estate agent was cheaper than having an appraisal done."

"I see. And did you?"

"Did I what?"

"Did you take out the home-equity loan?"

"No, I made other arrangements." He put the fingernail clipper away. "So when do you think I'll be getting my check?"

"Well, as I said, the investigator is waiting on the police report, and he still has a few things to check out."

"Your commercials show your agents at disaster sites cutting checks with hurricanes still spinning in the background."

"Mr. Riley, disaster relief is a little different situation."

"What's the difference? I've paid my premiums faithfully for years, and now my house is gone, my fully insured house."

"Yes, I appreciate that. The difference is that with a natural disaster, we don't have to go through the necessary steps to make sure fraud isn't involved."

"Did you say fraud?"

"It's just a matter of policy, I meant nothing personal by it."

"Listen lady, I want a check for the replacement value of my house on my desk by the end of the week or you'll hear from my lawyer."

"Mr. Riley, is your cell phone number 555-9009?"

Arthur glanced at his cell phone sitting on his desk. "Yes, it is. Why do you ask?"

"I received an anonymous call this morning from someone who said you might have called your own house yesterday and caused it to blow up."

"That's absurd." He loosened his tie.

"Would you have had any reason to call your empty house?"

"Lady, I spend my entire life on the phone, calling clients, talking to analysts. Sometimes I think I ought to just have a phone surgically attached to my head. If I called my own house it was probably by mistake."

"So you're not sure."

"I'm sure I did not blow up my own house."

"We'll be in touch with the police to see if they found any caller ID boxes in the rubble. In the meantime, the investigator will probably want to check with your cell phone company—"

"Anonymous calls are a very convenient way to drag out an investigation and avoid paying a settlement check. The police were just here, and they feel as though the explosion was an accident, so—"

"The police don't have quite the financial incentive we have to do a thorough investigation, now do they?"

"I'll tell them you said so." He leaned back in his chair and took a deep breath. "Look, I spent the morning picking through the rubble that used to be my house, and then I had to go to the morgue where I identified the body of my father-in-law that had been soaking in the river for several days. You just can't imagine. . . ."

"I'm sorry, I didn't know."

"How could you have? Anyway, to say I'm not thinking clearly at this point would be an understatement. If you need my cell phone records, I'll see that you get them, and I'm sorry if I've been hostile. It's just with everything going on. . . . Just call me if you need anything else."

"I'd appreciate your cooperation so we can get this matter closed."

"I'll make sure you have the information you need as soon as possible."

They said their goodbyes and Arthur hung up.

So much for a settlement check. Now he just wanted to get out of town with Cleon's money before he was arrested.

He called Mr. Smith.

"What was Maggie Connors doing at my sales meeting this morning?"

"If you would have called your house when I told you, she wouldn't have made the meeting."

"I didn't think this was such a difficult task. Maybe I need someone else to do the job."

"You don't know anyone else to do this job."

"The hell I don't. But I've paid you enough already, I might as well see this through. Where is she now?"

"I'm not sure. After the explosion this morning I got trapped in your neighborhood and couldn't get out without attracting attention."

"Look, she'll probably be back here soon, I told her to move her shit out of her office and into a cubicle by the end of today. See if she can have an accident crossing the street from the parking garage. If that doesn't work, get her tonight at her condo. Don't forget, this has got to look like an accident or you'll have one of your own."

There was a long pause.

"Don't threaten me, Arthur. You're not paying me that much."

Arthur leaned back in his chair feeling more confident than ever. "Smith, perhaps I have forgotten my place. Forgive me."

"This job is getting more complicated with this IRS agent hanging around. If he causes one more glitch we're going to have to reevaluate my fee."

"Let's see how things go this afternoon. I'll wait for your report."

Arthur hung up. When this nasty business was finished, Smith would be dead as well.

He walked to his outer office to see if his secretary had found Cleon's dentist.

Chapter **27**

Ed Granger swallowed the last of his Maalox. His week was going from bad to worse. Everyone from the mayor of St. Louis to the president of the United States was using the Gallen scandal to take potshots at the IRS and make statements about how the whole tax system should be overhauled. Then, when Channel 8 broke the news that Gallen and a female companion had been seen Wednesday afternoon at Cleon Cummings's former taxidermy business, a second wave of calls from reporters clogged the IRS phone lines. It had taken an hour for Ed's boss to reach him on the phone and deliver his own boat-load of shit.

Ed was afraid to watch TV that night for fear he'd be in Leno's monologue.

But the news about Gallen being spotted was hopeful. If the detectives were wrong about their original theory, and Gallen was still in St. Louis, then there must be a reason he was sticking around. Maybe the woman Gallen had been seen with could lead them to some answers.

Unfortunately, a call from the detectives had informed him that neither Gallen or his friend had left any fingerprints in the store. The shop owner had said the two kept their arms folded or had their hands in their pockets most of the time. Additionally, the shop owner's description of her was iffy at best. They promised to fax over the police artist's rendering the moment it was finished.

What was Gallen looking for? And how could Ed find out?

Ed left the mayhem in his office and walked down the hall to Gallen's former office. The detectives had searched the place yesterday and they weren't delicate—what was usually a fastidious work space was now in complete disarray. Files were strewn everywhere and books littered the floor. He had asked Dwight to try and restore some sense of order to the office but apparently Dwight hadn't had time.

Ed sat at Gallen's desk. Had Gallen really been sitting here just days ago putting the final touches on his grand scheme? A scheme that involved murder?

He buzzed Dwight and asked him to come to Gallen's office.

"Gallen would have a fit if he saw this place," Dwight said as he closed the door behind him. "Sorry I haven't had a chance—"

"Don't worry about it," Ed said. "The media's picked up the news that Gallen is now working with a woman. Any idea who she could be?"

"I thought that might be why you called me in here. I've been thinking about it since I heard the report but I can't come up with anyone."

"What happened to that airline attendant Gallen used to date?"

Dwight chuckled. "Boy, talk about a body to write home about. I think Gallen said she switched airlines and St. Louis was no longer a hub for her. She only came in town about once a month. They kind of drifted apart, and

I haven't heard Gallen mention her since before the holidays."

Granger absorbed the news. He had hoped for more but didn't really expect it. "When you guys discovered the Cummings character had liquidated all of his assets, did you check all of his accounts?"

"All but the Hamilton Securities account and an account at a bank in Kirksville. I called both of those places yesterday and they each confirmed the accounts were closed and paid out."

"Do you have written confirmations from them?"

"I got a fax from Kirksville. I haven't seen anything from Hamilton yet."

"And Hamilton is the brokerage firm Cummings's son-in-law manages. Is that right?"

Dwight nodded.

"Perhaps I'll swing by there and talk to Cummings's broker," Ed said. "Do you remember his name?"

"Her name, and I can get it for you. But I thought you had specific instructions from on high not to interfere with the police investigation."

"Hey, I'm just following up on the tax case investigation of Cleon Cummings. Why don't you track down that name for me. By the way, the police are supposed to fax over a rendering of the woman Gallen was spotted with. I'd like you to take a look at it and see if it rings any bells. If not, maybe somebody will recognize her from the news broadcasts. One way or another we need a break on this case."

"You mean the police do."

"Yeah, that's right. The police, who have stopped pursuing any other leads and are concentrating solely on Tim Gallen, need a break on this case. Not that I'm editorializing."

"That sounded pretty unbiased to me." Dwight left to get the broker's name at Hamilton Securities.

Ed's next call was to Henry Blake, the medical examiner at the South County coroner's office.

"Henry, this is Ed Granger."

"Long time no hear."

"Yeah, how long has it been?"

"Last December at your Christmas party."

"My, how time flies when your ass is in a sling," Ed said. "Henry, I need a favor."

"You're calling about the Cummings autopsy, I suppose?"

"Yeah, I was hoping you could tell me who is doing it. I'd like to talk to them when they finish."

"I just completed it myself."

"Already?"

"Every reporter in the free world has been calling us since that fisherman snagged the body. Hell, I even caught a reporter trying to sneak in dressed in scrubs. I thought I'd get it over with so life could get back to normal around here. We're not used to this much attention."

"So are you ruling it death by poisoning?"

"It's too early for that. I won't have the toxicology test findings back for awhile."

"But he did drown."

"He drowned, but not in that river."

"How can you tell?"

"When a person's submerged in water longer than he'd like, eventually he breaks and starts inhaling the water until his respiration stops. It's just not physically possible to hold your breath and die under water."

"So how can you tell he didn't drown in the river?"

"Ed, think about all the shit that's in a river. There's sand, bits of plant debris, all sorts of rubbish floating around. When a person drowns in a river, part of that crud gets sucked into his lungs. I didn't find anything like that in Cummings's lungs."

"So where did he drown? In a pool or something?"

"Could have been a pool, a bathtub, or even that big fountain in front of your office."

"Very funny. If it was a pool, couldn't you check for chlorine?"

"Chlorine doesn't last long enough in a body to be detected."

"So what does this tell you?"

"That I'm glad Tim Gallen wasn't under my supervision."

on a golf course or gone for the day, so there were few spectators around. She opened the front door and scanned the lobby. Only the cashier's windows across from the main office had any security cameras, since that was the area where money and securities were kept. There weren't any cameras aimed either at the main boardroom or inside it.

She retrieved an empty box from the mail room and went to her office to begin moving her things to her cubicle. In eight years she had collected a lot of stuff. It was going to take all night to move everything to that little cubby hole, and half of it probably wouldn't fit.

She'd just picked up the phone to let Tim know she was going to be later than she expected when Bill Farley stopped by her office. It didn't take much for him to convince her she desperately needed at least one alcoholic refreshment before undertaking an office move of this caliber. They quickly relocated to The Trading Pit, four floors above Hamilton Securities. The Pit was a common Alcoholics Anonymous meeting place for financial types without the cumbersome twelve-step program and with all the alcohol your liquid assets could buy.

Three margaritas later, Maggie tried to convince Bill she had to get back, but he ordered another round of drinks, explaining that the buy-one-get-one financial incentives of happy hour prohibited them from leaving. She didn't make much of an argument, sensing this would be the last time she had drinks with her closest friend. By the time she finished her fourth drink and walked back into the Hamilton office, it was five-fifteen. The office was empty except for three or four people milling about.

She strolled nonchalantly to her new cubicle via Arthur's office. His door was closed, thank God. The little twerp was probably out trolling for Girl Scouts. She studied his outer office out of the corner of her eye as she went by. The main ceiling in the bullpen area was probably twenty feet high, but the ceiling dropped to eleven feet in the private hallway leading to Arthur's office.

She'd been in Arthur's office a hundred times but had never looked at it from the perspective of breaking in. It would just be a matter of Tim boosting her up and over to get inside. With Tim's height they wouldn't even need a ladder.

She continued to her cubicle and set her box down on the desk to survey her new surroundings. The furniture was mismatched, there was an ugly stain in the middle of the carpet, the desk corners were badly worn, and she could hear some guy taking a piss in the bathroom only three feet away. The fumes that would emanate from the restrooms after one of the office's Mexican brunches would probably wilt her spider plant. No, this was not going to work.

She went back to her office and packed up her personal items. A framed copy of her first buyer's order. A slinky—a gift from an old boyfriend who had promised her something slinky for her birthday. A hand-blown glass bull. She loaded her prized possessions into her small box, then closed it up and ducked out before she started crying. The alcohol was making her way too sentimental. Arthur could take care of the rest.

Maggie waited at the corner of Baxter and Hartley to cross the street to the parking garage. She steadied herself against a no-parking sign. The noise and bustle from rush hour combined with the heat was making her feel more drunk than she was. While she waited for the traffic light to turn she passed the time listening to a group of secretaries complain about a new supervisor.

An instant later she dropped her box and flung her arms in front of her to absorb the impact of her body hitting the burning pavement. The sounds of blaring horns and screeching tires exploded in her ears. She could feel the vibrations of a bus bearing down on her, but she couldn't get herself out of the way.

Then a pair of hands pulled her back onto the sidewalk, where she fell in a mangled mess.

She opened her eyes and saw Tim's face.

"Are you all right?" He bent down to her. He was wearing running shorts and a sweaty T-shirt. In her absence he had dyed his hair, developed a tan, and was now wearing glasses. The three little changes altered his appearance surprisingly.

"Did you push me?" she said.

"If I'd pushed you, I wouldn't have pulled you back."

"You've got to wait until it's clear," said an elderly man standing next to her. "You young people have got to be more careful. Are you okay? Did you break anything?"

"I did wait," she said. "I think somebody pushed me."

She tried to get to her feet but her knees wouldn't support her weight.

"Want me to get an ambulance?" one of the secretaries said.

"No, just let me sit on that bench for a moment. I'll be all right."

Tim carried her to a nearby park bench while the secretary collected the box's contents. Tim assured the little knot of bystanders who had gathered that Maggie would be fine and they dispersed.

She sat on the bench trembling. "What are you doing here?"

"I got worried when you didn't come home. I called, and your secretary said you'd left for the day. That was two hours ago, so I decided to jog over and see what was going on. By the smell of your breath I'm guessing you haven't been at the library reading financial reports."

"I'm sorry. I should have called." She covered her eyes with her hands. The sun seemed so bright. Usually when she felt this drunk it was the moon she had to contend with.

"It's a good thing you didn't call, otherwise I wouldn't have jogged over here. Are you sure someone pushed you, you didn't just have too much to drink?"

"Yes, I'm sure, and I haven't had that much to drink."

She looked down at the box of treasures that summarized the last eight years of her life. Everything was destroyed.

Police sirens drowned out her sniffling. Three patrol cars converged and pulled into the parking garage across the street. Tim grabbed a nearby newspaper and hid behind it while the police circled their way up the garage ramps. They stopped on the fifth floor in the same area she had parked Tim's car.

He grabbed her box of now worthless mementos and dumped it into a trash can, then he yanked her to her feet and started walking her home.

"This is our last public appearance," he said. "Let's hope those garden gloves worked and there aren't any fingerprints in the car. Otherwise, the police will probably get to your condo before we do."

Chapter 29

Arthur stared out his office window, mouth agape. Was he cursed or something?

A couple of hours earlier, he'd been standing at that same spot trying to shake the image of Cleon's body and wishing his window would open so he could get some fresh air. That's when he saw Maggie pull into the garage driving a beat-up piece of shit.

He'd waited about ten minutes and then circulated around the office. By then, she was upstairs with Farley having drinks. He went back to his office and spotted Smith parked nearby, also waiting.

Two hours later, the IRS agent Gallen jogged by several times, and Arthur realized he might foil Smith's latest attempt on Maggie. So he waited until Gallen jogged around each floor of the parking garage and stopped at the car Maggie had driven in. Then Arthur walked to a pay phone around the corner and anonymously reported seeing the wanted IRS agent driving into a Clayton parking garage. It was only after he was back in his office that he realized he hadn't told the police which Clayton garage he'd spotted the agent at. By the time the men in blue got there, Gallen had managed to save Maggie from becoming mush in the bus's tire treads.

He yanked the curtain back in place. Why had the two paired up? It would be much easier to kill Maggie without Gallen around.

On the other hand, Gallen might know too much about Maggie's embezzlement, soon to be his embezzlement. Maybe it was better they had escaped the police. He didn't want the agent focusing any extra attention on Maggie that could lead back to Cleon's account. At least while she was alive.

Now he was going to have to add the IRS agent to the casualty list. This venture was getting expensive.

He answered his cell phone on the first ring. "What?"

"I'm going to need at least seventy-five grand to finish this job," Smith said.

"Are you out of your mind?"

"Hey, look, *The Dispatch* is offering fifty for Maggie's companion, and I don't have to kill him. If you won't pay me seventy-five, I'll take *The Dispatch*'s money and probably get my picture in the paper for being a good citizen."

"All right, all right. I can get you sixty thousand, but that's the best I can do. And that takes care of both of them."

"You're talking like this is negotiable, Arthur. If I'm going to risk taking care of your two birds in the bush I need it to be worth my while. Seventy-five thou or I go to the paper."

"Fine. I'll have your money for you tomorrow."

"Half before and the other half when I'm done."

Arthur hung up on him.

The problem was, he was tapped out. If someone discovered him pawning any of the items he had smuggled out of his house before it blew up, it would cause more problems. That left the 1964 Mercedes, since the Vette had been repoed. He reached into his pocket and fondled the familiar key fob. The classic blue convertible had driven him to his wedding fifteen years ago and to his wife's and mother-in-law's funerals five years ago. Maybe it was time to close that painful chapter. The insurance settlement was iffy at best, but control of Cleon's millions was only days from being a reality. If he liquidated his last asset then he wouldn't leave any money on the table.

He locked up his office and drove to the Mercedes dealership on Olive Boulevard. In less than an hour he sold his prized convertible for a half-decent price. He would have negotiated harder on the deal but with so many millions of dollars so close he didn't feel like haggling over thousands.

When he finished at the Mercedes dealership he walked across the street to the BMW dealer and test drove a Z3 and a Beamer sedan. He preferred the Z3 convertible Roadster and arranged to rent it for $75 a day for six months. He would only need the car for another week or so, but had suggested the six-month term since renting Z3s wasn't the norm. The contract provided enough time for the BMW boys to more than cover the car's depreciation and still make out when they resold the vehicle.

It would have been a good deal, if Arthur had any intention of honoring it.

Chapter **30**

A full summer moon lit the Clayton financial district like daytime, but the empty streets and dark buildings betrayed the actual 3:00 a.m. time. Unlike the suburbs with the occasional barking dog or howling cat, the sleeping business zone was absolutely silent. Maggie thought their footsteps could be heard a block away as they climbed the Hamilton Securities steps.

She unlocked the deadbolt on the front door with a loud metallic thud, and she and Tim strolled into the main lobby. They were dressed in jeans and T-shirts, and each carried several boxes of assorted sizes and a half-empty bottle of champagne. If they bumped into anyone, they planned on saying they were having a late-night office move/demotion party. Once they turned the corner of the lobby and walked into the main boardroom, they scanned the office for any signs of life. No one. They unloaded the boxes and champagne in Maggie's former office and walked to Arthur's.

At the far end of the boardroom was a hallway that led

to Arthur's reception area. Arthur's secretary was positioned here during the day as a buffer between the chaos of the boardroom and Arthur's inner sanctuary. The floor plan hid Tim and Maggie from anyone entering the Hamilton office but at the same time limited their escape.

Maggie's stomach was in its now routine state of volcanic bile, threatening to erupt with each passing moment. What if the penniless parasite was sleeping in his office since his house blew up? They had circled the parking garage searching for familiar cars and hadn't found any, but what if they missed his car parked on the street? She listened at Arthur's door for sounds of gale force winds being sucked through his deviated septum, but all was quiet. Arthur was probably snoring peacefully at some hotel.

His door was locked.

Tim pulled a chair next to Arthur's door, climbed onto it, and removed the overhead ceiling panel. They were in luck. Through the two-foot by two-foot hole they could see there was no fire wall above separating Arthur's office from the outer area. The ceiling panels were supported by the office wall below. Like most construction in the Hamilton building, every expense had been spared.

Tim stepped onto the arms of the chair and balanced himself against the wall with one hand while he reached into the ceiling and pulled out the adjacent panel above Arthur's office. He handed it to Maggie and climbed down. "Everything looks good. Make sure the coast is still clear."

Maggie checked around the corner one more time. The boardroom remained black. She returned to Tim, who bent over with cupped hands to boost her into the ceiling. Although she wanted to finish their breaking and entering before she vomited on her partner in crime, she hesitated before stepping into his waiting hands. Had he saved her life this afternoon or was he the one who pushed her?

"Come on," he whispered. "We haven't got all night."

He was right. She tucked the small flashlight into her

back pocket and settled her right foot into his hands.

He lifted her before she locked her leg and almost flipped her over backward.

"Stop, stop, stop!"

They regrouped and tried again.

"Slower this time. I'm not the springing Wallenda."

Tim cupped his hands again. She put her foot back in his hands and placed a hand on each of his shoulders. She felt him tense under her touch. Was that just a reaction to breaking and entering or was it about her?

"Ready," she said.

He lifted her almost effortlessly, and moments later her head was in the ceiling.

"Use the wall to pull yourself up," Tim said.

She gripped the wall but she couldn't pull herself onto it. This was why she was always picked last for sports as a child.

"I'm not strong enough," she said after several attempts. "This isn't working."

For the third time they reorganized on the floor.

Tim studied the ceiling. "I'll bust a panel if I do this. Let's try it one more time. This time I'll stand on the chair and boost you up from there."

The new arrangement worked much better. The extra two feet from the chair put her well into the ceiling. She pulled herself onto the wall and tried to peer through into Arthur's office below.

Although Arthur's curtains were open it was still too dark to see. That was probably Arthur's love seat just below her. Or was that the end table? Well, she'd find out.

She wedged her body around in the cramped ceiling space and swung her legs into the opening over Arthur's office. Then she tried to lower herself slowly inside but her upper body strength failed again. She crashed half onto the love seat, half on the floor, with two more ceiling panels and their framing smashing down around her.

"Shit!" she yelled and then froze. There was a police

car waiting at the intersection just twenty feet outside Arthur's window.

"Maggie, are you okay?" Tim whisper-shouted. "What happened?"

She didn't respond. She waited for the police car to move on while she rubbed her left leg, which had absorbed the brunt of her misguided landing. At least she hadn't broken it. The ceiling panels hadn't fared as well. They were in a zillion pieces.

"Maggie?"

The police car left, and she hobbled to the door and unlocked it for Tim.

"My perfect landing was a little less than perfect," she whispered.

Tim focused his compact flashlight on the destruction. "Holy shit, what did you do?"

"I lost my grip. Those ceiling panels aren't as sturdy as you would think."

He shook his head. "We'll deal with this later. Let's see if this was worth the effort."

"Yeah, thanks for asking, I'll be just fine." She shined her flashlight on her ankle, which was turning most of the colors in the rainbow.

He paused. "I guess you'd be the unlucky prisoner who breaks his leg during the prison escape and his buddies have to shoot him."

She rubbed her ankle. This was why she had stayed away from men. They were always too self-absorbed to think of anyone else. Tim was no exception.

He turned his back on her and the mess she created and walked over to close the curtains. Then he went to Arthur's filing cabinets to begin his search.

"These cabinets are locked. So is the desk."

"Can't you break into them?"

"Not without being noticeable." He paused and stared at the cabinets. "God, all we need now is the sound track to *The Pink Panther* playing in the background and this fiasco would be complete."

Maggie's shoulders slumped. She was tired and suffering from post-hangover lethargy. She didn't want to hear how almost breaking her leg was going to be in vain.

"Wait, I've got an idea." She pulled out her key ring. "There are only about a dozen different desk locks in this entire brokerage office. It's pretty common knowledge that if you have something of value, like a new country club membership directory, you have to take it home with you or everyone in the office will have a copy of it by the end of the week. Maybe my key will fit Arthur's desk."

She limped to Arthur's desk but didn't even bother to try her key once she got a closer look at it.

"So much for that idea," she said. "Looks like Arthur's desk didn't come from the office supply close-out-blow-out like the rest of ours did."

They stood in the darkness and stared at the locked office furniture.

"Give me your keys," Tim said.

She handed the keys to him, not sure what good it would do. He took the keys and walked out into Arthur's reception area. Minutes later he returned, jingling a new ring of keys.

"Your desk key worked on his secretary's desk. Let's see if the keys I found in her bottom drawer work here."

He tried each of the five keys on the filing cabinet without luck, but when he tried Arthur's desk drawer it slid open on the first try. "And what do we have here but the keys to the filing cabinet. Tah dahhh."

Maggie forgot her nervousness and cracked a smile. It seemed crashing from the ceiling and risking arrest weren't going to be a total waste.

"You check the desk, I want to take a look at these files. Let me know if you find anything. And don't let your flashlight shine on the windows."

Maggie made herself comfortable in Arthur's two-thousand-dollar customized chair and began rummaging. She found sales reports, broker evaluations, memos from the main office criticizing Arthur's performance, budget projections, and financial statements for the office. All information she would have loved to devote some time to, but nothing that connected Arthur to Cleon's death. She did run across two AOL discs, which she laid on the desktop.

"You got anything?" Tim asked. He had searched three of the file drawers and was already working on the bottom drawer.

"Just some AOL discs. I set them aside for you." She swiveled Arthur's chair to the left side drawers and began searching them. They were filled with junk. Two phone books, Hamilton stationery and envelopes, a baseball, an extra telephone headset, fountain pen refills, and some other miscellaneous office supplies. She cringed at the discovery of some condoms waiting to get lucky. Nothing of any use.

She looked over at Tim, who now had one of Arthur's files fanned on the floor for a closer inspection. This was back to looking like a waste of time. She should be getting a good night's sleep before facing Arthur tomorrow over why she hadn't cleaned out her office.

She leaned back in Arthur's chair. "If I were Arthur where would I hide something?"

She tapped on the side of the desk. No hidden panel. She would have been surprised if Arthur was that elaborate. No, Arthur was more simple, more obvious. She checked under his leather blotter but still nothing. She stood and checked behind the pictures hanging on the wall behind her and then searched his credenza. Still nothing. She flopped back in Arthur's form-fitting chair. She brushed her hand underneath the desktop, expecting to find old wads of gum.

Instead she felt the smooth surface of two envelopes taped to the underside.

"Hey, I think—"

"Not now," Tim said.

Maggie crawled under the desk to get a look at what

she had felt. It was a Hamilton Securities postage-paid
return envelope, and next to that was another envelope
from a travel agency. She focused the flashlight on the
Hamilton envelope and ran her fingers over it again. It
felt as though another envelope was inside.

She peeked at Tim, who was still engrossed in the file.
She started to remove the Hamilton envelope and then
stopped. Before she went any further she measured the
envelope's distance from the right-hand corner of the
desk, one thumb width.

The tape pulled away willingly in one long strip.

The envelope was sealed but she ripped it open without
hesitation. She could easily replace it with another Hamilton envelope from one of Arthur's desk drawers. Inside
she found a sealed window envelope. Through the return
window was the familiar Hamilton Securities return address as it appeared on a check. In the address window
was the printed name of the check's recipient.

Terry Stevens.

Her hands quivered as she opened the envelope. Here
was the $3,209,422.59 check she was waiting for, com-
plete with her fake Mail Boxes Etc. address. But what
was Arthur doing with it? She chewed her thumb nail and
looked again at Tim, who was still oblivious. The air conditioner clicked off, causing her to jump. She bit her lip
and carefully removed the other envelope taped to the
underside of the desk.

The envelope's return address was AAA World Travel.
This envelope was also sealed, but it was a gummy seal
that had already been opened several times and then
pressed together. She pulled out the contents.

Tickets in Arthur's name to and from the Cayman Islands this weekend.

The blood drained from her face. Arthur knew everything. He must have killed Cleon and intercepted her
check. He clearly planned on opening an account in Terry
Stevens's name in the Caymans. Just her luck to pick a

false identity with a genderless name. But why hadn't he confronted her? What did—

Her near-drowning at the health club. Her close brush with becoming roadkill. Arthur wasn't going to confront her because he planned on killing her.

Sitting under Arthur's desk in the darkened room she felt like the baby-sitter in a bad B-movie who just discovered there was a serial killer in the house. She exhaled and only then realized she had been holding her breath.

A flashlight shined on the check and tickets, and she jumped.

Tim kneeled in front of her. "Looks like you found something."

He took the envelopes from her and examined their contents, then pointed his flashlight at Arthur's wall calendar. "I can't imagine our buddy Art is going to the Caymans to vacation when he arrives on Saturday night and returns on Monday. My guess is he's planning on opening up a three-million-dollar account there. So much for your plans with Cleon's money."

She was speechless. Arthur was trying to kill her.

"Who did you tell about your Terry Stevens plan?"

"No one. I haven't told a soul." She shook her head to try and snap out of it. "I'm not in the habit of sharing my felonious intentions with my friends and family."

"Can you—" Her voice was trembling. So were her hands. "Can you use this to arrest him?" Her life would be much safer with Arthur in jail.

"This is probably not in line with Hamilton Securities' policy, but even if we catch him cashing this check, it won't prove he killed Cleon." He smiled. "After all, Arthur's just doing what you wanted to do."

The air conditioner clicked on again and Maggie rubbed her arms, trying to make her goose bumps go away. "Did you find anything in Arthur's files?"

"Maybe. I've got two different sets of tax returns for last year. One version shows he owes twenty-eight thousand and change, the other shows the IRS owes him thirty-one hundred. You can guess which one he filed. From the looks of Arthur's financial records, he was in no position to plant two million dollars in my bank account. I did find a receipt for a paper shredder and a receipt from the messenger service that delivered it to Cleon."

"Cleon told me Arthur sent him one. That's what gave him the idea to shred everything."

"But you said Arthur writes off everything he buys. Then where is the receipt for the poison he used on Cleon?"

"Well, maybe he knew better than to try to write off Cleon's murder. Even Arthur has his limits."

"I'm not so sure Arthur is the one who killed Cleon and framed me."

Maggie was, and almost said so. But then she remembered Tim's statement about excluding her if she was in danger. Apparently gas explosions and breaking and entering didn't count, but attempts on her life probably did.

Tim was still looking down at the files. "I must have missed something."

She walked toward the door. "Why don't you make copies of Arthur's files. We'll look at them more closely at my place. It's late and I don't want to be here any longer."

"Where do you think you're going?"

"I need to put those two envelopes back the way I found them, but Arthur doesn't have any windowed envelopes in his desk. Only Operations uses them to mail checks. I'm going to see if I can find one in the supply room. On my way I'll turn the copier on for you, it's right outside the door."

Tim nodded and started collecting files.

Outside Arthur's office she flipped on the copier and hurried to the mailroom and the doorway that led to the office supplies. She rushed past boxes of new account forms, IRA brochures, and mutual fund brochures and tripped over a smaller box she didn't see with her flashlight. Finally she reached the corner that held the Hamilton stationery. Perched on a bottom shelf was an entire case of window envelopes. She pulled out two, and two regular Hamilton envelopes from another nearby box.

She then darted through the darkness to her office and began digging through her recycling trash can. This was the first time she was glad Arthur instituted his money-saving idea of having the cleaning people come every other day. She found what she was looking for near the bottom of the trash—a five-cent dividend check an irate client had brought in.

She placed the five-cent check into one of the new window envelopes, sealed it, and put that envelope into a Hamilton envelope. It looked and felt exactly like the Terry Stevens check. She tucked it into her back pocket and was about to go back to Arthur's office when she heard the familiar sound of the front door opening.

She turned off her flashlight and dove under her desk. There was no way to warn Tim.

She listened to footsteps walk through the main lobby and into the boardroom. She strained but couldn't hear any more. Should she stay where she was?

No. If it was another one of Arthur's killers, they would check her office first.

She crept out from her desk and crawled to her office doorway. There was a man's voice coming from the center of the bullpen. She sneaked past her assistant's desk and down the hallway toward the maze of cubicles, then she stood up halfway.

A desk light was on at one of the center cubicles, and a man was talking on the phone. His back was to her. She inched closer.

"I wanted to catch you before you left," he said, his back still to her. "No, I'm not home. I came into the office so Arthur could pay for this call." There was a long pause. "I miss you, too. I can't wait for you to get home."

It was Richard Mooring placing a long distance call on Arthur's nickel. His wife was a lobbyist who was usually in D.C. or out of the country. Maggie wanted to kill him for scaring her. She could faintly hear the copier running at the other end of the building, but Mooring wasn't paying any attention.

She waited until he began talking again and crawled around the edge of the bullpen. By the time she reached Arthur's office, Tim had finished making his copies and was picking up the ceiling debris.

"What took you so long?"

"Shhhh! We've got company."

She described the visit from Mooring and she handed him the empty window and postage-paid envelopes. Tim put the Terry Stevens check into the envelopes the way it was originally and watched Maggie tape the envelopes back under Arthur's desk, one thumb's width from the right corner. Then they crawled to Arthur's outer office and waited for the broker to finish his call.

Twenty minutes later Mooring hung up and left the building. It was almost 4:30 a.m. They needed to finish and get out of the office.

"I'm going to replace these ceiling tiles with tiles from some other corner of the office," Tim said. "While I do that, will you use some scotch tape and pick up any ceiling shit that I missed?"

"Sure, no problem."

She retrieved a tape dispenser from Arthur's desk, then tiptoed to Arthur's outer office to make sure Tim had left. She stuck her head around the corner and saw the light from his flashlight moving away from her.

She raced back to Arthur's desk and exchanged the envelope with the Terry Stevens check with the impostor from her back pocket. If Arthur was trying to kill her she had more bargaining power controlling the three million dollars than if he did. She folded the Stevens envelope in thirds and slid it into her back pocket.

By the time Tim returned she had finished collecting the last ceiling remnants. He hoisted the new ceiling panels in place and when he was done, no one could tell what had happened.

"I got these from a section near the lobby behind that overgrown ficus tree. It could be weeks before they're missed."

Tim put Arthur's original tax returns back in the filing cabinet and locked everything. Maggie watched him double check under Arthur's desk to make sure the envelopes were still there. She thought about pretending to be insulted but decided to let it pass without comment.

Tim tucked the AOL discs into his back pocket, and before they left he put Arthur's keys back in the secretary's desk. At 5:09 a.m. they walked out of the Hamilton office and went back to Maggie's to get some sleep.

Chapter 31

Before Maggie closed the front door of her condo to leave for Hamilton Securities Thursday morning, Tim had already started her computer and was connected to the Internet using one of the AOL disks from Arthur's desk and Maggie's credit card number. He had ten free hours and planned on using most of it.

His first stop was the UPS Web Page, which offered him his choice of options including tracking, quick cost, drop-off, and pickup information. He clicked on the tracking button. A new page appeared explaining that any UPS bar-coded shipment could be tracked any time, anywhere in the world, instantly. All a person needed to do was enter the tracking number. It was as simple as the television commercials proclaimed—thank God—and it wasn't even pass code protected.

By inputting a package's tracking number the Web page returned the package's status, time and date it was delivered, the last name of the person who signed for it, what date it was sent on, the city and state it was shipped to, but not the street address. The Web site also included a warning that stated UPS authorized the use of the UPS tracking system solely for shippers and receivers to track their shipments. Any other use by anyone else was expressly forbidden. Would men in brown trucks show up to arrest him? Probably not.

Using the four preprinted shipping forms he had stolen from Stuffing Stuff and some trial and error, he broke the code used to create UPS tracking numbers. He rubbed his hands together and started to type. Knowing the sequential code for tracking numbers meant he could work backward from the four numbers he had to get a complete log of Stuffing Stuff's prior shipments.

Within two hours Tim had documented Stuffing Stuff's shipments for the last thirty days. About fifteen packages were shipped out-of-state to various places around the country. Another twenty-nine packages were shipped within Missouri. But last Monday eight packages had been shipped to the Caymans. Nine more had followed on Tuesday, seven each on Wednesday and Thursday, and four on Friday. The packages sent last Tuesday and Wednesday had taken five business days to deliver. The packages sent last Thursday would be received today, which meant the packages shipped last Friday would arrive tomorrow. All the packages that had arrived had been signed for by someone named Nealey.

But why so many packages? It was time to call UPS.

"Thank you for calling UPS," a perky voice said. "This is Jennifer Lowery, how may I help you?"

"May I speak with someone in your international division?"

"I'd be happy to transfer you, but first I'll give you the number in case we're disconnected."

Tim wrote down the number, and a moment later a second perky voice was on the line. "Thank you for calling UPS. This is Donna Cortez, how may I help you?"

"I'm calling to get some information on a package I

would like to ship to the Cayman Islands."

"I would be happy to help you with that, sir. From what zip code will you be shipping?"

"63122."

"And the zip code you are shipping to?"

"I'm not sure. It's in the Cayman Islands."

"Okay, and how can I help you?"

"Can you tell me how long it will take to get there?"

"If you use our Express delivery, it should take three business days once it clears Customs."

"And how long does Customs take?"

"If all your documentation is in order, it usually takes up to three business days."

"Could you tell me if there would be any problem shipping a stuffed grizzly bear? Not a stuffed toy, but a real animal?"

"Grizzly bears are kind of big, and most countries won't accept packages of more than 150 pounds. Let me see what the Cayman restrictions are." Tim could hear the customer service rep type a few key strokes on a computer. "The Caymans will only accept packages up to 70 pounds and there are size restrictions. The maximum length is 108 inches long. The maximum size is 130 inches. You get the maximum size by adding the length plus the girth. To give you an example, a box that is 26 inches cubed would meet the maximum size restrictions."

"Yeah, that sounds a little small for a grizzly bear. But how about . . . say, a fox." Tim could imagine the rep's eyebrows raising on the other end. "Is there any problem shipping a fox?"

"If you can hold for a moment, I'll check that for you, sir."

Tim rubbed his temple. He was close, he had to be.

"No, I'm afraid fox is not an approved animal fur or skin, and it cannot be accepted by UPS for international delivery."

"Even if it's dead?"

"Yes, I'm sorry, sir. I'm not sure if it is a UPS rule or a Customs rule, but the only animal skins or furs we can accept are domestic farm animals."

Tim couldn't recall seeing any of those at the Stuffing Stuff showroom. Damn.

"Thanks," he said. "You've been very helpful."

He went to the refrigerator to get a soda. He really needed sleep, but he only had time for a caffeine fix and a quick break. He flipped on the television and channel-surfed past the morning offering of trashy talk show subjects, the weather channel, and several premium channels that were scrambled. He stumbled on an old episode of *Green Acres* and watched enough to remember why it was taken off the air. He continued on to the local news, which was now reporting that dental records had been used to positively identify Cleon Cummings as the drowned man found in Silver River. The story also stated that Cleon was believed to have shredded close to $152 million before his death. The station had a local calculus teacher explain how the amount was determined based upon weight, volume, and an inspection of the shredded cash. Tim switched back to *Green Acres*.

Of course!

He ran to the phone and called the international UPS division again.

"Can you tell me where your office in the Caymans is located?"

"We use a service partner on Grand Cayman by the name of Starkar. They're located on Eastern Avenue. I don't have their hours, but I can give you their phone number if you would like."

Tim wrote down the number and called Starkar. He learned their hours were from eight to five. According to the woman, most incoming UPS packages arrived around 1:30, took a half hour to pass through Customs, and then were sorted for delivery. The deliveries went out by 3:30 and were done by 5:00.

Tim thanked the woman for her help. He had one more piece of the puzzle.

Chapter **32**

Maggie opened the Hamilton Securities front door Thursday morning to see two receptionists furiously pointing her in the direction of Arthur's office.

"He wants to see you now," one said. "Right now. Before you do anything else."

"Do not pass go, go directly to his office," the other receptionist echoed.

"Tell him I'll be there in a minute," Maggie said. "I'm getting a Pepsi first."

The two women spewed objections in stereo while Maggie limped to the Hamilton cafeteria. She dropped two quarters into the soda machine and was rewarded with her morning Pepsi. With only an hour or so of sleep she needed the caffeine. She went to the sink to wipe off the can's top and then continued to her former office.

Surprisingly, everything in her office was where she had left it. She dug out two Oreo cookies from her bottom desk drawer and sat down to enjoy her breakfast. Her intercom beeped when she bit into the first cookie.

"Maggie?" Arthur said. "If it's convenient, would you please come to my office immediately?"

Maggie looked at her intercom, expecting syrup to ooze through the speaker from Arthur's voice. "I'm eating right now, Arthur. I'll be there in a few."

She clicked off the speaker and took the phone off the hook to prevent any more interruptions. She couldn't tell from his tone of voice if he knew about the missing check or was just looking forward to firing her.

There was no way he could prove she broke into his office, but could he prove her transfer of Cleon's money? And what if he could? Any evidence that could implicate her would implicate him too. She forced herself to eat another cookie, occasionally taking a swig of Pepsi, and let the crumbs fall where they pleased.

And what about the fact that he was trying to kill her? Should she let him know she knew?

She took one last look around her office and began the walk to Arthur's office. She'd have to play it by ear.

With each step she reviewed the responses she had practiced with Tim this morning. She yawned from the lack of sleep although her adrenaline was pumping on overdrive. She nodded at Arthur's secretary as she passed by and opened his door, not bothering to knock.

"I guess you called me in here to fire me?"

From Arthur's manner on the intercom she half expected to be greeted by a group of patrolmen. Instead, Arthur sprang from his chair and gently guided her to the love seat she had crashed onto only hours earlier.

"No, Maggie. Where did you get an idea like that? I called you in here because I've been very concerned about you."

Of all the ways Arthur could have begun their conversation, this is one she didn't expect. "Concerned? About me?"

"You seem to be acting out of character lately, and I just wanted to make sure everything was all right. Sadly, we don't get much time to talk these days and I regret that."

"Excuse me, Arthur, but did the ghost of Christmas past visit you last night?"

Arthur feigned shock a little too theatrically. "I told you, I'm just concerned."

"You didn't seem concerned yesterday when you gave away my office in front of everyone."

Arthur pursed his lips and nodded his head. "Yes, well, I believe I overreacted. Even bosses make mistakes. But don't worry about that. You still have your job, and it will probably be just a matter of time until you're back into your regular production numbers and have a private office again."

Maggie looked at Arthur as if he had grown a third eye. She scanned the room for signs of *Candid Camera*.

"Business goes in cycles," Arthur said. "You're just in a down curve, but I don't care about your production numbers. What's important is that you're okay. Meanwhile, I think you should take a little time off. I think it would do you some good to get away from things for awhile."

"Actually, taking off a few days would help me sort out some private matters I need to take care of."

"Say no more. Take a week, two if you need it. I'll make sure your accounts are covered. Just come back to us with that vim and vigor we always adore about you."

Maggie used the arm of the love seat to help her to her feet. Was this the same man that was trying to kill her? She couldn't be wrong about that, could she?

Maggie could almost feel the secretary straining from her chair outside to overhear their conversation. Before everyone finished their morning coffee the gossip about this conversation would be around the office.

Arthur stuck out his hand, and Maggie automatically reached to shake it. Feeling his clammy paw envelop hers reminded her of George Bailey shaking Mr. Potter's hand after Potter makes his lavish employment offer. Arthur must have sensed her revelation because he ushered her out of his office before her tired mind could react.

It hit her when Arthur's door closed behind her with the finality of a coffin lid. It was obvious by the secretary's expression that Maggie had just given her killer a witness to his concerned act. She had also probably delayed the search for her soon-to-be-missing body since no one would be expecting her back for a few weeks.

She walked toward the exit with no idea of what Arthur was up to. Did he or didn't he know? When she first barged into his office she thought Arthur had his hand under his desk, as if feeling for the envelopes. But knowing Arthur, he could have just as easily been feeling himself.

Chapter 33

Arthur knew every tactile detail of the two envelopes taped beneath his desk. The worn corner on the left edge of the travel agency envelope. The familiar smoothness of the Hamilton number ten envelope. The way they almost, but not quite, butted up against each other.

He ran his hands over them once more, lovingly. He wanted to rip the envelopes open and fondle their contents, but once he started indiscriminately opening them, he wouldn't stop, and someone would eventually see him. Instead he struck a bargain with himself. He would view the check and the airline ticket three times a day. That should be enough to gratify himself while not endangering his secret.

He had held off on the morning's first viewing until the business with Maggie was over. And even now he wanted to prolong the pleasure.

Yes, he would first make a ceremonious walk around the boardroom to solve a few problems, dole out some wisdom, and motivate his troops. Then he would stop by the cafeteria and pick up a doughnut. With doughnut in hand, he would return to his office, lock the door, and enjoy the day's first exhibition.

After that, he would call Smith, and they would discuss their new plan for Maggie's and Tim's demise.

Chapter **34**

Maggie stepped outside into the morning heat. What next? At a nearby pay phone she called Tim to see how his project was going.

"Hello, you've reached 555-4557. Please leave a message," she heard her voice say.

"Tim it's me. Pick up. I'm calling from a pay phone."

"I'm here," he said, stopping the machine.

"Did you come up with anything?"

"Did I ever." Tim explained his discovery of Cleon's shipments to the Caymans.

"What's so big about that? You don't know what he shipped or the address where he shipped it." The summer sun was beginning to cause small sweat marks on Maggie's silk blouse.

"I have a hunch. Between the shipments and Arthur's travel plans, it tells me I'm going there, too."

"But how does that prove Arthur's involvement?"

"It doesn't. I'm really getting the feeling Arthur isn't involved."

"But what about the check we found last night and the Cayman brochures and lists of Cayman banks and attorneys at his house?"

"Let me rephrase that. I don't think Arthur is involved in Cleon's murder or in framing me. We certainly didn't find any evidence of it, either at the house or the office. As for the check and the Cayman stuff at his house, I think he stumbled onto Cleon's plan and is trying to embezzle the money for himself."

"You really don't think Arthur killed Cleon?"

"It just doesn't add up. I'd say he's capable of stealing millions but not murder."

If she was right, Arthur was capable of murder, he just wasn't very good at it.

"Remember the receipt for the shredder I found?" Tim said. "The one he sent to Cleon last Wednesday? That would have meant that Cleon worked around the clock to get all of his money shredded by Monday. But the guy at Stuffing Stuff mentioned that Cleon was working a full day up until the end."

"So when did Cleon find the time to shred the money?"

"Exactly. He must have had some help—some help that double-crossed him. And Arthur certainly wouldn't have helped shred cash, so who did? Someone close to Cleon. Someone he trusted. Someone who knew about his IRS problems and had the resources to frame me with two million dollars. That certainly doesn't sound like Arthur."

Maybe he had a point.

"So who does it sound like?"

"I'm hoping it's Nealey, the person who's been signing for the packages in the Caymans."

She could tell by the sound of his voice how desperate he was becoming to solve the mystery of who framed him, and get his life and career back. And she really hoped he did. Straight-laced as he was, he didn't deserve having his life ruined.

Still, she doubted his trip to the Caymans was going to

accomplish anything except to get him out of her hair before the police found him and arrested them both.

"Speaking of Arthur," Tim said, "did you get a chance to talk to him this morning?"

She reviewed her Arthur encounter with him.

"You see," he said, "that doesn't sound like a murderer to me."

"It doesn't sound like the Arthur I've come to know and love, either."

"He had three million bucks taped under his desk. Maybe he felt magnanimous."

"It would take a personality transplant to make Arthur magnanimous. This is the man who—"

"Please deposit another twenty-five cents to continue your conversation," a recorded voice said.

Maggie fished in her pockets for some change but came up empty-handed. "I'm out of change. I'll meet you at home in about an hour."

She was about to say goodbye when she noticed the front page of the local newspaper on sale in a newspaper box. It featured a big picture of Tim along with a police sketch of Maggie. The headline read "IRS Agent Spotted In South St. Louis."

"Wait a minute, we're on the front page of this morning's paper. Let me see what it says."

"Give me the pay phone number and I'll call you back."

She read the number off the phone and hung up. Then she waited at the newspaper box until another buyer arrived and caught the door before it closed. She was scanning the article when the phone rang.

"Tell me you didn't just steal a newspaper," Tim said.

"Okay, I didn't just steal a newspaper."

"Maggie, how can you do that?"

"Excuse me, Pope John Paul, I don't have any change. Now would you mind shutting up for a minute so I can see what the article says?"

She picked out the major points of the story. "Let's

see . . . you were sighted at Stuffing Stuff with an uniden-
tified companion. . . . the shop owner says you're threatening and dangerous."

"Me? Must have been the way I ran when he spotted
me."

"You had me scared enough in the motel room."

"What about your hairy legs, they could have
terrified—"

"Do you want to hear the rest of this story or not?"
she said and then didn't bother to wait for his answer.
"Local law enforcement officials are stepping up the
search for you with a promise from the mayor that St.
Louis would give the FBI their full support. Congratulations, you've got a whole bunch of government
branches after you."

"Thanks. Anything on you?"

She studied the artist's drawing. With her hair stuffed
into her hat and wearing sunglasses, not even her own
mother would recognize the drawing as her.

"Not really, just a drawing of a psycho-woman wearing
a baseball hat. I think I'm okay. But, you better stay at
the condo today until we figure out how to get you down
to the Caymans. I've got a few stops to make, I'll be home
in an hour."

She hung up. It was time to decide. Was Arthur really
a killer? Even if Tim was right and Arthur wasn't trying
to kill her, he might try if he knew about the switched
checks. Would she be walking into a trap he had set? If
so, she could be framing herself for Cleon's murder as
well. But if Arthur knew about the checks, would he have
been so nice to her this morning?

She closed her eyes. "Dear God," she whispered,
"please send me a sign if I'm to do this or not. I don't
want to go to jail but I don't know how else to get the
money for my Visa bills."

She waited.

A bus drove by with a billboard on its side advertising Roto-Rooter. The headline screamed, "Adios, Hair-ball!"

So even God thought Arthur was a hairball.

She walked across the street to the Harris Bank.

Chapter 35

The inside of the Harris Bank office was a reassuring oasis of marble and glass compared with the bustle of Type A commuters outside in the Thursday morning traffic jam. The bank tellers were sequestered to the left of the stately lobby. Since Maggie didn't see any customer service representatives in the glass offices lining the parameter, she waited her turn for an available teller. She tried not to fidget.

A security guard walked in, nodded at what was probably the head teller, and left. Maggie's heart raced at the sight of him.

An elderly man ahead of her complained he had been cheated out of one day's interest on his last statement. The teller tried to explain that the statement cycle was different from the calendar cycle and that his interest would be credited on his next statement. This concept was beyond the man's comprehension. Getting no satisfaction for the dollar-and-eighty-cent adjustment he wanted, the man launched into a tirade on the outrageous fees the bank charged. The teller listened for a few more minutes and then referred the gentleman to the assistant manager.

Another teller became available and motioned for Maggie to approach. Maggie glanced around—still no Arthur—and walked over.

"My name is Terry Stevens," she said. "I'm here to cash a Hamilton Securities check. I would like to have nine thousand dollars of it paid out in cash and the balance in a cashier's check."

"Are you a bank customer?"

"No. But the check is drawn on your bank."

She handed her the check and hoped the teller didn't notice her hand shaking. There was no need to worry. The teller's eyes widened and focused solely on the check's amount.

"May I see some identification?"

"Of course." Maggie gave her the Terry Stevens driver's license.

"I need to verify the availability of funds to cash a check of this size. Would you mind waiting in one of those chairs over there? This may take a little while. We'll also need to check with Hamilton."

Maggie sat down and waited.

Chapter **36**

Arthur took a big bite of his doughnut. Doctors and cholesterol be damned, there was nothing like dough fried in lard, drizzled in chocolate, and drilled with cream. He took a second bite while he ran his hand under the desk to reassure himself his two precious envelopes were still there. His office door was locked and his secretary had instructions to hold all calls.

It was time.

He started with the travel agency envelope. The gummy seal had lost most of its adhesiveness and opened easily. He extracted his ticket to the Caymans. The air conditioning blew overhead, and he imagined his plane landing on the tropical island. He would spend Saturday night and Sunday relaxing, drinking rum, and fraternizing with the local females. Then Monday morning at nine o'clock he would meet with a Vincent DeMarique, esquire, at the Bank of Grand Cayman. Vincent assured him it would take less than an hour to make the necessary arrangements. The Caymans were still happy to accommodate American money.

He slipped the ticket back into its envelope.

He closed his eyes and prepared for his moment of ecstasy. He could feel the check envelope still within the Hamilton envelope. He opened his eyes again and removed the interior envelope.

His utopia shattered.

He ripped the envelope open. In his hands he held a five-cent check from Hamilton made payable to Mrs. Carrie Howat.

A dizziness hit him and he realized he was hyperventilating. He deliberately slowed his breathing.

He scrolled through the account information to see who her broker was.

Maggie Connors. Of course.

He reached for his phone and dialed information.

"Harris Bank on Baxter in Clayton!"

A recorded message gave him the phone number and offered to connect him for an additional thirty-five cents.

"Yes!" he yelled into the phone and the number rang through.

"Thank you for calling Harris Savings. Please hold."

"Answer the goddamn phone!"

He wanted to hang up and redial, but since information connected him directly he hadn't written the number down.

"Thank you for holding," a sugar-coated voice said. "How may I help you?"

"This is Arthur Riley, chief operating officer of Hamilton Securities. Get me your goddamn manager on the phone and do it now!"

"I'm sorry, sir, our manager is at a creativity retreat."

"Then put whoever is running the goddamn bank on the phone. You're wasting time."

"Yes, sir. Please hold."

"This is Dave Luby, assistant manager. How can I help you?"

"Mr. Luby, Arthur Riley, chief operating officer of Hamilton Securities. I need to stop payment on a Hamilton Securities check made out to Terry Stevens for over three million dollars. It's been stolen."

"I'd like to help you, Mr. Riley, but we've just cashed that check."

"What? How the hell could you cash a check that size without checking with our office first? Isn't there some kind of holding period or something?"

"We did call your office, and everything was cleared. There were enough funds to cover the check, and so by banking regulations we cashed it."

"You just handed her three million dollars? Do you always keep that much money on hand?"

"Well, when I say we cashed it, I mean we debited the account. Nine thousand dollars was paid in cash and the rest was paid out in a cashier's check."

"Who was the check made payable to?"

"I'm sorry, Mr. Riley, I don't think I'm able to divulge that information. I really don't have any proof of who I'm talking to."

"You want proof? Look out your goddamn window, you idiot, my office is right across the goddamn street. I suggest you divulge that information now or you can kiss our account goodbye."

"Just a minute, sir. I'll check."

Arthur's hand tightened around the telephone.

"It was made out to Janey Fitzgerald Securities."

He slammed the phone down.

Chapter **37**

"**H**ello, you've reached 555-4557. Please leave a message," Maggie's answering machine said.

Tim stopped pecking on the computer to see if Maggie was calling.

"Hi, Ms. Stevens. This is Joe Michaels from Janey Fitzgerald Securities. Our appointment was thirty minutes ago, and since you haven't arrived I'm calling to see if you need to reschedule. I'm a little concerned because I won't be able to hold these bearer bonds after today."

There was a long pause.

"Never mind, my secretary just informed me you have arrived."

Tim went to the answering machine and erased the call. Interesting.

Chapter **38**

Maggie was positively buoyant. Getting the nine thousand and the cashier's check had been as easy as cashing a weekly payroll check. Evidently Arthur had not discovered her switch.

It took forever to find a cab that would take her to the Fitzgerald office in Ladue, and by the time she arrived she was almost a half hour late. She apologized for her tardiness and Joe Michaels assured her it wasn't a problem. And given that she was about to drop three million dollars on them, it probably wasn't.

She and Michaels exchanged the typical introductory pleasantries and she followed the young broker back to his office. He had a remarkable composure. If the roles were reversed and she was sitting on three million dollars in bearer bonds waiting for a late mystery client, she would have been calling the client every five minutes and gnawing on her knuckles by now.

The Fitzgerald office was decorated in typical financial style, with framed stock certificates on the walls, plush carpeting underfoot, and beautiful, overpaid people scurrying around. Joe motioned for her to have a seat. With a twinge of jealousy she noticed this rookie broker's office was much nicer than the one she had just been demoted from at Hamilton.

"I'd like to begin by first giving you some background information on our firm and the different client resources that are available to you."

He reached for an overproduced brochure to emphasize the points he was about to make. She grabbed his arm.

"Before you get started," she said, "I should tell you that I only have a few minutes. My car is in the shop and I have a taxi waiting for me outside. Perhaps you could give me the company introduction another time."

"Yes, of course. Let's just walk over to the cashiers where they have the bonds waiting for you."

He escorted her to a private office behind the cashier's counter. A clerk came in, asked her for some identification, and they then began the process of endorsing the bonds into Terry Stevens's name. After Maggie signed the last certificate, the clerk handed her the bearer bonds, neatly tucked inside two Janey Fitzgerald legal envelopes. The $3,200,422.59 cashier's check transformed into seventy-five different bond issues from eight different countries, with maturities ranging from one to thirty years.

Her next stop was the Federal Express office. There she filled out a shipping label addressed to her parents. She borrowed a pen and paper and made detailed notes on how the bearer bonds were to be sold and reinvested. She dropped the note, along with $500,000 in bonds, into the shipping envelope and sealed it. She then repeated the process with another $500,000 in bonds going to a different address. The Federal Express clerk assured her both packages shipped by second-day air would arrive at their destinations on Monday.

At 10:30 she was back at her condo with the cash and the remaining bonds tucked discreetly in her purse.

"Hi, honey, I'm home," she said as she walked in the

front door. "You'll be glad to know I rented a car on my way home so I can give you a ride to the airport."

Tim met her at the doorway. "You're just in time. Pack a bag. I've reserved us a flight out of Kansas City at 3: 40 to the Caymans. Do you have a valid passport?"

"What? I'm not following you and Arthur down there. That's the last thing in the world I want to do. And besides, I don't have a passport."

He pursued her into the kitchen. "Maggie, you promised you would help, and it will be a lot easier for me to fly out of the country if I'm traveling with someone."

"I said I would help if you let me keep Cleon's money from the Hamilton account. Since Arthur has it, the deal is off. And for the second time, I don't have a passport."

"Well, do you have $5,000?"

She felt her front pockets. "No, I must have left my walking-around money in my other pants. Not that it matters since I'm not going with you."

Now that she had financial independence, the last thing she was going to do was risk losing it by helping him any more. Arguably, she had made her money unconventionally, but that was no reason to piss it all away by making decisions with her heart instead of her head. Tim had become too much of a hazard, and it was time to end their alliance.

"You have to help me with this one last part." He stood in front of her and lifted her chin up so she looked in his eyes. "Without you, my plan won't work. I might as well turn myself in and get railroaded for something we both know I didn't do."

She pushed his hand away. "That's not fair."

"When the money is gone, so is your help. Is that it?"

Maggie didn't answer. It was just the opposite. Now that she had the money, she didn't see the point in taking the risk to keep helping him.

Tim bent toward her. "Didn't you learn anything from Cleon? He had millions, but it didn't mean anything to him after his wife died. And now here you are, a single-minded, unemployed workaholic who hasn't probably been laid, much less in love, since, when—a year? Two years? And where has it gotten you?"

Maggie's face flushed. Even with her secret bonds his comment still hurt.

"I thought there was more to you," he said. "I thought you might care about something other than yourself just long enough to see justice served. I can't believe Cleon was such a friend to you and you're letting his murderer get away."

He turned from her and sat down at the kitchen table, his head in his hands.

She watched him without saying anything. She had sacrificed so much to finally reach this point. But so had Tim. Seeing him with shoulders slumped, hopeless, reminded her of the ache she had when Cleon had first called and said he was dying. Maybe it didn't matter if she helped Tim a bit more. She just hoped she wouldn't regret it.

The phone interrupted the silence. Maggie walked past him and answered it.

"Good morning, my malignant Maggot, have you missed me?"

It was Arthur back in his old form. She leaned against the counter for support. Tim looked at her for some sign of whom she was talking to but she kept her face blank.

"You've been a very bad girl, haven't you?" Arthur said. "I happen to know you embezzled $3,207,422.59 from Cleon's account and transferred it into a bogus Terry Stevens account. I also know that you had a check issued to Terry Stevens, forged her name, and used the money to purchase bearer bonds from Janey Fitzgerald."

Maggie didn't say anything.

"It just so happens that I received a call from your IRS agent's boss. He's coming over in a half hour to discuss my father-in-law's account. If you're not here before he is, I'm telling him and the police everything I know. You'll be arrested for falsifying a driver's license application, embezzlement, and forgery. Best of all, you and your IRS pal will be charged with the murder of Cleon. What will your parents say when this hits the news?"

Maggie remained silent.

Arthur let out a dramatic sigh. "This whole situation has me rather fuckstrated. Of course, if you bring me the bonds before he gets here I think we could work out a very special arrangement. I'd be happy to give you the details at my hotel tonight. But first, you need to get those bonds back to me. I'll see you soon."

He hung up.

"I'm not interested in switching my phone service," she said and hung up. She ducked her head into the refrigerator and pretended to look for something to eat while she regained her composure. "How are we supposed to pay for tickets to the Caymans? Buying and flying the same day has got to cost a fortune."

Tim looked up and met her eyes. "I was hoping you could put it on a credit card. I've only got about four thousand dollars, and I need that to buy a passport."

"What about the two million in your bank account? You didn't go on a shopping spree without me, did you?" She closed the refrigerator door and walked to the sink to wipe off the top of her Pepsi can. She lingered at the sink with her back to Tim.

"If I tried to make a withdrawal on that account I'd be in lockup before the teller wished me a nice day."

"But the two million," she said over her shoulder.

"The money isn't mine and I'm not going to use it. The account is probably frozen anyhow."

She turned and faced Tim. "Oh, so you're too pure to use any of the money sitting in your account, yet it doesn't bother you that I'm almost bankrupt and you want me to pay for this trip. Do you have any idea how expensive airfare is going to be without a fourteen-day advance purchase?"

"I'm sorry, Maggie, but I don't know how else to do this. You'll be reimbursed by the IRS once this mess is all figured out. I promise." He smiled.

"Right."

"Maggie, if there's another way to do this, I'm open to suggestions. I'm sorry for getting you so involved in this, but remember you were a little tangled when we met."

If he was going to get righteous, at least he had the grace to be apologetic about it.

"Okay," she said. "But how do you plan on getting on the plane? They've got to have your picture posted at every terminal within five hundred miles. Then there's that awful sketch they're running of me."

"I've already got it figured out. I know a guy in Kansas City who can make fake passports for us, but they're five thousand dollars each and I only have four."

Maggie went to the bathroom and returned with six thousand dollars. It only left her with three thousand dollars, but it would have to do.

"You can explain to me where this money came from while we drive," he said. "Look, we don't have much time. It's a four-hour trip to Kansas City and there's two places we have to stop at on the way. We've got to get going."

She checked her watch. He was right. Given what Arthur had said, the police would be showing up at her door in half an hour with a warrant charging her with Cleon's murder. Finding the real killer had suddenly become very important to her.

She stuffed a few things into a bag, was glad she didn't have any pets, and walked out of her condo for the last time.

Tim got into his normal traveling position in the back seat with a blanket over his head. Maggie hit the automatic door opener for her garage door. When the door opened, she saw in her rearview mirror a man standing in her driveway pointing a gun at her. She hit the button again to close the door but the opener didn't respond fast enough.

"Get out of the car," the man said.

She stayed in the driver's seat and locked the car doors.

She was afraid to look and see if any of Tim's appendages were sticking out.

The man approached her window and displayed a badge. "My name is Ed Granger. I'm with the IRS and I'd like to talk to you. Please step out of the car."

She unbuckled her seat belt and did as she was told.

"Is there a problem? I have my post office return receipts showing I filed my taxes by the extension deadline."

"Why would you think there is a problem?"

"Because you're pointing a gun at me."

He holstered his weapon. "Sorry. I was expecting someone else."

"And who did you expect to find backing out of my garage?"

"Would you mind if we went inside for a moment? I'd like to ask you a few questions."

"I'm kind of in a hurry. What's this about?"

"I promise this won't take long. Would you mind?"

She locked her car and escorted him in the back door of her condo. She noticed that his eyes scrutinized everything he walked by. They stopped in the living room. She surveyed the room for traces of Tim's stay, but everything looked okay.

"You still haven't told me what this is about," she said, with her hands on her hips.

"I have a few questions regarding Cleon Cummings. I'm actually on my way over to your office to talk with Arthur Riley. When I called, your secretary said you were going to be out the rest of the day. Since your place is on the way I thought I would try my luck and see if I could catch you at home."

"My secretary gave you my address?"

"You're in the book. I understand Cummings was your client."

"I've already talked to someone from your office. What else do you want to know?"

"Who did you talk to?"

Oh, Tim was already on the run when he met her in her office. "Can I get you something to drink?" she said over her shoulder and walked to the kitchen.

"No, I'm fine. So who did you talk to?"

She returned with a soda. "I think it was that agent that's in the news."

"When did you talk to him?"

"Monday, I think. Yes, I'm sure of it because it was before Cleon died."

"What did he want to know?"

"He just wanted copies of Cleon's statements. That's about it."

"And that was Monday?"

"Yes, Mr. Granger, it was Monday."

"Did he seem to be acting strange?"

"I don't know how he acts normally so I couldn't say. Really Mr. Granger, I have to be going."

"That's right, you said you were in a hurry. Where are you off to?"

"I have my annual pap smear at my gynecologist's if you must know."

"Sorry." He blushed slightly. "Would you mind if I used your bathroom before I go? I just had a Big Gulp, and those things go right through me."

"It's this way."

She led him to the bathroom and then returned to the living room to wait. A few minutes later she heard the toilet flush, and the manager returned carrying an empty box of black hair dye.

"Forgive me, Ms. Connors, but I noticed this box in your trash can. Your hair looks auburn to me and I'm curious."

"I decided to experiment and I ended up looking rather evil in black so I switched back. Is there anything else?"

"Then why wasn't there an auburn box in the trash?"

"Because you're not supposed to dye your hair twice in the same day. I went to my hairdresser to have the red done so my hair wouldn't fall out."

He rubbed his receding hair line. "You wouldn't want to have that pretty hair fall out. I'm really sorry for the intrusion. I guess I'm just grasping at straws." He walked to the door and she followed. "Tim Gallen, the agent you talked to, was under my supervision, and it doesn't look good on a resume when one of your best employees kills a citizen and makes off with millions. I've always worked for the government and I can't imagine there are too many companies in the private sector who will be dying to hire a fifty-three-year-old screw-up." He looked at the floor. "I've got two girls in college and another who's a senior in high school right now. I was just looking for any answers you might have."

God, another hard-working innocent. Why couldn't she go back to the days when IRS agents were faceless bureaucrats?

"How can you be fired when he hasn't even been convicted yet?" she said. "What if he's innocent?"

"I think you're the only person in St. Louis who has raised that possibility."

They walked back into the garage, and he peered in the car window.

"What do you have under the blanket?" he asked.

"Just some stuff."

"Mind if I have a look at it?"

"Mr. Granger, if I miss this appointment it will take a month to get another appointment and I'm out of birth control pills."

He put his hand on his gun. "Just a quick peek."

Maggie unlocked the car and stood back. Granger leaned into the car and pulled the blanket back to expose a small white wicker end table. He put the blanket back the way he found it.

"Sorry, Ms. Connors. I'll tell your boss you've been very helpful."

"Yes, Arthur will appreciate that." Maggie waited beside her car until the man drove away. "Tim?"

"I'm under the car."

"Let's get out of here."

She tossed the wicker table into the corner of the garage with the rest of the ensemble and Tim crawled back into his hiding place.

"What did Ed want?" he said.

"Some answers. I made the mistake of telling him I talked to you, but I said I did it on Monday."

"Anything else?"

"It sounds like he's getting the axe for his prize student flipping out."

"Damn. Ed's got a couple of girls in college," he said.

"Yeah, and another one in high school."

"Let's just find Cleon's killer. It'll be best for all concerned."

Maggie pulled out of her garage and turned left, headed toward their first stop—Columbia, Missouri. When she was halfway down the block, Smith pulled out and dropped in behind her.

Chapter 39

The sign for Hiram's Make Believin' was large enough for only the very dedicated to see. Maggie parked the car behind the building and they entered from a door in the rear. A pasty-faced old man greeted them.

The man put down the bagel he was gnawing on. "Can I help you?"

"We've been invited to a costume party tonight and we need some disguises," Tim said.

"I see." The man stared closely at Tim's unshaven face and wrinkled clothes. "Well, come on in."

He led them into a small shop so packed with masks and costumes that Tim felt he was in a crowded elevator.

"Now," the old man said, "do you want a disguise or a costume?"

Maggie stopped admiring a case of wigs and hats. "What's the difference?"

"A disguise will take your identity and alter it, using makeup and false attachments. A costume, on the other hand, will totally conceal your identity. It's the difference

between changing into a couple in their eighties and
changing into Cookie Monster and Big Bird from *Sesame
Street*."

"Ahh, I can see we don't know much about the nuances
of the theater," Tim said. "Which do you think offers a
better surprise at midnight when true identities are revealed?"

The man looked into Tim's eyes as if trying to read his
mind. "I think, young man, that you two want disguises."

Tim took a step backward. "A disguise it is."

The owner led them to a corner of the store where a
rack of robes hung. He flipped through robes of every
color and material until he came to a black suit.

"You have the face of an honest man, how would you
feel about walking as a man of the cloth?" The timeworn
man held up an outfit, complete with white collar, for Tim
to inspect.

"But won't people be able to recognize my face?"

"Not when I'm done with you."

He fitted Tim with a gray wig, matching gray mustache,
a pair of spectacles, a Bible, a cane, and a five-pound
weight that hung from a cushioned necklace.

Tim fingered the weight before tucking it into his shirt.
"What's this for?"

"It will help you walk slowly and with a stoop, but
don't wear it too long or you'll screw up your back. For
you, Missy, how about going as a pixie?"

"I'd like us to be a couple," Tim said while he ap-
praised his new look in a mirror.

"All right, sister, come with me."

Ten minutes later Maggie came out wearing a long,
black habit. "I'm going to sweat to death in here, and I'm
not sure this is really disguising my face."

The shopkeeper removed her headpiece and put a gray
wig on her so the bangs would stick out under the headpiece. Next he gave her a pair of black sunglasses and a
blind person's cane. She put the sunglasses on and looked
in the mirror again.

"Wow, that makes a big difference," she said.

"Would you like to rent these ensembles or would you prefer to purchase them?"

"Perhaps we should buy them," Tim said, still admiring their new look. "No one's going to recognize us in these. I'm sure we can use them again for Halloween."

The man rang the outfits up and, after a moment's hesitation, Maggie paid him. Tim noticed she still had a sizable wad left in her wallet.

"Tell you what," Tim said, "why don't we wear these disguises back to the office and test them out."

Maggie smiled. "Sure."

The storekeeper nodded his head and placed Tim's street clothes into a bag, and the newly ordained priest stepped onto the streets of Columbia feeling more relaxed than he had all week. He tucked his Bible under his arm, and helped the now blind Sister Maggie carefully to her car.

"Maybe you should drive," she said.

"Thanks, but I don't want to trust my new outfit any more than necessary."

"But, Father." She ran her fingers over his face. "How can I possibly drive?"

On impulse, he kissed her fingertips.

Maggie let her hands slide from Tim's lips and clasp his neck. She pressed against him and tilted her chin upward, expecting Tim to kiss her. Instead, he stiffened and pulled back.

"I don't think this is a good idea," he said, unlatching her embrace.

"You're kidding me!" Maggie said, thrusting her hands onto her hips.

"I think we should keep things professional."

"Oh you're a professional all right, a professional asshole."

"I think you are misinterpreting—"

"I'm misinterpreting nothing. But have it your way."

"I'm sorry, Maggie. I didn't mean to offend you."

"You're giving yourself too much credit."

Tim stepped away, not wanting to meet her eyes. He climbed into the car and back under his blanket. They drove in silence, a few miles below the speed limit down I-70 toward Kansas City. Every few minutes the tires slapped through the tar patches in the pavement that had softened under the blazing sun. The rhythmic noise was comforting.

After fifteen minutes, Tim broke the silence. "Guess how I know where to get fake passports?"

Maggie ignored the question.

"I prosecuted a guy for skimming cash from his chain of restaurants about a year ago," he said from his hiding place. "Several of his restaurants were in Kansas City, and his brother did the bookkeeping. His brother also dabbled in forgery and money laundering, but not very effectively. The brother did keep good records, which we confiscated to help prove our case. Anyway, I'm hoping he doesn't recognize us."

Maggie didn't respond.

"We should probably come up with a story explaining why a priest and a nun need fake passports."

She continued her silent treatment.

"How about if we tell him that our passports were confiscated because we tried to sneak into Cuba and do missionary work?"

"Oh that ought to be good."

"Nice to hear your voice again. Does this mean we're talking?"

"You know what happens when you assume. . . ."

"Come on, Maggie. I'm sorry about what happened. Could we put that behind us and just concentrate on getting this Cleon mess figured out?"

"You're the boss," she said flatly.

"Could you flip on the radio? I'd like to hear what's happening with Cleon's case."

She dialed in a news-talk radio station, and they didn't have to wait long.

"The body found by two men fishing on the Silver River has been identified. Dental records were used to positively identify the body of Cleon Cummings," the broadcast said. "Sources close to the investigation say the multimillionaire shredded $160 million dollars before being poisoned and then drowning in the river behind his home. Authorities continue to look for Tim Gallen, the IRS agent, and an unidentified female accomplice in connection with the case. The agent is believed to have taken over two million dollars from Cummings before disappearing."

Maggie turned the radio off.

"Cleon's net worth is growing," Tim said. "This morning the news claimed it was $152 and I only made it to $139 million."

"And you ought to know."

"Nah, the IRS is always the last to know. Next to the ex-wife." He paused. "You know, the reports aren't mentioning anything about the poison being English nightshade. The police must be holding that back."

The car made a sudden lurch and horns blared around them.

"Hey," Tim yelled, "what's going on?"

"English nightshade? That was the poison?"

"Yeah, I think somebody laced Cleon's tea with it."

"Tea?"

"I think so, Maggie. Why, what's the matter?"

Maggie was silent for a long time. Then, "I was right. He was going to try and deduct it."

"What are you talking about?"

"When I was searching the office in Arthur's home, I found a file labeled 'CC' in his briefcase that contained receipts for a tin of tea and an English nightshade plant."

"What? Why didn't you tell me?"

"Because I didn't know it was important, that's why. How was I to know English nightshade could be a poison? When you told me he was poisoned I thought you meant something like arsenic or rat poisoning or something. But there's more."

Tim lay huddled under the blanket while Maggie told him about her near drowning in the hot tub and then reminded him about being pushed into the street.

"Why didn't you tell me?" he said when she was done. "Why didn't you tell somebody for God's sake?"

"You were there when I got pushed."

"I thought you had just had too much to drink and lost your balance. You should have been in protective custody long before now. I can't believe you didn't tell me."

"I didn't think it was important, and you said if I was in any danger that you'd cut me out."

"Not important—"

"Look, I lead a quiet, peaceful, moderately law-abiding life. I don't assume someone's trying to kill me every time I have a little accident. And when I did finally figure out Arthur was after me—"

"I talked you out of it," Tim said. "I'm sorry, Maggie."

"You didn't know. But what do we do now?"

"Just what we're doing. Go to the Caymans, track down this Nealey person, and find out what's going on."

"Right."

Tim felt the car surge forward. He had a feeling they were no longer under the speed limit.

"Besides," he said, "Arthur will be in the Caymans this weekend to deposit his three million. If all else fails, we can follow him and get some answers then."

The car slowed, and he guessed they were back under the speed limit.

When they reached the city limits, Tim gave Maggie directions to a small shop located in a seedier section of town. They parked in front of an unmarked door.

"I hope the car is still here when we're done," she said.

Tim knocked on the door.

No answer.

He knocked again.

An intercom crackled to the left of the door. "What is it, Padre?"

Tim looked around to see how they were being seen, but the painted-over windows offered no clues. "Hello, my son. We have come to you for help."

"We gave at the office, come back another day."

There was silence. Tim pounded on the door again.

"I told you Padre, we're not interested."

"We came for passports," Tim said. "My brother is the priest at the St. Charles Correctional Facility. He counsels your brother Jerry. That's where we got your name. Please help us, we don't know where else to go."

Silence returned and they waited.

The door opened slightly. A voice came out of the darkness. "Jerry's found God. That's all he talks about anymore. Your brother is the one who did it?"

"Jerry is the one who did it. My brother only facilitated the process, my son."

"So your brother is a father? That's pretty funny."

The man opened the door and invited them in. In the darkened stairwell they couldn't see him but they followed his odor up the creaky wooden staircase.

At the top they went through a doorway and the world completely changed. When Tim's eyes adjusted to the bright lights he saw the latest desktop publishing equipment, complete with several digital cameras, color printers, and a darkroom. Everything a forger needs, including a stack of passports that had been liberated from their previous owners.

"Padre, this service is expensive. Do you have ten thousand dollars?"

Tim handed him the money.

The artist wiped his hands on his dirty T-shirt before counting the money. "I guess business at the church has been good."

Tim didn't answer.

"How long will this take?" Maggie asked.

"Quicker than getting a driver's license."

He was right. Thirty minutes later Tim and Maggie left with their new passports in the name of Father Joseph Charles and Sister Emily Parker.

Now they were ready for the airport.

Chapter 40

Smith waited until he was sure Maggie took the airport exit before calling Arthur.

"It looks like our friends are going to do some traveling," he said.

"Hold on just a minute." He could hear Arthur throwing someone out of his office before he returned. "Where are you?"

"I'm pulling into the long-term parking lot at the Kansas City airport. The lady is still traveling with her friend. On their way from St. Louis they stopped at a costume place, and now she looks like Mother Teresa. Her friend is dressed as a priest. They made one other stop in downtown Kansas City. They were in there for half an hour, but I'm not sure what they did."

"Sounds like they're trying to get past airport security and get out of the country."

"I think it would be best if I followed them and concluded our business at their destination."

"Perhaps you're right. Tourists are always getting themselves killed in the most unlikely manner. I believe the local government usually goes out of its way to keep that kind of publicity to a minimum. Go ahead and follow them. Let me know where you're headed. If you get a chance to kill them tonight, do it. Just don't let anything happen to Maggie's stuff until I get a chance to go through it. And you know, if it's out of the country, I don't think it has to look like an accident anymore. You could make it an old-fashioned rape and murder if you like. Do what you want with the other one."

Smith shook his head. The fool should know better than to make comments like that on a cellular phone. He was surprised Arthur hadn't long ago been committed to an institution for people who needed to be protected from themselves.

"I'll call you later to let you know where we end up," he said and hung up.

This woman had something Arthur wanted badly, which meant he could kill her, find whatever it was, and either blackmail Arthur with it or keep it for himself if it turned out to be valuable. Luckily he was prepared. He had packed an overnight bag, including his passport, since he planned on skipping the country himself when this job was done.

He ran for the shuttle bus.

There would be ample opportunities to kill the two before they got on a plane, but he liked the idea of having Arthur pay for his vacation, wherever they were going. He climbed on the long-term parking shuttle bus and took a seat a few rows behind Sister Maggie. He was dressed in a preppie long-sleeved Oxford and wearing a pair of khakis. With his hair cut, and his beard and mustache shaved, she didn't recognize him from the hot tub encounter. She even smiled at him when he passed her seat.

Rape and murder? He couldn't keep himself from snickering at how enjoyable and profitable this assignment was becoming.

Chapter 41

Maggie's bladder felt like an overfilled water balloon. She sat jiggling her leg in hyperdrive and praying for a quick takeoff, but the plane remained parked on a side entrance to the runway where it had taxied ten minutes ago. She should have gone to the bathroom before she got on the plane, but by the time they reached the gate, the announcer was calling for final boarding.

At least the ticket agent had processed them without a second thought, and they sailed through security without a problem. The disguises and passports had worked perfectly. Maggie had wanted to get rid of her nun's outfit as soon as they made it to the gate, but Tim had said they still needed to clear customs in the Caymans and it would be better if she waited. She had convinced him to let her stop using the sunglasses and cane, which were tucked by her side.

Now as the plane sat on the tarmac without its air conditioning working, Maggie wished she had changed. The plane was completely filled, so they weren't able to get

two seats together. Tim was four rows back in the last
row. Beside her was a stressed-out mother who was trying
to help her husband sitting in the row in front of her keep
control of their screaming two-year-old.

"Ladies and gentlemen," a flight attendant announced
over the speaker, "the Captain has just informed me that
we will be returning to the gate to correct a minor problem. Please stay in your seats while the Captain has the
seat belt sign on."

Maggie hastily unbuckled her seat belt and crawled
over her row companions, trying not to trip on her long
robe. She clambered to the back of the plane, accidentally
bumping a few of her fellow passengers when the plane
occasionally pitched in its lumbering maneuvers to return
to the gate. She reached the micro bathroom and opened
the door, which attracted the attention of the flight attendant in the rear of the plane.

"Excuse me, Sister, you'll have to take your seat while
the Captain has the fasten seat belt sight on," the attendant
said.

"Forgive me, my child, but it's an emergency. Too
much holy water before leaving the rectory."

Maggie closed the door and slipped the "Occupied"
sign into position. In record time she emptied her bladder
with a feeling more satisfying than any recent orgasm she
could remember. She dressed again and washed her hands.
She was about to leave when she felt an itch on the top
of her head she couldn't get to through her headpiece and
wig. She took them both off and scratched furiously. The
plane lurched; Maggie lost her balance and almost fell
into the toilet. When she recovered, she looked down to
see her gray wig sitting in blue liquid at the bottom of
the silver toilet bowl. *Terrific*.

She ignored the posted warnings not to flush personal
items and sent the wig off to Tidy Bowl Heaven. She
pulled her headpiece down as low as it would go and
stumbled back out into the aisle.

•   •   •

Father Tim Gallen put down the magazine he had been reading and looked toward the window for signs of the police, but he couldn't see very well from his aisle seat. The flight was probably being called back to the gate so he could be arrested. Buckled in seat C, row thirty-three, there was no escape. He waited for his moment of reckoning to arrive.

Something knocked him in the back of the head. It was Maggie returning from the bathroom. He was furious when he saw she had gotten rid of her wig. Maybe it didn't matter since the police were waiting to board.

Ten minutes passed and nothing happened.

The airplane's phone in front of him invited him to check in with his office, the wife and kids, and anyone else worthy of a two-dollar-a-minute phone rate.

Do planes get parking tickets?

Not planes, but Cleon did!

He removed the plane's phone from the headrest and slid his credit card down the phone's side. Nothing happened. He tried again. Still nothing. Either the phone was out of order or it only worked during flight. He decided to wait until they took off and try again. If they took off.

The airplane's loudspeaker clicked on.

"Ladies and gentlemen, I'm happy to tell you that the problem is almost fixed and we should be ready for take-off in a few minutes. Thank you for your patience."

The vacationers Maggie passed were glaring back and forth from their watches to the flight attendants, looking anything but patient.

When she dropped back into her seat she noticed that the woman who had been sitting beside her had switched with a guy in the row ahead of them so the woman could travel with her husband and daughter. The guy next to her was the same cute guy from the shuttle bus. Maybe it was a good thing an act of God had caused the demise of the gray wig.

"Welcome back, sister," he said. "You don't look like you're a fan of flying."

"As a matter of fact, I hate it."

"Perhaps this will help." He reached into his briefcase and removed two airplane-sized bottles of gin and tonic. "When I got my seat assignment and realized I was so far back that I almost qualified for another flight number, I decided to bring a few refreshments with me. I figured it would be a good hour before the attendants made it to me with any alcohol."

Maggie stared at the bottle. Tim would kill her if he saw her drinking alcohol while impersonating a nun. But then again, she was ready to kill Tim for the way he had rejected her.

"That's very nice of you," she said, "but I really shouldn't."

"I recommend it to smooth out the air turbulence." He poured the first gin and tonic into a red plastic cup. "Look, you can't even tell what it is. And we're so far back on this plane no one is even paying any attention to us."

Her new friend was right. The man sitting in the aisle seat was already asleep.

The plane taxied away from the gate. A few minutes later the engines erupted and the plane climbed into the air. They weren't getting arrested after all.

"Now that we're in the air you definitely need to join me," he said, handing her the cup.

Maybe it was finally time to loosen up and get back into the social scene. If Tim was hell-bent on being "Mr. Professional" then so be it. She'd enjoy this guy's company instead. Besides, Tim was probably back in his seat fantasizing about new IRS regulations. "Well, I guess it wouldn't hurt since today is my last day as a nun."

"You know, that doesn't surprise me." He mixed the second drink. "I bet you can serve God better outside the confines of the Church."

"That's exactly my thinking."

•   •   •

Once the plane reached its cruising altitude and the Captain turned off the seat belt sign, Tim walked to the back of the cabin. The phone at his seat wasn't working, which was just as well. On the wall by the flight attendants' serving galley was another phone—this one offering more privacy than the one at his seat. He removed the phone from its cradle and slid his credit card where instructed. He called information and got the number for the Baltimore police. He dialed again, and when he heard the phone ringing, he tucked himself into the wall to keep his conversation as private as possible.

Tim spent the next ten minutes transferring from one department to another, trying to locate an officer named Jennifer. He didn't have a clue what her last name was but did remember her unforgettable figure, which he tried to politely describe to each person he was switched to. He finally found her on the sixth transfer.

"Jennifer? It's me, Tim Gallen from CID. We met at a drug trafficking conference about a year ago."

"Who?"

"Tim Gallen from the Dallas conference. You said if I ever needed anything. . . ."

"Like the underwear you left in my hotel room?"

Tim laughed. He'd found the right Jennifer.

"I need a favor. My sister's father-in-law is missing. He suffers from Alzheimer's and they think he got himself lost. One of your officers gave him a parking ticket about three weeks or so ago. Could you check on where it was issued? I'd really appreciate it."

"Hey, is this the same Tim Gallen that's all over the news?"

"Would you believe that he's my evil twin brother?"

No response.

"Please, Jennifer, I need your help. I didn't do it."

"What do you need exactly?" She spoke cautiously as if her words were being recorded.

"I'm trying to track down the location of a parking

ticket one of your officers issued to Cleon Cummings in Baltimore about three weeks ago."

"Is this considered aiding and abetting a known fugitive?"

"Only if you do it."

"Give me one of those sweet smiles and I will."

"I'm doing it," he said.

"So am I," she said.

Tim gave her Cleon's name and social security number.

"All right, on April 15th at 10:12 a.m., Cleon was given a parking citation at the corner of Cornell Drive and First Avenue. He must have returned to his vehicle just as the officer was completing the ticket," she said.

"How do you know that?"

"Because the vehicle is listed as a Ryder rental truck. If Cleon wasn't there, the officer wouldn't have known who the truck belonged to."

"I don't know my way around Baltimore. Any idea what's around Cornell Drive?"

"Mainly government buildings. I think the court house is also near there."

Tim thanked her profusely, hung up, and dialed information for the Federal Reserve Bank of Baltimore.

"Good morning, may I help you?"

"Yes, where are you located?" He crossed his fingers.

"We're at 3994 Fourth Street."

"Is Cornell Drive and First Avenue near there by any chance?"

"That's around the corner. First Avenue is right behind our building."

Tim hung up with a wide grin on his face. Everything now made sense.

Maggie spent the plane trip tossing back gin and tonics and listening to her new friend tell hilarious stories about running a women's undergarment business he inherited from his father. She almost regretted it when the plane landed four hours later in Georgetown, Grand Cayman.

By then Arthur, the SEC, the police, and Visa all seemed like distant worries from a former lifetime. Even the fat kid who had been kicking the back of Maggie's seat for the duration of the flight ended his torment.

"Where are you staying on the island?" The man's voice was full of promise and as confident as if he had asked the time of day.

"I'm not sure, this trip was kind of unexpected."

"So was mine! Perhaps we can get together tonight for a late dinner. I'd hate to spend my birthday alone."

"Your birthday! You should have said something sooner. I would have baked a cake." They both laughed. "Should I just refer to you as birthday boy, or do you have a given name you prefer?"

"Yes, I'm sorry. Hello, my name is Larry Smith."

"It's a pleasure to meet you, Larry. My name is Maggie Connors."

"Sister Maggie, that name suits you."

She winced. Her name was suppose to be Sister Emily Parker. She looked over her shoulder and couldn't see Tim. Oh well, it was a harmless mistake.

"So how about it, Ms. Connors, formerly Sister Maggie? Will you meet me for a late dinner, drinks, and maybe a little birthday cake?"

Maggie stared at his face, searching for some sign that she might be sitting next to a serial murderer, but she only saw his boy-next-door grin. On the other hand, he was coming on to a nun. Should she take him up on his offer? He seemed familiar, but in a way she couldn't place. She guessed he was in his late thirties; and for all the perils of women's underwear, the business seemed to be doing well.

"I'd love to," she said, "but after the morning I had, all I want to do right now is have a glass of wine and soak in the bathtub. It's been such a hectic day. I'm afraid I'm not up to a late-night celebration."

"Did I ever tell you what a turn-on wrinkled fingers and toes are?"

"My, you're terribly forward with a woman who has taken her vows."

"Must be that virgin aura you have about you."

She hadn't heard that in a long time. If ever.

They walked down the steps to the tarmac. The sticky, tropical heat baptized her soul. Her new life in the Caymans was starting better than she expected.

"I've got to get some luggage I checked," he said when they reached the terminal. "Perhaps we'll bump into each other again."

"I hope so. Until then, happy birthday."

Larry waved goodbye and followed the crowd of people en route to retrieve their luggage.

Suddenly someone jerked her aside. It was Father Tim.

"Are you out of your mind?" he said. "What kind of a spectacle do you think you made getting drunk on the plane when you're supposed to be a nun?"

She stared at him, then smiled. The gin and tonics had been too effective for his criticism to make an impact.

"Father Gallen, I mean Father Charles, everything is fine."

"No, it's not fine. We still have to make it through Customs and you're staggering all over the place."

"Then take my arm and walk with me."

The Customs agent didn't even make eye contact with them and waved them through. Maggie thought Tim almost seemed disappointed that they weren't discovered. She could tell he hated for his perfect plan to be altered in any way, and her getting drunk with Larry Smith definitely wasn't part of his strategy.

They found their way to the taxi stand and waited for an available cab. Next to them, four uniformed stewards tried to corral a throng of arriving passengers for a Windjammer cruise. A cab finally arrived, and Maggie told him to take them to the best hotel on the island. Tim sulked in the corner of the cab and didn't say a word. She relaxed in the back seat with her envelope of two million dollars in bearer bonds taped to her stomach.

The cabbie drove into downtown Georgetown and then out past a Hilton, a Marriott, and several other chain hotels before stopping at the Trade Winds Village. The driver had probably picked the accommodations because of the cab fare it fetched rather than for its one-star rating. She tipped him anyway.

They registered and checked into two adjoining suites connected by a common door. Maggie's suite was surprisingly clean, but the view did not match the brochure the hotel manager had shown her moments earlier in the lobby—unless the dumpster directly below her balcony was a new, added attraction. Across the alley was the restaurant with the rooftop dining area that the manager had mentioned. The far end of the cafe probably offered diners a panoramic view of the ocean.

After checking in, Tim had dropped his bag in his suite and then told her he was going out. Undoubtedly to pout, but she wasn't going to let him ruin her first night on the island. She flung her black robe and headpiece on the bed and then took off her shoes. Wearing just a T-shirt and shorts she walked out onto the balcony to have a look around.

The trash smell below easily overpowered the few wild flowers clinging to the balcony's wrought iron fence. The balcony offered two chairs and a small table but everything was covered with a fine layer of dirt, so she walked back inside and closed the sliding glass doors behind her, but left the curtains open. The few tourists dining on the restaurant's balcony were looking at the ocean in the other direction, so she undressed.

She went into the bathroom and turned the hot water on full blast in the bathtub. The bathroom had an entrance from the hall and from the bedroom, which combined to make the room almost as big as the kitchen. An old clawfoot bathtub stood majestically on one side of the bathroom; a pedestal sink balanced the room on the other side.

While the bathtub filled, Maggie went to the kitchen to get an overpriced bottle of wine from the stocked refrigerator. She poured herself a glass and took several long drinks. The bath had a few more minutes before it was filled, so she turned on the television to a local station and refilled her glass.

She sat on the bed drinking her wine and watching a review of four local reggae bands, then turned her attention to the envelope of bearer bonds lying beside her on the bed. It was time to find a safe hiding place for them.

Unlike the rest of the suite, the kitchen had a drop ceiling. Since the kitchen area was out of view from the windows, she took the envelope and crawled on top of the kitchen counter with it. She gently pushed one of the ceiling panels aside—another fringe benefit of her breaking and entering experience with Tim—and placed the bonds inside. She stood there naked, with a glass of wine at her feet and two million dollars over her head, and laughed. It was a wonderful feeling. If only she had an eight-by-ten glossy of the scene to send to Arthur.

She jumped down from the counter to check on her bath. The mirror in the bathroom was completely fogged and a steamy mist hung in the air. With balmy, ninety-degree weather outside, the bathroom had rarely been converted into a steam bath.

She turned the water off and poked her toe into the tub. It took several minutes for her to inch the rest of her body into the hot water. The reggae music from the television drifted in and lulled her overworked nerves. She took another sip of wine and closed her eyes to let the water boil away any last remaining worries of St. Louis.

Following Maggie from the airport had been easy. Getting past the old lock on her hotel door was even easier.

The man slipped inside before anyone noticed.

Chapter 42

Tim stared at the hickey on the back of the waitress's neck as he trudged up the stairs to the restaurant's rooftop cafe. She led him to a table with an oceanfront view, but he asked instead for one closer to the center of the restaurant. The waitress shrugged and told Tim to take any table he wanted. It was late and the dinner crowd had come and gone.

He sat with his back to the ocean, reading a newspaper and sucking down a Red Stripe with the passion of a man no longer governed by a religious disguise.

The waitress reappeared with a menu and another beer. He was scanning the day's specials when he noticed Maggie standing on her balcony, directly across from the cafe. She looked in Tim's direction and he ducked behind his menu. He waited a few moments and peeked again. She had vanished but had left the curtains open, which provided an encompassing view of her hotel suite.

She made a fool of herself with that guy on the plane. He had gotten more pissed off with each giggle and toss

of her head. Her careless attitude toward compromising
their covers put them both at risk, especially if she was
right and Arthur was trying to—

Oh hell, even he knew it was more than that. He was
jealous and might as well admit it. He swallowed some
more beer.

He looked again at Maggie's sliding glass doors and
saw that she had undressed and was walking around her
room naked. He glanced at the few other diners to see if
anyone else was enjoying the peep show, but they were
staring at the ocean. Tourists usually did miss the best
local attractions. He turned back just as she walked out
of view into what was probably her bathroom. He lifted
his beer again and waited for her to reappear.

The waitress picked up the empty bottle from his table.
"Eh man, why you want to stare at that ugly hotel?"

Before Tim could answer, Maggie sauntered into view
again, this time with a bath towel draped over one shoulder.

The waitress slapped him on the back of his head. "You
are very wicked."

She confiscated Tim's half-full beer and his menu before stomping away. His act of voyeurism had evidently
caused him to forfeit his dining privileges.

He threw a couple of dollars on the table and was about
to leave when he took one last look at Maggie's room.

The man from the plane was walking around Maggie's
suite. Had she invited him over so quickly? He watched
as the man stopped every few steps and turned his head
as if to listen for someone or something. Then the man
shut all the curtains.

Oh well, if that was how Maggie was going to spend
her night then Tim could find someone to amuse himself
with as well.

He started down the stairs. Where did one go if one
were looking for company on a tropical island night? He
might have thought about this on the plane like Maggie
did, but he had been seated next to an attorney from Des

Moines. And he'd been dressed as a priest. Although being dressed as a nun hadn't slowed Maggie down.

Actually, it was pretty strange the way that guy came on to Sister Maggie. Almost as if he was going to stick with her no matter what. And the way he was so nervous in her room, almost sneaking around—

Tim began to run.

Chapter 43

Larry Smith first checked to make sure Maggie was in the tub as she had planned. He snickered. She was asleep. It was the perfect opportunity to search her room and see what he could find.

He rummaged through her one piece of luggage and in, under, and around the bed. Nothing. He searched the cabinets in the kitchen and then the inside of the refrigerator. Still nothing. What was Arthur so hot for?

He rolled his head to stretch the muscles in the back of his neck and that's when he noticed the footprints on the countertop. He looked at the ceiling. Everything looked normal.

He climbed up, removed the ceiling panel directly above the footprints, and set the panel on the counter. Then he reached his hand into the ceiling and felt an envelope. He pulled it out and climbed down off the counter to get a closer look. Before he opened the envelope he tiptoed to the bathroom door to make sure Maggie was still resting in the tub. She looked more wrinkled but still asleep.

He walked back to the kitchen. He leaned against the counter and opened the envelope. What was so special about a bunch of foreign documents?

He paged through the contents. They were bonds of some sort, and according to the face values printed on the elaborate pages there was well over a million dollars worth of paper. No wonder Arthur had been so emphatic about needing to search Maggie's stuff. This was going to be a successful night after all. He put the bonds back in their envelope and set the envelope on the counter. He pulled Arthur's business card from his back pocket and placed it on top of the envelope as a reminder. When he was finished, he would give Art a call and tell him some island punk had robbed and killed Maggie before he had a chance to.

He rolled up his sleeves and walked to the bathroom door. Killing her first and then having his fun was a quieter option than the reverse. He could hear faint voices from the adjacent room, and if Maggie started screaming she would quickly have the entire hotel's attention. He stood in the doorway and watched her soak. Her toes had poked out of the water and were resting on the edge of the tub. Her eyes were still closed. And her legs were the hairiest he'd ever seen.

One of his previous cell mates was a self-proclaimed expert in drowning women in bathtubs without leaving any signs of a struggle. Dank Hank, as he liked to be called, had killed two of his wives that way and was living lavishly off the insurance money when he got too greedy and decided to go for a third. The third victim's father became suspicious, and soon the police did, too.

Hank's method was to yank the woman's feet up by the ankles, which drove her head under the water. According to Hank, if you did it right, the water entered her mouth and nose before she had a chance to react, even to hold her breath.

He nudged the bathroom door open and more steam escaped. Over the noise of the TV he could hear Maggie's rhythmic breathing. He crept to the edge of the bathtub without waking her and stared down at her naked body. Even without her buying dinner it was going to be a very enjoyable night.

He grabbed her ankles and pulled them up and apart as Hank had described. Her head was under water before her eyes bulged opened in horror. He stood there relishing the improved view and watching her struggle for air when the bathroom door flung open and the IRS guy tackled him.

The mirror above the sink shattered when the two of them collided with it. Smith struggled, but the IRS guy had him pretty well pinned. Maggie erupted from the bathtub, screaming and gasping for air and her shrieking distracted the IRS guy enough for Larry to land a solid punch.

The IRS guy fell to the tile floor and Larry fled the bathroom. He grabbed the envelope of bonds he had left on the kitchen counter and then escaped out the balcony door. He jumped onto the garbage dumpster below and was down the alley and into the night before anyone noticed him.

Tim slowly got to his feet just as Maggie screamed again and bolted out of the bathroom. He had to tackle her onto the bed and clamp his hand over her mouth to quiet her. This was getting to be a habit.

"Be quiet, calm down," he said. "You're safe, everything's going to be all right."

Maggie bit into his hand as hard as she could.

"Jesus Christ!" He let go of her mouth.

"What kind of psycho prick agent are you?" She grabbed her nun's robe lying on the bed to cover herself.

"The kind that just saved your life, although now I'm not sure why I did."

Tim left her on the bed and went to the kitchen to put

his bleeding hand under running water. Maggie wrapped the robe around herself and followed him.

"But I thought you. . . ." She looked back toward the bathroom, not sure what had happened.

"Trust me, this wasn't my elaborate plan to do another horizontal twist and shout with you on the bed."

The ceiling panel lying on the countertop grabbed her attention. "Oh my God!"

Tim sighed. "Let me guess, he got your bearer bonds too."

She clutched the robe and crawled onto the counter. The ceiling space was empty. The bonds were gone. She jumped off the counter and ran to the bed, where she buried her face in the pillow and sobbed.

Tim strolled in after her. "By the way, you're welcome."

Maggie's crying got louder.

"Now I'm probably going to need a tetanus shot."

There was a knock on the door.

"This is the hotel manager. Is everything all right?"

Tim opened the door partway. "Yes, my wife just saw a huge cockroach in the bathroom and it scared her."

The manager noticed Tim's bleeding hand.

"I'm afraid I accidentally broke the bathroom mirror trying to kill it. The roach put up quite a fight."

The manager motioned to gain entrance to the room. "Perhaps I should—"

Tim continued to block his entrance. "Would it be possible for you to come back in the morning after my wife calms down?"

"Of course, and please accept my apologies for the insect's intrusion into your room. We use a very reputable insect service but bugs are a part of life on the island."

"I see," Tim said. "Thank you."

After the manager left Tim slid the deadbolt into place. He also shut the balcony doors and dropped a wooden brace into the track to prevent them from being opened. Next he went to the bathroom and tried to clean up as much of the mess as he could. When he returned to the kitchen he found Arthur Riley's business card, which the attacker must have dropped. He called the handwritten phone number scrawled on the back.

"Riley," came the answer after only one ring.

"Arthur Riley, this is Tim Gallen. I'm calling to let you know the guy you hired to kill Maggie Connors botched up again, only this time he made off with several million in bearer bonds. I don't think either one of us is going to see him again. And if you or anyone else tries to harm Maggie I am going to have you arrested for tax fraud. I have a copy of both of your returns from last year—the one your accountant signed and the one you filed with the forged accountant's signature. Have a nice night."

He hung up and went to sit beside Maggie, who was still crying on the bed.

"Look, Maggie, I'm sorry about your bonds, but at least you're still alive. Arthur isn't going to try and hurt you anymore."

Maggie tightened the robe around her. "Please just go away and leave me alone."

"Fine. I'll go but I'll leave the door between our two rooms open. If you need anything during the night, just yell."

She rolled away from him and continued to cry.

He left her to it. If he was right, he'd have plenty of chances to straighten things out between them.

Chapter **44**

It was 10:00 a.m. Friday morning before Tim knocked on the open door of Maggie's room and invited himself in. She was grateful that he'd waited—it was after midnight before she had cried herself to sleep. She had showered, unfortunately without the razor she'd forgotten to pack, and was now dressed in a pair of jeans and a black T-shirt.

He brushed a strand of hair away from her face. "You look better this morning."

"Thanks." It wasn't true. Her eyes were puffy and her face very white. She pulled away and walked to the refrigerator for a bottle of water.

He nodded at the suitcase sitting near the door. "Where are you going?"

"Home. I've reserved a flight out this afternoon."

"You can't leave yet. I still need your help. Don't leave now just because your bonds were stolen."

She paused from drinking her water. "How did you know about the bonds?"

"Your broker called Thursday morning wondering why you were late for your appointment. On his message he said you had just arrived and to disregard his call. I erased it before you got home."

She might have known. One more glaring example of her inability to play cops and robbers.

"I'm sorry, Tim, but I've had enough. I figure if I go home tonight, I can work on my resume tomorrow and be prepared for the want ads on Sunday."

"Maggie, I know things didn't work out as you planned."

"That's the understatement of the day." She walked to the window and pulled the curtain back. Another brilliant, tropical day was beginning. The sun hurt her eyes so she dropped the curtain back in place and turned to face him. "For the last eight years, while my friends were out partying, getting married, having kids, I was reading financial reports, making cold calls, and putting up with Arthur's crap. I didn't mind because I knew it would all eventually pay off. But then all my best clients started dying—which was not part of my master plan—and my one salvation becomes Stanley Goldwyn, the world's most adorable, little old man, who is supposed to have millions for me to invest. And I think that finally, maybe, it's my turn." She paused to swallow some more water. "That this account is the break I've been working so many years for, but then Stanley turns out not to have any money after all. Now I'm not back at square one, I'm buried below it."

"It's not that bad."

"Oh really? As you so eloquently pointed out earlier, I'm almost thirty years old, in debt, unemployed, a criminal, and the first guy I flirt with almost drowns me and steals my stolen bonds."

"I guess you should have taken me up on my invitation for lunch; I wouldn't have taken your bonds."

"You only asked me out because you wanted information from me." She hoped he would deny it.

"I guess I too tend to have a one-track mind," he said.

"You'll have to be obsessed all by yourself then. I'm officially ending my career as a white-collar criminal. I think I finally understand what Emerson meant when he said 'Money often costs too much.' "

Tim raised an eyebrow at her.

"It's one of the few quotes I remember from English Lit classes," she said.

"So that's it? You're just giving up and going back to St. Louis?"

"I'm not cut out to be a fugitive. Besides, I can't afford it. Maybe Arthur didn't turn me in for stealing Cleon's money. Don't companies sometimes look the other way to avoid bad publicity?"

"Yeah, but do you want to do jail time for killing Cleon?"

"I didn't kill Cleon."

"Look at today's *USA Today*."

He handed her the paper, opened to an article stating that Maggie Connors was now wanted in connection with the murder of the millionaire who had shredded all his money. She was believed to be working with Tim Gallen, the rogue IRS agent still sought for questioning. Arthur was quoted several times.

She laid the paper aside and rubbed her temples.

"Besides, I need your help to finish this investigation," he said.

She didn't look up. "What exactly is your plan?"

"The UPS center here receives their packages around 1:00 p.m. With an island this small, there can't be that many delivery trucks. My guess is that there are probably only a handful. And I remember from my last vacation down here that the trucks are really tiny too, about the size of a squashed Volkswagen bus. I figure we rent two mopeds and stake out the office. Once the trucks leave, we follow two of the bigger ones. You could follow one and I'll follow another."

"That's your plan? We randomly follow little brown

trucks and see which one delivers Cleon's packages to someone named Nealey? That plan sucks."

"Excuse me, Sherlock Holmes, but we don't really have that many options. Why don't we go get some lunch and discuss it. You'll feel better after you have something in your stomach."

He was right. She put on a pair of white tennis shoes, and when Tim wasn't looking, tucked the last of her remaining cash into her pocket. She had stashed the money under a corner of the bathroom rug when she first arrived.

They locked their rooms and went to a restaurant down the street. It had open-air dining, and they sat at a table near the ocean. Maggie found it hard to keep moping with the sun so bright and the ocean so beautiful. Tim kept the conversation going and by dessert she was laughing at the mess they were in. Oddly enough, she was beginning to feel relaxed, like a cloud of anxiousness had finally been lifted from her.

"If we're going to be fugitives from the law, isn't it better that we're here than say, oh, I don't know, Wisconsin?" Tim said.

"You're right, Clyde. Let's go get our mopeds and get this plan on the road."

They rented two red mopeds for twenty dollars. Maggie started her bike and immediately crashed into the side of the store.

The brick wall was undamaged, but her jeans were smeared with black streaks and blood began soaking through from her knee. She turned from Tim so he wouldn't see that she still hadn't shaved and rolled up her pant leg. She pushed down on the gash until it stopped bleeding, gently replaced her pant leg, and began picking pieces of gravel out of her elbow.

"This isn't a good omen," she said.

But after a few minutes and a couple of practice laps around the parking lot, she felt more comfortable. Maggie continued circling the lot while Tim went back inside the store for two helmets and directions to the UPS center.

"Okay, this place is about ten minutes away," he said. "Are you ready?"

She gave him the thumbs up and put on her helmet.

She trailed behind Tim as their mopeds climbed a small paved road. At the top of the hill they began their descent down into the valley until they were near the airport. It was a beautiful ride, but the coolness of the tropical forest ended and they found themselves in an open gravel lot. At the center was a faded brown shack surrounded by nine brown mini-UPS trucks. The sun had forced everyone inside, making the place seem abandoned.

"Now what?"

Tim turned off his moped. "That's a good question. Let's wait here and see what happens."

They waited for thirty minutes. No one came in or out of the building.

"We can't just sit here all afternoon," she said.

"Sooner or later those trucks will move. We just have to be patient."

"I'd like to, but I have to go to the bathroom."

"You have a whole tropical rain forest at your disposal. I promise not to look."

"Sorry, Tim, the one thing I don't do is piss in the woods. I'm going to just ride up to the office and use their bathroom."

"But what if one of the trucks pulls out while you're in there? The whole plan will be ruined."

"I wouldn't really worry about that, it's not much of a plan. But I promise I'll hurry."

She started her moped and drove to the building's entrance and parked the bike in what she guessed was a parking space. She opened the front door and was assaulted by more hot air. So much for air conditioning.

In the reception area Maggie found a woman sitting on a chair with her back to her watching a *Northern Exposure* rerun on a small black and white television. The screened windows didn't seem to let in any breeze, and Maggie felt like she was in a hot box.

The woman turned down the volume on the television. "Can I help you?"

"Could I please use your bathroom? If I go over one more bump on my moped I think my bladder will explode."

The woman pointed to a door behind her. "Through there and follow the hallway back to the far corner. The women's bathroom is the last door on the right, it's not marked." She lowered her voice. "Be careful not to use the men's. They're such pigs."

Maggie thanked her, went through the door, and realized she was right in the middle of their shipping operation. Groups of about a dozen boxes were piled in different stacks, ready to be sorted and loaded on the waiting trucks. Four men shuffled back and forth between the piles. From the look of things the workload could have easily been handled by one man, but who was she to criticize island rhythms?

She approached the man holding a clipboard.

"Excuse me, may I talk with you for a moment?"

"Sure." He gave her a smile that exposed more gum than teeth. "How can I help you?"

"Two things. First, I'm trying to locate an address of some packages that have been shipped here from St. Louis, Missouri—in the United States. Secondly, I need to use the bathroom."

"I'd love to help locate your address lady, but we get so many packages in here. . . ."

She pulled out a fifty-dollar bill. "These packages have been sent from a St. Louis company called Stuffing Stuff. There have been about four or five shipments each day for the last several days to someone named Nealey."

"Maybe I do know which ones you're talking about. But I can't give out that information. It's confidential."

"Look, I don't think anyone's national security is going to be compromised." She pulled out another fifty. "What if you just suggested a pile of boxes I might walk by?"

"Very good, lady." He took the hundred dollars. "I'll show you the way to the bathroom."

He led her on a circuitous route to the bathroom. When they approached a stack of boxes he ripped off a corner of the paper on his clipboard and handed her a stubby pencil. "You might want to take this paper and pencil with you if you see something you'd like to write down."

She smiled and took the items she had just bought for a hundred dollars.

"When you're done," he said, "just turn down that hallway and the bathroom is on the right. Make sure you go to the second bathroom 'cause they're not marked and the first one is the men's room."

Maggie thanked him and walked to the stack of boxes. The first box she looked at was addressed to Helen Nealey at 500 Oceanway, Georgetown, Grand Cayman. The return address was Stuffing Stuff. Three other boxes sitting nearby were also addressed to Nealey. She scribbled down the address and then went to the bathroom.

When she returned to the front office, Tim was sitting in a chair waiting for her.

"Did you fall in?" he said. "I was starting to worry."

"I don't think those oysters from last night agreed with me."

The woman behind the counter smiled at Maggie and seemed to make a mental note not to venture to the bathroom for a while.

Tim and Maggie returned to their mopeds. Maggie began to tell him her discovery, but he motioned her to be quiet. He started his moped and she followed him out of the parking lot and back to the street. They rode about a mile until Tim pulled over and parked under some trees in a seafood restaurant's parking lot.

"While you were leisurely spending your morning in the john," he said, "I did a little snooping. All the UPS trucks come this way before separating so we can wait here and be less conspicuous. Better yet, only three trucks are making deliveries this afternoon so the odds are in our favor."

"Why Tim, you found all that out by yourself? You must have gotten gold stars in detective school."

Tim beamed. "Well Maggie, really it was—"

She handed him her piece of paper.

"What's this?"

"The address Cleon's been shipping the packages to. I bribed one of the package handlers."

"Oh."

"Oh? That's it, oh? Not even a 'Well done, Watson?' "

He grinned sheepishly. "I suppose I deserved that. Well done, Watson." He paused and then began dancing around the mopeds. "And thank you, Jesus! You have delivered us from evil. Thank you, Jesus."

His evangelistic yelling and dancing provoked stares from a group of tourists coming out of the restaurant, which Tim ignored.

"Shall we go before someone commits you to the nervous hospital?" she said.

"But of course." He bowed and motioned for Maggie to mount her moped. "Let's go see what Helen Nealey has waiting for us."

The two drove off to Oceanway as an oversized woman on a rented scooter followed them out of the parking lot. Several small stains covered the front of her blouse where she had dribbled sauce from her mahimahi lunch. Her back end completely engulfed the moped's seat, and the small motor labored up the hill, but Mary Hodgkins simply gave the bike more gas.

When she left work yesterday, she had given up hope of finding someone who had fraudulently applied for a driver's license. Especially now while she was enjoying her free vacation. But there was no doubt about it. The little redhead who had just taken off on the moped was the same woman who had applied for the Terry Stevens license. What luck! It was a good thing Mary had decided against a second dessert, otherwise she would have missed seeing the woman and her companion at the far end of the parking lot.

Mary would gladly interrupt her vacation to seek retribution. She had until five o'clock today to get the evidence to her supervisor and plenty of sunny days after that to enjoy her victory.

"Thank you, Jesus!" She laughed as she increased her speed. "I don't think I'll be working Saturdays when I get home."

Chapter **45**

Tim had left his government-issued nine-millimeter gun locked in the trunk of Maggie's rental car. He knew he wouldn't be able to smuggle it onto the plane, but en route to Helen Nealey's house he realized he needed some kind of weapon. He motioned for Maggie to stop at a weather-worn dive shop. Since guns are illegal in the Caymans, even the police didn't carry them, Tim thought a speargun purchase would be quick, easy, and legal. Of course, nothing lately was ever quick, easy, and legal.

The dive shop owner explained that spearfishing was against the law in the Caymans, which made spearguns illegal as well. Tim convinced Maggie to donate her cash reserve to help their situation. Once the store owner saw the American's wad of cash, he produced a brand new speargun from behind the counter. It took all of Maggie's money to purchase the gun, which thankfully came disassembled in a convenient carrying case.

Helen Nealey's home sat atop a luscious hillside as nonchalantly as the rest of the wealthy neighborhood. The front of the home maintained the traditional white stucco exterior and clay roof, but the back of the home revealed a more American touch. Maggie and Tim crouched in the bushes and stared at the two-story glass atrium that overlooked the small harbor below.

They crept back to the side of the house and found an open door. Tim went in first with Maggie right behind him. The door let them into a kitchen. They stopped to listen for a sign that their infiltration had been discovered. The house remained quiet.

Tim could smell dinner baking. Maggie peeked into the oven.

"Fish," she whispered. "It looks like it's almost ready."

"The diners can't be too far away, then," he said.

Tim inched into the adjacent dining room with his speargun pointed straight ahead. He was about to move into the living room when he heard two people talking as they came down from the upstairs. He and Maggie backtracked to the kitchen.

Maggie pulled on his shirt. "Maybe this isn't such a good idea," she said.

"Don't worry," he said. "Trust me."

He motioned for her to stay in the kitchen, and he walked through the dining room to the living room with the speargun cocked. "Pull your arm out of that pig's ass right now or you'll be the one squealing."

The old man removed his arm from the stuffed pig. When he did, bundles of money dropped out onto the piles of cash already littering the floor. There were fifteen other pigs stationed around the room. From the amount of money on the floor, it looked as though most of the pigs had been relieved of their stuffing.

"And you," Tim said to the man's female companion, "I want you to put your hands in the air where I can see them."

"I've got arthritis in my shoulders," she said. "I can't get my hands up high."

"Come on, Timmy," the man said. "Helen isn't going to hurt anybody."

As soon as the man spoke, Maggie burst out of the kitchen. "Cleon!"

"Magpie, I never expected to see you here."

"Me? I thought you drowned!"

"Him drown?" Tim said. "A trained scuba diver?"

"Nicely done, Timmy," Cleon said with a grin. "I did just happen to have two well-placed air tanks hidden below my dock."

"But," Maggie said, "the body they found, and your dental records confirmed. . . ."

"When you're as rich as I am, it's amazing what can turn up floating in a river when you make a cash payment to a funeral director with a failing business," Cleon said. "As for the dental records, a quick payoff to an underpaid dental receptionist and shazam, that guy's dental records were in my file. A little more money to someone else and lo and behold—my ring was on the body in the morgue when Arthur went to identify it."

"But what about your heart problem?" she asked.

He pounded his chest. "My ticker's never been better." He reddened slightly. "Sorry for putting you through that, Magpie, but it was part of my perfect plan. I created the perfect tax deduction. My death."

"Your death is not tax deductible," Tim said.

"What do you mean, my death isn't tax deductible? Of course it is. With my estate shredded and me presumed dead, why should the IRS pursue my case? That's the perfect tax deduction if you ask me. And Maggie, while you're here, maybe you can tell me what happened to that three million dollars that was never wired to the Bank of Cayman?"

"Be quiet," Tim said. "That money is the least of your problems."

Maggie's face contorted with confusion. "But I don't get it. How can all of this money be here when the news showed pictures of it shredded?"

Cleon looked at him. "Timmy?"

"He didn't shred his money," Tim said. "There's no way he could have in such a short time. He would have needed a small army of shredders. Besides the money in all the bags we found was shredded into bits and pieces. The kind of shredder you buy at an office supply store shreds paper into strips. My guess is that on Cleon's way back from delivering a stuffed animal to a senator in Washington, he stopped by the Federal Reserve Bank in Baltimore. He must have made arrangements to purchase bags of shredded money from them."

"You can buy shredded money?" Maggie said.

"Yeah, when money is taken out of circulation for being worn or damaged, it is shredded. The Baltimore Federal Reserve happens to be one of the few Federal Reserve Banks that still sells the money it shreds."

"Very good," Cleon said, "but how did you find me and my pigs?"

"Maggie had told me about your fake barnyard, but the investigating sergeant at your drowning Monday night said they searched the place and didn't find anything unusual except for all the shredded cash. I would call a fake barnyard with thirty-five potbellied pigs a little unusual. Then, your manager at Stuffing Stuff said you thought computers were worthless, yet you had installed a modem and UPS tracking software on yours. A little detection and some Internet surfing, and I discovered you had shipped thirty-five packages here and that pigs are one of the few animals that can be shipped to the Caymans. It didn't take much to put the two together. As for locating your address, you have Maggie to thank for that."

Maggie shrugged. "Sorry, Cleon, I didn't know it was you. I thought it was someone named Nealey."

"And by the way, Cleon, getting my fingerprints on the poisoned tin of tea was brilliant, as was putting the two million in my bank account."

"So they found the deposit slip I put into your trash can?"

"They must have," Tim said, "or Inspection could have checked my bank balances."

Cleon chuckled. "You might want to check that balance again. I pulled it back out."

"By framing me and mentioning Arthur on the 911 call, you gave the police two suspects to pursue, although Arthur never really came under much scrutiny."

"Timmy—"

"Quit calling me Timmy!"

"You've a right to be angry," Cleon said. "I'm sorry for what I put you through. If I'd known you better I wouldn't have done it. But bear in mind, with you and Arthur both implicated, chances were very good neither of you would be convicted."

"I was going to lose my job, Cleon. As an agent with the Service, my integrity means everything. I would rather have people think I murdered someone than have them think I took a bribe. You framed me for both."

"Sorry, but I really thought you'd take the money. Two million would have been a comfortable severance pay."

Tim didn't answer for a moment. Cleon was right. He'd had two million dollars handed to him and he'd never thought of keeping it because of the minor technical point that it didn't belong to him.

"What can I say?" he said at last. "I love my work. I like being one of the good guys."

"I guess you do, and I'm sure your career will be fine," Cleon said. "If I was doing it again, I'd leave you out of it and just let Arthur hang." Cleon gestured at the pile of cash on the floor. "And, of course, I'll gladly pay you the monies I owe. You did what I didn't think a government employee could do, you actually did some creative problem solving."

"Sorry, Cleon, it's a little late for that. Maggie, would you please call the police and ask them to join us?"

"We don't have a telephone," Helen said. "It's one of the pleasures of living on an island."

Tim rolled his eyes. Nothing was ever easy.

"Fine. Maggie, why don't you go start the car that I saw parked in the driveway. Then we can all drive down to the police station together."

Maggie took Cleon's keys. She came back moments later. "Two of the tires are completely flat."

"I read in the newspapers about that bag lady putting a curse on you," Cleon said. "Looks like you haven't shaken it yet."

Tim handed Maggie the speargun. "Be careful, it's heavy."

"What am I supposed to do with this?"

"Just stand here for a minute and keep an eye on them."

Tim ran upstairs and came back with a sheet, which he began ripping in strips.

"Hey, that's a new sheet," Cleon said. "It's got a 275-thread count."

"Oh please, don't even start."

Tim kept on ripping, then he retrieved two chairs from the dining room and positioned them in the middle of the living room. He tied Cleon's hands behind his back and bound him into a chair. He repeated the process for Helen. Then he picked up a camera from a side table. "Does this have film in it?"

"Almost a full roll," Helen said.

Tim laid Cleon's copy of yesterday's Wall Street on Cleon's lap so the front page was visible, then he picked up the camera and started taking pictures.

"Say cheese." He circled the room snapping pictures from every angle of Cleon, Helen, and all the cash.

"What are you doing?" Maggie said.

"Just a little career insurance in case the local police screw up the crime scene. How much did you have stuffed in those pigs anyway? About five million each?"

"Something like that. You're not really putting me away, are you?" Cleon said.

Tim finished the roll, popped it out of the camera, and scribbled an IOU for one roll of film.

"I'm sorry, Cleon. I really don't have a choice. After

all, we're not talking about a misplaced decimal. We're talking major fraud." Tim sighed. "You really broke the rules I'm afraid."

"Just thought I'd ask."

"Maggie," Tim said, "I'll run down to the main road and try to get some help. It shouldn't take too long, and you don't have to worry about them trying anything. I'll be back as soon as I can. I'll lock the door behind me."

After Tim left, Maggie sat down on a satin Queen Anne and began her vigil.

"I don't suppose I could talk you into untying us, could I, Maggie?" Cleon said.

"I'm afraid not. I like you a lot, but—"

"You like Dudley Do-Right more." Cleon leaned his head back, dramatically. "I suppose I'll get used to prison food. In fact, once I've lost my few remaining teeth—"

Maggie laughed. "Oh come on, Cleon. You know as well as I do that you'll probably get probation and six months' community service."

"And a hefty bill."

"For money you really owe. Besides, you can write a book about the whole experience and make some of it back."

"Hey, I never thought about that."

"Of course, you'll be creating another tax liability."

"Speaking of liabilities, how did Arthur take my death? And what happened to my Hamilton money?"

"Arthur faked grief very well. As for your Hamilton money, I'm sorry, but when I thought you were dead I tried to embezzle your balance. Arthur discovered what I was doing and tried to have me killed."

"He always was a poor loser. The fool thought he could make arrangements to kill me. The simp couldn't even do that right, as much as I tried to help him."

Maggie thought about her second near-drowning and shuddered. "Yeah, but he came a little closer to killing me than I would have liked."

"Well, I'm glad he missed. What happened?"

"Arthur had some lowlife follow me down here, and he broke into my room last night and nearly drowned me while I was in the bathtub. Tim saved my life."

"He is Dudley Do-Right."

"As for your money, I had converted your account into foreign bearer bonds and the guy made off with them before he got away."

"I wonder if I can write that off as a loss?" Cleon said with smile.

A smoke alarm shrilled from the kitchen.

"Our dinner's burning!"

Maggie ran into the kitchen and turned off the oven. She pulled out the charred fish and dropped the pan into the sink. Then, she opened the back door to give the clouds of black smoke an escape route.

She was trying unsuccessfully to silence the alarm with a broomstick when she was struck from behind. Her head hit a corner cabinet and she collapsed onto the floor.

Chapter 46

Tim bolted through the door with a small squadron of police at his heels. He found Maggie bound and gagged on the living room floor. A huge woman towered over her with the speargun in her hand. Cleon and Helen were gone.

"What the hell have you done?" Tim said.

"I'm glad you're finally here." The woman pointed the gun at Tim. "Arrest that man and his accomplice."

"Are you out of your mind, lady? Who are you?" Tim untied Maggie. "Where are Cleon and Helen?"

"My name is Mary Hodgkins," the fat woman said, "and I am with the Illinois Department of License and Registration."

"Excuse me, Miss Hodgkins," one of the police officers said. "Before we go any further, would you mind giving me your weapon?"

"Of course," she said and handed the speargun to the officer. "Now, as I was saying, this woman applied for an Illinois license using fraudulent identification, which is a felony in my state. I would like to have her arrested and extradited back to the States for prosecution." She nodded at Tim. "I'm not sure what his story is."

"My story," said Tim, "is that I'm going to wring your fat neck if I can get my hands around it."

Tim lunged toward the woman. Two of the officers jumped in to restrain him. Once he calmed down, one of the officers tipped his hat to the fat lady.

"Miss Hodgkins, is it?" he asked. "That man is a federal agent, and he has explained that Maggie Connors was working under his direction. What happened to the two people who were being detained here?"

"You mean the banker and his friend?"

"Cleon wasn't a banker!" Tim yelled.

"He told me he was opening a bank, which is why he had so much cash here. Anyhow—I apologized for slashing his tires—I didn't want that woman to escape. He said these two had broken into his home to rob him. When I untied them, they grabbed all the cash that was lying around here and they fled down the hill toward a yacht in the harbor. I'm sure they're way out to sea by now."

The police turned to Maggie for a second opinion. "That's right," she said. "We've been working undercover, and this woman just freed a major fugitive."

"Applying for a fraudulent license is a felony in Illinois."

"And assault is a crime here," one of the officers said. "So is breaking and entering, having a speargun, and impeding an investigation." He turned to Tim. "Do you wish to press charges, sir?"

"It depends. Will Maggie ever have to hear about that stupid license again?"

The woman glared back. "No charges will be filed."

"Then no charges will be filed," Tim said.

"Well," the officer said, "that certainly saves a lot of paperwork. Now let's see what we can do about your mysterious missing banker."

The police hung around for about twenty minutes, but

without the hundred-plus million dollars that had been piled in the living room, they quickly lost their interest. Miss Hodgkins badgered them into taking her back to the station and calling her supervisor to confirm that she had caught a fraudulent application, although no charges were being filed. Tim told the police they were going to look around awhile longer and would lock up before they left.

As soon as the police left, Maggie and Tim collapsed into chairs.

"At least you've got the pictures," she said, "and neither of us is going to jail for Cleon's murder."

Tim closed his eyes and sank back, listening to the waves breaking outside the window. It was almost over.

"You know," he said, "I'm almost glad Cleon got away. For a cheat and a fraud, he really wasn't a bad guy."

Maggie walked to the window to look at the view and discovered an envelope on the ledge addressed to Tim. She handed it to him.

He opened it and found a brief confession, absolving him of all blame and admitting his tax liability. It was signed by Cleon and witnessed by Helen. At the bottom was a note: *In case the pictures don't turn out.*

"Well, I'll be. Good old Cleon."

They sat quietly for a moment.

"Tim, I'm sorry about the money."

"Oh, I wouldn't worry about that."

"Well, how much does Cleon owe?"

"I'm afraid I can't discuss Cleon's taxes. All taxpayer files are confidential."

The door bell rang.

"Who the hell is that?" Maggie said. "Probably Hodgkins back to do a citizen's arrest for my unpaid parking tickets."

"I think it's probably a certain UPS delivery."

Maggie looked at him in disbelief. "My God," she said, "The last shipment, I'd forgotten all—"

"There are only thirty-one pigs here. You said there were thirty-five in Cleon's fake barnyard."

He went to the door and returned with a brown man in a brown uniform pushing a hand truck laden with four large boxes.

Tim handed her the clipboard. "Would you care to sign, Miss Nealey?"

When the UPS man left, Maggie ran to the kitchen for a carving knife. By the time she got back, Tim had torn the packaging away from one of the pigs. He took the knife from Maggie and plunged it into the pig's stomach. He carved out a six-inch hole, and cash came pouring out. They both dove in and started counting. The pig contained just over five million dollars.

"Well, that was fun. I'm going to ship the other three pigs back to my boss without opening them. That's more than enough to cover Cleon's tax bill."

"Does that mean that we get to keep this cash?" she said, pointing at the floor.

Tim sighed. How could he make her understand?

"Maggie, I can't. Consider it a moral quirk," he said. "I know there are a lot of people—like Miss Hodgkins, for instance—who just follow the rules because they don't know any better. And I don't have a lot of respect for them either. What you don't understand is that we, as a people, make these rules up for ourselves. They're our own rules. However indirectly, we get the government we decide we want, and trying to make an end run around the system, like Cleon did, is lazy and irresponsible. Does this make any sense?"

"Oh beautiful, for spacious skies. . . ." she sang.

"Knock it off."

"Yeah, it makes some sense, but enough to give up twenty million for?"

"Well, I've been tempted, believe me. But it really does matter that the money doesn't belong to me. As an employee of the Treasury, I'm not eligible for any reward. I can't get paid millions for just doing my job. It wouldn't be fair. It's—"

"I know," she said. "It's just not right. But like I said,

faced with the choice between twenty million and the satisfaction of being part of a self-governing system, it would be hard to pass up the cash." She bent over and started stacking the bundles of money. "Let's get this money packed up before I regress and accidentally kill you and keep all the loot."

Tim stared at her a moment, then broke into a wide grin. "Why don't you?"

"What?"

"I don't mean kill me, I mean why don't you keep the money from the pig we opened?"

"Are you having an ethical crisis? Should I call 911?"

"You found this address, not to mention your help back in St. Louis. You probably didn't know the IRS has a policy of rewarding honest citizens for helping to identify persons who have cheated on their taxes. It's the 'Money Talks' law, more formally known as the Internal Revenue Code Section 7623. The District Director is the one who usually determines the amount of the award paid. One hundred thousand is the max, but since the Director isn't here, and there's no way we'll be able to repatch this pig and get the money back through customs, I think I can make a managerial decision and give it to you."

"Are you sure?" She paused, with a confused look on her face. "Did I just ask you if you're sure? What the hell do I care if you're sure or not. Of course I'll take the money."

"For the record, I am sure. If I try to work with the local police, this money will somehow disappear into a bureaucratic black hole, and they might even seize the other three pigs. I'd rather you have it. Consider this the IRS's payment for your services rendered."

"So what do I do now?"

"I'd say you laugh all the way to the bank."

Chapter 47

A woman from room service at the Marriott woke Maggie Saturday morning when she came in to deliver a basket of flowers. Maggie sat up in bed, prompting a five-minute apology from the woman for not realizing Maggie was in the room. The woman put the flowers on the table and switched the "do not disturb" sign to the outside doorknob before closing the door behind her.

Maggie dropped her head back on her pillow, but it was too late. The morning sun filled the room and there was no getting back to sleep. She opened her eyes and cringed. Her head pounded as if she had been on a college drinking binge. Must have been when she hit it, yesterday.

She climbed out of bed and stopped to look at the arrangement. The card said *Arthur is in jail. Have a nice day*. Interspersed among the flowers were a dozen women's razors. She smiled, despite her headache, picked up one of the razors, and went to the bathroom and took some aspirin.

She stood in the shower with a cold can of Pepsi

pressed against the back of her neck. Once her headache began to subside, she drank the Pepsi and finally shaved her legs.

When she emerged from the shower, she felt refreshed and grateful. For the first time in what seemed like a week, she had completed her bathing without being attacked by a strange man.

She had transferred from the Trade Winds Village to the Marriott last night. Somehow, being located on the fourteenth floor of the resort felt reassuring. She dressed in an overpriced designer shirt and matching shorts she had purchased yesterday in the hotel's boutique. It was already ten o'clock, so she removed the beach bags of cash tucked under her bed. It was time to get the money deposited in a safe place.

At the hotel's entrance the doorman whistled for a cab, and Maggie tipped him before climbing in. She instructed the cabbie to take her to the First Bank of Cayman and to stay while she went inside. Maggie waited her turn in line. When a teller became available Maggie explained she wanted to open an account with a cash deposit and was escorted to a waiting area.

Maggie sat in one of the leather chairs and scanned the *Wall Street Journal* that was sitting on a coffee table. It seemed every twenty-four hours, her life got turned around in a different direction. She would have been more comfortable if Tim were there, but he had decided to fly home early this morning to try to save his career.

A woman in her midthirties came in. "Ms. Connors?"

Maggie nodded.

"My name is Renee Adopa. I understand you wish to open an account." She led Maggie back to her office and began filling out the paperwork. "Have you been on the island long?"

"No, not really."

"What should I use as your address for the account?"

"Right now I'm staying at the Marriott. Would it be possible to use the bank's address for now?"

"Of course, whatever is convenient for you." Renee smiled. "How much will you be depositing with us today?"

"Four million, seven hundred and fifty thousand dollars." Maggie couldn't help but smile as she said the amount.

"That is a nice sum of money. After we deposit the cash would you like me to prepare an investment plan for you? Our savings account is only paying about 2.5%. We could do much better by investing some of the money in stocks and bonds, which I could help you with. I could recommend some investments that would provide a steady income, or are you more concerned with growth opportunities?"

"For now, why don't you just put the proceeds in a money market account. I'll decide what to do with it later."

Renee gave her a copy of the paperwork and thanked her for opening the account.

By noon Maggie was lying on a secluded section of beach listening to the waves crash against the sand. She deserved at least a week's moratorium from deciding what to do with her new life. The deserted oasis encouraged her to completely relax, for once in her life.

She felt a shadow pass over her face and opened her eyes to see if the cloud was very big. Instead of seeing a cloud, she saw Tim Gallen blocking her sun.

"What are you doing here?" she said, with a smile.

"I went to the airport and tried to buy a ticket home, but for some reason my credit card was canceled. I'm not sure which arm of the law I have to thank for that but I've got no way to get home. So, I called Ed collect and explained everything, our visit to Arthur's house, the UPS shipments, and our discovery of Cleon alive and well in the Caymans. I told him I was overnighting Cleon's confession and photos and to be on the lookout for three little pigs."

"I bet he was pretty happy to hear from you."

"He was. He also said an agent from Inspection who had been on vacation got back and had my message about Cleon's bribe in his voice mail box. I must have dialed the wrong number for John Corbin."

"What are you talking about?"

"Forget it, it's a long story and it doesn't matter now. I told Ed to call me once he got the packages and I was no longer on the firing line. Until then, I said I wanted to spend some time with Little Red Riding Hood."

"My, Mr. Wolf, you do have a way with mixing your storybook characters."

Tim sat down beside her. "Just think, Arthur has probably been strip-searched by now."

"That's how he prefers to begin his day. What were the charges?"

"Blowing up his house, tax evasion, hiring someone to try and kill you. Ed said he would call the Clayton police and give them a list of options. Did everything go all right at the First Bank of Cayman?"

"Jesus, will I ever be able to tell when I'm being followed?"

Tim shrugged and shook his head. His shoulders were no longer bunched up by his ears and he seemed more relaxed. He took his socks and shoes off and rubbed his toes in the sand. "Looks like you finally got a chance to shave those legs. They look nice."

Maggie smiled again.

The waves crashed against the sand and both were quiet for a while, not sure what to say.

Tim spoke first. "Since I'm broke, and you're sitting on almost five million dollars, how about buying me lunch?" He stood up and brushed off the sand.

"I suppose you'll want to discuss my tax situation?"

She took his hand. He helped her to her feet and then pulled her into him, both of his arms around her waist.

"As a matter of fact, I do have a taxing situation in mind I'd like to discuss with you," he said into her ear, "but it's more personal than financial."

Before she could react, Tim's mouth found hers and he kissed her with a kiss that wasn't in any IRS rule book.

She pushed him away.

"I thought I wasn't your type."

"I lied." He bent down and kissed her again.

She locked her arms against his chest to prevent another kiss.

"Slow down, tax man. You said you had a one-track mind for those beloved tax regulations." She tilted her head and raised a questioning eyebrow. "Are you sure there's room for me in your life?"

He grinned. "I was assessing my love life this morning—"

"You? Assessing something other than taxes?"

"Unfortunately, I realized I had no love life to assess." He paused. "I'd like to change that." His tone was sincere.

She studied his face for a moment. He looked confident but vulnerable.

Maggie moved one hand to his shoulder and used her other hand to guide Tim's face down to hers.

"I'm from the government and I'm here to help you," she whispered, and kissed him back.

Chapter **48**

The UPS driver drove up to a small stone bungalow
off Delmar. The home was typical of St. Louis's West
End, with eighty-year-old architecture and eighty-year-old
residents.

The driver knocked on the door, heard a shuffle of footsteps, and then an elderly man appeared. His eyes were
puffy and bloodshot. He looked like a lost child.

"May I help you?" he asked, sniffling.

"I have a two-day air package for Stanley Goldwyn."

"That's me. Won't you please come in?"

"I'm kind of in a hurry, sir. If you'll just sign right
here."

"Oh, please come in and have some lemonade. It's so
hot out and you look thirsty."

The driver agreed. It was his last Monday delivery and
he was dying of thirst.

The heat inside the home was almost suffocating. Even
the childhood pictures of several sons and daughters hanging on the walls seemed to be sweating. Mr. Goldwyn

explained that it was cooler in the kitchen, and he followed him across well-worn orange shag carpet to the back of the house.

A woman he assumed was Mrs. Goldwyn sat clipping coupons at the kitchen table. She set her scissors aside when he and Mr. Goldwyn entered the room.

Mr. Goldwyn set the package on the counter and proudly introduced his wife to the driver.

"We were childhood sweethearts," Mr. Goldwyn said. "We survived the poverty of the Depression. Now it looks like we're back there again for our retirement."

The elderly woman frowned at her husband for mentioning their financial condition. Then a smile quickly returned to her face and she poured the driver an ice-cold glass of homemade lemonade as promised. The driver gulped it down and thanked them both, then escaped the home before he could become entangled in one of the never-ending stories old people love to tell.

"What is in the envelope?" Jean said when Stanley returned from showing the driver out.

"I assume it's some more papers from our attorney. In fact, when the doorbell rang I thought it was the real estate agent who was listing our house."

Jean's lower lip trembled at the reminder that Stanley's gambling was forcing them to sell the home they had lived in since they were first married. She rubbed the space on her finger where her wedding ring had been before it was pawned to pay for some prescriptions.

Stanley tugged on the envelope's tab several times before he got it to open. He pulled out a stack of ornate legal-looking papers. Confused, he handed them with the cover note to his wife, then wrung his hands while she interpreted the package's contents.

She put the glasses on that had been dangling by a chain around her neck. "It's from that Maggie Connors at Hamilton Securities." She read the note, looked up at her husband and then read the note again. Tears streamed down her wrinkled face.

"What's wrong? I told her I was sorry. Does she want money, too? Am I in trouble?"

The woman reached over and held her husband's hand. "No. She's giving us $500,000 in bonds to help us get back on our feet."

Bio

Malinda Terreri is married with two beautiful daughters. Her husband is ecstatic that she executes her schemes in writing rather than in reality. This is her first novel, which she finished during her daughters' naps.

Ms. Terreri is a professional sales trainer known for her fun, interactive training exercises. Her articles on sales training have appeared in publications around the world.

She is currently working on a sequel to *A Tax Deductible Death*. You may visit her at her Web Site: www.MalindaTerreri.com

Your purchase of this novel helps grant the wishes of children with life-threatening illnesses as 20 percent of the author's proceeds will be donated to the Make A Wish Foundation.

EARLENE FOWLER

introduces Benni Harper, curator of San Celina's folk art museum and amateur sleuth

❑ FOOL'S PUZZLE   0-425-14545-X/$6.50

Ex-cowgirl Benni Harper moved to San Celina, California, to begin a new career as curator of the town's folk art museum. But when one of the museum's first quilt exhibit artists is found dead, Benni must piece together a pattern of family secrets and small-town lies to catch the killer.

❑ IRISH CHAIN   0-425-15137-9/$6.50

When Brady O'Hara and his former girlfriend are murdered at the San Celina Senior Citizen's Prom, Benni believes it's more than mere jealousy—and she risks everything to unveil the conspiracy O'Hara had been hiding for fifty years.

❑ KANSAS TROUBLES   0-425-15696-6/$6.50

After their wedding, Benni and Gabe visit his hometown near Wichita. There Benni meets Tyler Brown: aspiring country singer, gifted quilter, and former Amish wife. But when Tyler is murdered and the case comes between Gabe and her, Benni learns that her marriage is much like the Kansas weather: bound to be stormy.

❑ GOOSE IN THE POND   0-425-16239-7/$6.50
❑ DOVE IN THE WINDOW   0-425-16894-8/$6.50

Prices slightly higher in Canada

Payable by Visa, MC or AMEX only ($10.00 min.), No cash, checks or COD. Shipping & handling: US/Can. $2.75 for one book, $1.00 for each add'l book; int'l $5.00 for one book, $1.00 for each add'l. Call (800) 788-6262 or (201) 933-9292, fax (201) 896-8569 or mail your orders to:

Penguin Putnam Inc. P.O. Box 12289, Dept. B Newark, NJ 07101-5289 Please allow 4-6 weeks for delivery. Foreign and Canadian delivery 6-8 weeks.	Bill my: ❑ Visa ❑ MasterCard ❑ Amex _____ (expires) Card# _____ Signature _____

Bill to:

Name _____

Address _____ City _____

State/ZIP _____ Daytime Phone # _____

Ship to:

Name _____ Book Total $ _____

Address _____ Applicable Sales Tax $ _____

City _____ Postage & Handling $ _____

State/ZIP _____ Total Amount Due $ _____

This offer subject to change without notice.   Ad # 523 (4/00)

SUSAN WITTIG ALBERT

__THYME OF DEATH   0-425-14098-9/$6.50

China Bayles left her law practice to open an herb shop in
Pecan Springs, Texas. But tensions run high in small towns,
too—and the results can be murder.

__WITCHES' BANE   0-425-14406-2/$6.50

When a series of Halloween pranks turns deadly, China must
investigate to unmask a killer.

__HANGMAN'S ROOT   0-425-14898-X/$5.99

When a prominent animal researcher is murdered, China
discovers a fervent animal rights activist isn't the only person
who wanted him dead.

__ROSEMARY REMEMBERED   0-425-15405-X/$6.50

When a woman who looks just like China is found murdered
in a pickup truck, China looks for a killer close to home.

__RUEFUL DEATH   0-425-15941-8/$6.50
__LOVE LIES BLEEDING   0-425-16611-2/$6.50
__CHILE DEATH   0-425-17147-7/$6.50

Prices slightly higher in Canada

Payable by Visa, MC or AMEX only ($10.00 min.), No cash, checks or COD. Shipping & handling:
US/Can. $2.75 for one book, $1.00 for each add'l book; Int'l $5.00 for one book, $1.00 for each
add'l. Call (800) 788-6262 or (201) 933-9292, fax (201) 896-8569 or mail your orders to:

Penguin Putnam Inc.   Bill my: ❑ Visa ❑ MasterCard ❑ Amex _____(expires)
P.O. Box 12289, Dept. B
Newark, NJ 07101-5289   Card# _____
Please allow 4-6 weeks for delivery.   Signature _____
Foreign and Canadian delivery 6-8 weeks.
Bill to:
Name _____
Address _____City _____
State/ZIP _____Daytime Phone # _____
Ship to:
Name _____Book Total $ _____
Address _____Applicable Sales Tax $ _____
City _____Postage & Handling $ _____
State/ZIP _____Total Amount Due $ _____
This offer subject to change without notice.   Ad # 546 (3/00)

Miriam Grace Monfredo

*brings to life one of the most exciting periods
in our nation's history—the mid-1800s—when the passionate struggles
of suffragettes, abolitionists, and other heroes touched the lives of every
American, including a small-town librarian named Glynis Tryon...*

__BLACKWATER SPIRITS__   0-425-15266-9/$6.50

*Glynis Tryon, no stranger to political controversy, is fighting
the prejudice against the Seneca Iroquois. And the issue
becomes personal when one of Glynis's Iroquois friends is
accused of murder...*

__NORTH STAR CONSPIRACY__   0-425-14720-7/$6.50

__SENECA FALLS INHERITANCE__
                                                          0-425-14465-8/$6.99

__THROUGH A GOLD EAGLE__   0-425-15898-5/$6.50
*When abolitionist John Brown is suspected of moving counter-
feit bills, Glynis is compelled to launch her own campaign for
freedom—to free an innocent man.*

Prices slightly higher in Canada

Payable by Visa, MC or AMEX only ($10.00 min.), No cash, checks or COD. Shipping & handling:
US/Can. $2.75 for one book, $1.00 for each add'l book; Int'l $5.00 for one book, $1.00 for each
add'l. Call (800) 788-6262 or (201) 933-9292, fax (201) 896-8569 or mail your orders to:

Penguin Putnam Inc. P.O. Box 12289, Dept. B Newark, NJ 07101-5289 Please allow 4-6 weeks for delivery. Foreign and Canadian delivery 6-8 weeks.	Bill my: ❑ Visa ❑ MasterCard ❑ Amex _____(expires) Card# _____ Signature _____

Bill to:

Name _____

Address _____ City _____

State/ZIP _____ Daytime Phone # _____

Ship to:

Name _____ Book Total $ _____

Address _____ Applicable Sales Tax $ _____

City _____ Postage & Handling $ _____

State/ZIP _____ Total Amount Due $ _____

This offer subject to change without notice.   Ad # 649 (4/00)

BETSY DEVONSHIRE
NEEDLECRAFT MYSTERIES
by Monica Ferris

FREE NEEDLEWORK PATTERN INCLUDED
IN EACH MYSTERY!

❏ CREWEL WORLD
0-425-16780-1/$5.99

When Betsy's sister is murdered in her own needlework store, Betsy takes over the shop and the investigation. But to find the murderer, she'll have to put together a list of motives and suspects to figure out the killer's pattern of crime...

❏ FRAMED IN LACE
0-425-17149-3/$5.99

A skeleton is discovered when the historic Hopkins ferry is raised from the lake. Unfortunately, the only evidence found was a piece of lace-like fabric. But once Betsy and the patrons of the needlecraft shop lend a hand, they're sure to stitch together this mystery...

❏ A STITCH IN TIME
0-425-17149-3/$5.99

A skeleton is discovered when the historic Hopkins ferry is raised from the lake. Unfortunately, the only evidence found was a piece of lace-like fabric. But once Betsy and the patrons of the needlecraft shop lend a hand, they're sure to stitch together this mystery...

Prices slightly higher in Canada

Payable by Visa, MC or AMEX only ($10.00 min.), No cash, checks or COD. Shipping & handling: US/Can. $2.75 for one book, $1.00 for each add'l book; Int'l $5.00 for one book, $1.00 for each add'l. Call (800) 788-6262 or (201) 933-9292, fax (201) 896-8569 or mail your orders to:

Penguin Putnam Inc.	Bill my: ❏ Visa ❏ MasterCard ❏ Amex _____ (expires)
P.O. Box 12289, Dept. B	Card# _____
Newark, NJ 07101-5289	
Please allow 4-6 weeks for delivery.	Signature _____
Foreign and Canadian delivery 6-8 weeks.	

Bill to:

Name _____

Address _____ City _____

State/ZIP _____ Daytime Phone # _____

Ship to:

Name _____ Book Total $ _____

Address _____ Applicable Sales Tax $ _____

City _____ Postage & Handling $ _____

State/ZIP _____ Total Amount Due $ _____

This offer subject to change without notice.   Ad # 901 (4/00)

NOREEN WALD

The Ghostwriter Mystery Series

❏ **Ghostwriter**　　　　　0–425–16947–2/$5.99

As good at detection as dreaming up whodunits, this gutsy,
single, wise-cracking New Yorker has a knack for spotting a
nice set of biceps, a great martini—and the devious turnings
of the criminal mind. Now she faces a plot much deadlier
than fiction: Who's killing Manhattan's ghostwriters?

❏ **Death Comes for the Critic**
　　　　　　　　　　　0–425–17344–5/$5.99

When Richard Peter, acerbic book critic and ghostwriter Jake
O'Hara's co-author, is stabbed in the back—literally—Jake is left
ghosting for the dead—and chasing down clues to a murder that
hasn't seen its final chapter....

Prices slightly higher in Canada

Payable by Visa, MC or AMEX only ($10.00 min.), No cash, checks or COD. Shipping & handling:
US/Can. $2.75 for one book, $1.00 for each add'l book; Int'l $5.00 for one book, $1.00 for each
add'l. Call (800) 788-6262 or (201) 933-9292, fax (201) 896-8569 or mail your orders to:

Penguin Putnam Inc. P.O. Box 12289, Dept. B Newark, NJ 07101-5289 Please allow 4-6 weeks for delivery. Foreign and Canadian delivery 6-8 weeks.	Bill my: ❏ Visa ❏ MasterCard ❏ Amex _____(expires) Card# _____ Signature _____

Bill to:

Name _____

Address _____City _____

State/ZIP _____Daytime Phone # _____

Ship to:

Name _____Book Total　　　$ _____

Address _____Applicable Sales Tax　$ _____

City _____Postage & Handling　$ _____

State/ZIP _____Total Amount Due　$ _____

This offer subject to change without notice.　　　　　Ad # 871 (8/00)